W9-AMB-891

PUTREFACTION LIVE

PUTREFACTION
LIVE

WARREN PERKINS

UNIVERSITY OF NEW MEXICO PRESS

ALBUQUERQUE

© 2009 by Warren Perkins
All rights reserved. Published 2009
Printed in the United States of America
13 12 11 10 09   1 2 3 4 5

LIBRARY OF CONGRESS CATALOGING-
IN-PUBLICATION DATA

Perkins, Warren, 1949–
Putrefaction Live / Warren Perkins.
        p. cm.
ISBN 978-0-8263-4776-3
    (pbk. : alk.paper)
1. Guitarists—Fiction.
2. Rock musicians—Fiction.
3. Navajo Indians—Fiction.
4. Self-actualization (Psychology)—
    Fiction. I. Title.
PS3616.E7483P87 2009
813'.6—dc22

2009010891

Interior book design and type
composition by Melissa Tandysh
Composed in 10.25/14 MinionPro
Display type is Roadkill

For Ellavina, Charlie, Daniel, and Mary

AUTHOR'S NOTE

For help with the manuscript in its various versions I would like to thank Ellen Lesser, Diane Lefer, Chris Noël, Xu Xi, Ellavina Perkins, Margaret Erhart, Ann Cummins, Steve Willis, Beth Hadas, Charles Callahan Perkins, Nancy Perkins, Nan Docherty, Emily Berg, Mary Lewis Perkins, Sarah Perkins, Stephany Brown, and Bill Burke. Thanks also to Dagoberto Gilb, Mik Jordahl, Ray Showa, and Florence Lynch.

Quotations are from Martha Blue's *Indian Trader: The Life and Times of J. L. Hubbell* (Walnut, CA: Kiva, 2000).

CHAPTER ONE

▨ **BEFORE THE SHARP** downhill curve at the Leupp compressor station, James had to slow way down because he knew it was a speed trap the Navajo cops made a lot of money on. He slowed further by the Nazarene church, and again at the school and the gas station/convenience store, and at the dirt lot where people sold hamburgers and fry bread and cheap beaded jewelry and old furniture from their pickups. Slow. A school crosswalk. Stop. A family tentatively stepped into it: two middle-aged women, a couple of teenage girls, and two grade-school boys, all fat. He could hardly believe how slowly they moved. Were Navajos getting slower because they were getting fatter, or had they always been slow? At Ganado Elementary in his day most of the kids were skinny, with maybe one fat kid per class, and he didn't remember how slow or fast they moved. Now, the supersized girls in capri pants snapped gum and looked around as if there might be something somewhere worth seeing, or not.

On the other side of the thin silver thread of the Little Colorado River, which was lying over the sand rather than flowing through it, stood a wind-blasted house, its roof dotted with tires to hold the shingles down. Nobody around. Miles down the road he passed another small house that waited in the breeze, two scabby dogs walking slowly in its shade. After six years in town, how long could he last out here?

He passed a pickup with kids laughing in the bed, their backs against the cab, hair flowing like a current in a stream, then an old man hauling hay, going half the speed limit, staring hard at the road in front of him, then a white Corolla with the seal of the Navajo Nation on the door, driven by a middle-aged, ramrod-scared Navajo woman with a perm, on some official nosey business tracking unvaccinated kids or youth at risk. He sped up as the landscape opened across the valley of the Little Colorado to the Hopi Buttes in the distance. He just kept his eye on these, and the car seemed to drive itself.

He fumbled with the radio, trying to get something he could stand to listen to, but all he found was seventies country-western: Waylon, Willie, Merle. Some powwow singing, the classic rock station, the same bad music day after day, year after year. Thousands came to metal concerts, and radio ignored them. He snapped a Regurgitate CD into his portable player and turned up the volume. He had to have sound.

An hour ago, when he was waiting for the train to pass the Flagstaff crossing, its sound was like bad thrash: a disciplined rhythm, loud, with unexpected grinds and screeches. A real train, the kind that runs drunks over. Not the lonesome-whistle melancholy bullshit country-western starlight on the rails.

Nor the wimpy new-age world music that seemed so safe, no stoned-out Peter Gabriel. His white cousin on his father's side almost died from Peter Gabriel! He was driving west, early in the morning in North Dakota, fifteen minutes into a didgeridoo solo, when he fell asleep and flipped the car, scattering five people over the plains.

At Greasewood James turned off the paved road and onto the graded track that snaked up the valley where three-hundred-year-old cottonwoods grew, along with big Chinese elms that had been planted seventy-five or a hundred years ago. He passed one old elm with its massive roots partially above the ground, covering a wide circle of dirt with shade, beside what was left of an old foundation, the house long since burned or blown away. It was early afternoon when he crossed over the mesa toward the ranch, high overcast, too cold for May, and dry dust rising thick in the air whenever a car or truck drove by.

At the ranch, no one was at either house. No surprise. It wasn't a ranch the way it was when his grandparents and his aunt Thelma lived here. His parents came out from Flagstaff every month or so for a weekend, and at the most someone came every few days to check on the cattle and the water and the houses and to give the dogs some food. Usually this was done by Thelma's son Max, James's cousin, who worked at the refinery on the other side of Gallup.

James and his younger brother Ben and his parents left the reservation after he graduated from high school. *Barely* graduated, and his father was the principal. They said they weren't making the same mistake with Ben, who enrolled at Flagstaff High and did well, while James made barely over minimum wage at Absolute Rental. Now he was back, not because he thought there was anything for him to do here, or that he belonged, but because he had a place to stay: his mother's empty house out on the ranch. Nobody to get in his face.

At Thelma's house, closer to the windmill, the two dogs barked at him as if he were a total stranger. Nearby, the white stucco hogan stood boarded up, used as storage since James's grandmother died. The cattle were nowhere around, probably over the hill near the other stock tank.

He walked down the hill to the well. The blades of the mill were turning in the high wind and the tank was flowing over, making a mess of mud around the troughs, which the cattle had trampled. James pulled the lever at the bottom of the tower, and it creaked to a halt. Then he let himself into his aunt's house. The key was always in the same place, on a long wire in the cross-pole of the clothesline, where she probably imagined no one would ever find it. He put out some kibble for the dogs, who stopped barking to eat greedily.

Up the hill in his mother's house he checked to see that there was water in the barrels and some food in the kitchen. When he shut the door he felt relief to be out of the wind, and sat. Back in the old house. It had the preserved look of a place where time moved more slowly. A pile of newspapers leaned against the wall by the woodstove, the top one opened to the veteran news. Against the far wall leaned his first guitar, the Gibson acoustic the tightness of whose steel strings he could still feel on the fingers of his left hand. A book abandoned on a table—a white book left by his white dad—stayed there for weeks. The same cans of fruits and vegetables lingered in the cupboards. His mother's upright loom stood on the living room floor by the couch, with the start of her Ganado-red rug, the warp two-thirds empty.

For two days James stayed alone in the house, and the wind blew steadily, dying down only long after sunset, then starting up again before the day had a chance to warm. Shingles blew off the roof. The pile of corrugated roofing rattled. The first afternoon, he walked down to check on the windmill, and when he got back to the house in a few short minutes his eyes burned with fine sand. Inside the house he was physically comfortable enough, though there were unending creaks and whistling noises from the wind. Now the ranch didn't feel so much like a place to rest and enjoy himself as an empty, lonely, even haunted place. He sat in the light of the window, which was warm, and read from the top of the pile of *Navajo Times* by the stove, meant for fire-starting.

From the page stared proud fools in uniform, already looking tortured. One of them was the younger brother of a high school friend. Once again he wondered why Navajos, after their years in *hwééldi* concentration camp, were so enthusiastic about fighting the United States' wars. As ignorant and unschooled as he was, how was it that he understood history better than everyone around him? Letters to the editor included prisoners asking for contact, tourists congratulating the tribe for being interesting, and confused rants against the tribal and federal governments. There was a lot of sports, high school games from the previous autumn.

He felt an eerie misery, as if everything were gone by, all sealed up and unreachable. The games had been lost and won, the Pfc from Kinlichee had been killed by a mine, the prisoner was on the other side of the wall, and time went on. He remembered the girl from his high school who had lost her arm in a car wreck a year after graduation. He remembered Rodney, stabbed beside the middle school track, pouring blood into the ground. "Teach him a lesson!"

He did thirty push-ups. He looked at his old Spider-Man comics. He played his guitar. He listened to CDs. He was not soliciting this nostalgia; he would have preferred to avoid it. But once he felt it, he was drawn in more and more deeply. Everything around him now spoke of the past. Too far back in the past to do anything about.

Even the recent past was uncorrectable. Terri was his first real girlfriend, and he had respected and trusted her. He treated her better than her family had, and better than those guys who came before him. And things had gone along nicely until that one night when he lost his temper and said things to her he shouldn't have said, throwing in her face her sorry past, her bitch mother and drunk-ass father, and left her in the pool hall all hot and red. And three nights later in Bunhuggers she was dry-humping some guy at the bar, trying to get him into a fight.

He walked down to his aunt's place to talk to the dogs. It was a little less crazy than talking to himself. They listened, they looked up at him, they thumped their tails and nuzzled up. Old dogs, if you feed them they wag and whimper for you, but what fakers. They heard his voice and tried to fool him into thinking they understood, that they were telling him, "Who loves you more than we do?"

Still, this was better than Flagstaff, with its racist cops and waitresses, tourists and trains, dick bosses and asshole contractors and idiot homeowners, tweaked-out musicians and Terri, shaking her slutty ass all over town. He could pretend this was a kind of vacation, a little break from all that.

He should stay away from women altogether for a while. It was like that thing that Groucho Marx said. He didn't know the right kind of women, because the right kind of women wouldn't want to know him. And he certainly was not going to meet them in Bunhuggers or the Redwood or at a Cannibal Corpse concert. They would have to have a lot more going for them than that.

On the third day the air was still, and he jogged around the place. He had about a three-mile route over the little hills and valleys that took him up to a rim of sandstone and gypsum thick with junipers and tall shrubs of cliffrose and mountain mahogany. A great horned owl sat on top of a dead pinyon, turning his head from behind one shoulder to behind the other, and back again. James's legs ached a little since he hadn't run in a couple of weeks, and he wheezed a little, not having remembered to bring his inhalers from Flagstaff. All that unhealthy town life, all that shit with Terri. Getting buzzed in a smoky bar and going home to argue.

At the windmill, he climbed the ladder to the top of the tank and pulled off the lid. The water was to the top. He grabbed the length of hose that hung by wires from the ladder and slipped the end in. On the ground he sucked on the hose and gave himself a cold shower almost as a punishment, then shaved and brushed his teeth. Much better. Maybe the wounds were healing. He had a lot of toughening up to do. In flip-flops and wrapped in a towel, he went back up the hill and put on clean clothes. Jeans and black Sepultura T-shirt with the dates of their tour in red. That was one kick-ass concert. He left out more dog food and opened the gate to the water in case the cattle came around, and drove off down the road to Ganado.

CHAPTER TWO

▨ **NOLAN LIVED IN** a house in the public school compound—known as Smurfville because all the buildings were painted dark blue—the same house that Nolan's parents lived in when James still went to high school there. The early afternoon was hot, and the door yawned open into the dark hallway. James called in. "Hello? What's up?"

But James didn't know if Nolan had recognized his voice. He sat in the dim living room on the couch in front of the blank TV. His baby girl was lying asleep beside him. "Hey, dude." Nolan laughed, as if it were a funny thing to see James. Nolan had slimmed down a little from the last time James had seen him, but he still had to hold his arms away from his body as he got up. He grinned and the dimples appeared in both cheeks, the gold-capped incisor glinting. Old-fashioned pirate elegance.

"Hey. So that's her, huh?"

"That's her." She lay face up, drool on her cheek. "The Beast."

A few weeks after the girl was born her mother took off to south Phoenix where some of her friends and relatives rented a house and partied. This was just before the baby's first-laugh celebration, which Nolan hosted alone.

"You getting good at cleaning up messes?"

"Spit and shit and puke. It's not like I got anything else to do."

"No work?"

"Hah. I can't if I'm going to babysit. Mom says that since Dad and her are working it's okay." He shrugged like, *I hate to depend on them but that's the way it is.*

"She's cute. Sure she's yours?"

Nolan gave him a look. While the Beast emitted little baby snores in the dusky room, they talked about old friends, which led Nolan to bring out pictures of his band, Putrefaction, taken before one of their gigs in Albuquerque. Leon, Zendrick, Nolan, and Muzz posed in their black T-shirts with scowls on their faces, trying hard not to look lame. Nolan's old girlfriend, the baby's mother, was giving the photographer the finger. They could have been in high school.

"I miss jamming, though. None of us seem to have much time. We are playing out at Redrock . . ."

There was a knock, and a teenage kid James didn't know talked with Nolan furtively at the door. Nolan went to the back for a six-pack of tallboys and a baggie, and the kid gave Nolan some bills.

The baby was starting to wake. "So you're bootlegging?"

"Doing folks a favor, helps feed the Beast. Innit? You hungry, Beast?" She made a sound of discontent, and he handed her the bottle. He went to the kitchen for a wet rag and wiped off her sticky face. She grimaced and struggled against him. "Let's go out, baby. Feel like going for a walk, dude?"

"Sure, why not? See if anything's changed."

Nolan plopped the girl in the stroller and fastened the straps. "Nothing much has."

Out on the cracked pavement the bright sun hurt James's eyes. A skinny boy shot baskets in the playground at the corner. James asked if school was out.

"Yeah, school-out was last week. Got quiet pretty quick." Nolan steered the stroller around a pile of trash: candy wrappers, paper cups, newspapers, and sticks and leaves from the unpruned elms.

There was a crack in the sidewalk that James remembered from his many walks to and from school years ago. They were heading toward the elementary school, past the low brick buildings of the staff housing. He saw that two of the houses had been boarded up, plywood instead of windows. "What's with that?" he asked Nolan, who shrugged.

The Beast shrieked when they walked by a house with another baby in the yard about the same age, stumbling around the shabby grass while her mother hung laundry to dry: women's shirts, jeans, and baby clothes. "Oh, there's your buddy," Nolan told his girl, who was leaning over in the stroller, reaching, aching with reaching. The woman looked up from her clothespins and smiled slightly. She had shiny black hair that hung to the middle of her back. "Hey," said Nolan.

"Hey," she answered, not stopping her work.

James nodded to her, then laughed as the baby in the yard toddled toward them, fell, and quickly picked herself up with a grin. She had her hair tied in one vertical ponytail, which poked into the air then fell like a fountain. Another Navajo baby dressed for laughs. She waddled, impaired by her diaper, fell frequently, but recovered with a goofy kind of grace.

When he and Nolan had gone a distance he asked if that was Angie.

"Yeah. Put on some weight, huh?"

Angie was someone James always liked, even in elementary and middle school. Well, not always: there was that time back in grade school when he fought a bully named Hector, and all the kids circled around, and he swore he saw Angie cheering for Hector. She denied it later, saying she hated Hector. After that they were friendly. He rarely said anything to a girl in those days, but somehow she was easy to talk to, pretty, but not stuck up. Now she was a few pounds heavier than in high school, but not bad, still looking good in jeans.

"That's her little girl?"

"She's got *two* kids already, man. Her husband's in the service. Quick on the trigger."

What had James thought, that everyone he had known before would be frozen in time? That all the slender girls he had craved had stayed slim and single and unburdened by kids and all the rest of life?

"Ah, man. I love kids and all that, but I'm not ready . . ."

"Feel free to babysit any time you like," Nolan said. James laughed but Nolan didn't.

They walked from the school to Montoya's, where James said hello to his old boss, Mrs. Montoya. He'd worked here after school with broom and mop, scooping ice cream and renting out bad videos: *Mercenary Women I, Mercenary Women II.* He remembered it as a busier place, where he was always rushing around for something. The post office, too, was quiet, and the hospital, and the hospital housing. The whole town seemed empty, inhabited by ghosts, as if a neutron bomb had been dropped. Maybe it had always been this way, and he hadn't noticed until he'd lived for years in the city. "Not much going on here, is there?"

"Probably *something* is going on somewhere," Nolan said, "behind closed doors. You should go with us out to Redrock tomorrow, for the Battle of the Bands. Help us set up, get in free. There's supposed to be twelve bands."

"Right on," said James.

They walked back into the school compound, the baby's head lolling against the stroller.

They went behind the middle school where the concrete playground met the grass and the cinder track. On the edge of the concrete James looked for traces of Rodney's blood. It had started out the same way all those little arguments started out. Lennerd was messing with Rodney at the edge of the track, calling him a punk, and Rodney, finally fed up, pushed Lennerd. Rodney's friends and Lennerd's friends yelled at them. Lennerd took out his knife—no one had seen or expected it—and got up close to Rodney and stabbed him in the belly. When the knife was in, Lennerd pushed upward with a TV flourish. "How do you like *that*, motherfucker?" Rodney knelt down, held his belly, his arms pooling with blood. They had cleaned it, of course, ten years ago, but for months the stain remained. Still, in the little pocks and cracks in the concrete there was bound to be some microscopic trace of him.

A shiver went through James, starting as a giddiness in his stomach then descending to his testicles as a tingling.

"I want to go home," Rodney had said.

When they got back to Nolan's house, his mother was home. She was the one who had passed on to Nolan his chubbiness, darkness, and round cheeks. She had a great big smile on her face and James was afraid he might be in for some teasing. She shook his hand and said how good he looked. "As handsome as you are, you must be married."

He blushed despite himself and she laughed, that loud high laugh that could have come from a high school girl.

"How's your mom?"

"Fine. Still teaching school."

"And your dad?"

"Still being the principal. He's so busy I hardly ever see him. Sometimes when she's lonely my mom calls me up to come over."

Nolan's mother unstrapped the baby and lifted her as she woke up, head bobbing. "*Íłhoshísh, shinálí. Óoshínee'*. Nolan, we're going to have hamburgers as soon as your dad gets back. You better wash this baby; look at her face. We're going to a bingo at seven. He says he's going to be lucky." She laughed again, sighing at the end. "James, eat with us. Are you still working in Flagstaff?"

"Well, I don't know. I just quit my job."

"Why don't you move back here and become a famous musician? A rock star."

"Okay," James said. They laughed. "Actually, I was thinking about that."

Nolan gave his daughter a bath. Happy splashing sounds came from the bathroom while James helped Mrs. Begay make supper. He sliced onions and tomatoes. She patted the hamburgers with her chubby hands and started them sizzling in the pan. She told him, "You know, I'm proud of Nolan. I wasn't sure he was really going to step up to it and take care of his girl. You know how bad he got with the drinking. He was never as bad as *she* was, but I thought I might have to take care of the little one all by myself. I can be a grandma, but I'm too old to be a mother again to a little baby. But he's doing real good."

"Yeah, he seems to like her."

"He *has* to like her."

"The mother has to, too," James said.

"The crazy mother? *Hóla. T'óó diigis.* I don't know, I don't know."

James got back to his mother's house before dark. The eight miles of sandy road went up and down over the low hills, passing by several ranch houses where no one seemed to be home. A lone man chopped firewood at Repent or Perish, which was what was painted on the piece of plywood nailed to the long shade-house where revivals used to be held. Now his aunt's dogs were again barking, and the air in the house seemed stale with a faint smell of mouse.

He was glad he had seen people, eaten in company. Nolan seemed a little sad, encumbered and trapped, and his father, when he was there, never said much, but his mom was always sweet. What was it about these mothers that made them so nice, made them care so much more about other people than they seemed to care about themselves? For a moment he wished his own mother were there, thumping on the loom beside him.

Rodney would be what, now? Twenty-four? Not that it really mattered. There are a lot of ways to go. A slit in the aorta is one way. James wanted to go on. He didn't want to have to go back to that, over and over.

In Putrefaction, Nolan was the lead guitar, and his brother Muzz played bass. Their drummer Leon, another kid from Ganado, was the fastest drummer on the reservation. They had recently added Zendrick, a new guy from Fort Defiance, as second guitar, and he was catching on. Muzz lived in Gallup with his girlfriend Zella, who would sing a few vocals for them when she felt like it.

James helped load their equipment into Leon's van in Ganado. It belonged to Leon's father, who used it in his work as an exterminator. Nolan was always laughing at the logo on the door, a dead mouse with its legs in the air, and threatened to alter the company name to "Putrefaction Exterminators," so it would look more like the band's own.

They met Muzz and Zella at the stage at the state park. The sponsors hadn't finished setting up. There was trouble with the sound, the stage, the lighting. A nervous guy with a little mustache told them there was a problem with security and he didn't know if the show could go on. He kept lifting himself up on his toes, as if trying to see over people's heads. "Our insurance won't let us do it."

"What happened?" asked Nolan. "I saw a couple of rent-a-cops here just a few minutes ago."

The man made a disgusted face; his mustache twitched. "You did, huh?"

Just then Leon came around from the other side of the stage with a big grin. "These two security dudes? They get each other all pissed off, then the one dude shouts something about the other dude's girlfriend, and then it's cunt and whore and pretty soon they're down in the dirt whaling on each other. They're still going at it."

They walked to where a crowd had gathered. A patrol car swung in from the highway with lights swirling and the siren blaring its short whuurr. James and the band moved closer in. The two cops looked at each other and at the two other uniformed men still writhing in the dirt, and, after a brief hesitation, cuffed the security guys one by one and took them away.

At last the show started when two other cops showed up for security duty. James didn't see that there was much need for them; despite the publicity, there were only four bands. And the audience was sparse and unfriendly, almost all of them boys. There was too much space between them, and they weren't screaming. A mosh pit had been set aside, but nobody wanted to dive in. A little group of guys slam danced up by the stage within a perimeter of long-haired heads banging. Everyone else was just standing there. The outdoor setting was wrong. Without walls, the sound just drifted to the stars above, and the crowd spread out, with none of that feeling of belonging to a strong and angry tribe.

"I sort of expected a bigger turnout," James said.

Nolan's band was the last to play, and by that time James was bored. The third band had played every one of their songs in 4:4 with only three chords. He was hoping his friends' music would pick up his spirits, but they too seemed distracted. It wasn't something he could quite put his finger on, because they were playing together for the most part. Not great music, not much earning potential.

The music ended a little over three hours after it started. Then the sponsor with the mustache got up on the stage with his applause-o-meter and called out the band names one by one, announcing the level of applause that registered on the machine. "Now let's hear it for band number four, Putrefaction!" James and the band and the few of their friends and relatives who had come to support them made all the noise they could, but they wound up third anyway.

They filed into the Mexican restaurant that stayed open late and had good *machaca* and carnitas with nice big thin tortillas. The waitresses there generally treated even Indians nicely, though they knew Indians didn't tip well. By the time the food arrived they had all downed their first beers.

James asked, "You get any prize money for third place?"

"Nah," said Nolan. "Sometimes they have prizes, but with this one you have to go up all the different levels to California, and then if you win all the way to the top—that is, if you're the shittiest band of the shittiest bands—some label is supposed to sign you."

"These sponsors are so full of it, man," Leon said. "And do you believe that fucking applause-o-meter?"

"Yeah, next time we need to bring a crowd," James said. "Your parents, brothers and sisters, cousins . . ."

Leon said, his mouth full of enchilada, "That's always who wins! Or if you've got a chick doing vocals, man, even if the band completely sucks, or even if the *chick* sucks, the audience always makes more noise, like they're trying to impress her, you know?"

Muzz scowled at his girlfriend. "Yeah," he said. Zella had refused to sing tonight.

She slammed her beer glass down on the table, glaring at Leon. "Yeah, well . . ." she started. "I don't *completely suck* and I don't plan on embarrassing myself with this loser band." She switched her glare from Leon to Muzz and stomped out of the restaurant.

"Jeez," said James to Nolan, taking a chance. "You guys sure have good luck with your women, don't you?"

CHAPTER THREE

HE COULD BREATHE again, away from the city with its lights and sound, but here at the ranch his eyes could barely make out the ground by starlight alone. He fell asleep with the windows open, the cool night air smelling of the white evening primrose, and just before the sun came up he woke to the sound of a vehicle he recognized. Sunday. It was his cousin Max down at his aunt's house. James brushed his teeth and washed the *nák'eeshchąą'* out of his eyes, put on the clothes he wore yesterday, and ambled down the hill.

Max had brought a box of doughnuts and the Albuquerque paper, and wore his long Carhartt. They shook hands. Max's calluses made his fingers seem a little stiff. "Good thing you're here," he said.

"Why?" said James.

"We have to go check on the cows. Especially my mom's bull."

James should have known Max would put him to work—he always had some project in mind.

"You still remember how to ride a horse?"

James glared at Max. What an asshole. He could ride fine, and the runt knew it. Walked around like he was six feet tall, but with a hat to hide his thinning hair. A balding Indian, imagine that.

"So what do you want?" said Max. "You want a safe, slow horse, or a good one?"

"How about a safe, fast one?"

"You got a horse like that around here?"

"Nope. I got no horse around here, good, bad, safe, or slow."

They saddled up, James on Blackie, the black gelding who was born here, would die here, worked hard for his retirement. He stood patiently, but Max's roan danced around like a grasshopper. "So your horse is the good one?" James said. In spite of himself he admired the way Max made the spunky horse obey him, not letting his head up until he would stand still. Max had ridden saddle bronc in high school rodeos.

They headed out to the southwest, where the beige grassland sloped slowly, without fences, toward the purple smudge of the Painted Desert, where cattle often wandered toward the water that springs up at the edge of the Chinle Formation. James's horse kept tugging to turn back until they were out of sight of the windmill. They wandered slowly along braided cattle paths that crossed and recrossed the rolling plain. At the top of a low rise Max dug the binoculars out from the saddlebag and scanned the bottom of the shallow valley, where James could make out a few dots of cattle.

They let the horses drink at the first well, where the water was a bit too salty for people. The galvanized troughs sat a little unevenly on the ground and dripped from one corner onto a pool of gray mud. The stock tank stood about seven feet high above them, uncovered, so that when James grabbed the rim and pushed up he could see the little waves across the top. Someone had tagged the tank in several colors of spray paint, but whoever painted it was trying to be too fancy. He couldn't tell if it really said anything.

"We used to scratch our initials," said Max. "Kids these days."

The morning was still cool, but it was May, and the sky looked like the day was going to warm up. "I wonder if we're going to get any rain this year."

"Not for a while yet, anyway. We'll be craving it from now till when it does come."

They met the graded road, which curved down near the middle of the valley, above the sandy bluffs and the dry wash. On the soft shoulder Max got his horse to lope a ways. James's horse reluctantly followed.

Ranch houses and hogans dotted the way down the valley, but from the look and sound of it, none were occupied. The fences around the buildings were falling down. Dust from dry stock ponds blew away.

The horses walked side by side down the road. "I remember when people lived out here," said Max. "We would come riding by and all these little kids would line up outside of their houses and wave. Or run into their houses and hide. Most of the ones who lived this far out would hide."

Far in the distance James saw the dark point on the horizon that was called Pilot Rock in English, a piece of black basalt on top of the middle of the vast clay badlands. The horses seemed to feel the weight of the distance and the sun and the drought and dragged themselves along with their heads down.

Max dropped back to ride alongside James. "So, do you like being out here again?"

"On the reservation? It's nice."

"Is it? It looks run down to me. There's plenty you could do around the place, especially if you don't have a job."

He ought to have told Max, "Then how come after all these years you haven't done it?" Instead, he said, "Yeah, there is plenty to do. Everything is falling apart. Maybe I ought to just stay out here for a while."

"I could get some roofing and have you start on my mom's house, do all the buildings. You got other plans?"

"I don't know. I'm checking things out. So far things don't look so encouraging for me to stick around."

"I might be able to get you a job at the oil refinery."

"No thanks. I'm scared of burning up." There had been an explosion at the plant a year ago, five people killed. The newspapers and radio kept at the story until the last worker died four days later.

There was no point in telling Max about his hopes for his music, vague as they were, since Max didn't play anything and had basic country-western tastes. And there was no reason at all to talk to him about breaking up with Terri and the scarcity of women in these parts. It wasn't like he was going to take his advice about any of that: Max had had two wives and three kids and none of them would speak to him.

The ground was all sandy with mounds of clay and gypsum here and there, and soft and crumbly reefs of beige and white sandstone, ancient lake deposits. There were little groups of cattle spread out in all directions. They spotted a brown bull, but when they got closer they saw it was not theirs.

James said, "I walked around the school compound with my friend

Nolan, and we went by the spot where Lennerd Jones killed Rodney Kinlicheenie."

"Who? When was this?"

"You know about this," James said. "I was in seventh grade, and Rodney was kind of a friend. You don't remember?"

"So, what, like ten years ago? I would have been in Malaysia then."

"I knew him since first grade, but we were just getting to talk about things."

"Who killed him, another kid?"

"Lennerd Jones. One of those Joneses from Kinlichee. He was like a year older than Rodney but in the same grade."

"Jesus. Things were already that bad back then. Did you see it?"

"Yes," James answered, riding ahead. He did not want to choke, so he kept his eyes dry, his head up like a stone balanced on a pillar, and his thoughts on the little herd of cattle far ahead. From somewhere beyond these barriers came the memory of shouting to Rodney, "Teach him a lesson!" Like pushing his friend into the knife.

He got Blackie to lope a bit, and even to run a short way, and he felt better.

"What's your hurry?" said Max when he finally caught up.

Max's experience at the same school in Ganado was of a different time, over a decade earlier. James's first memories of Max were of him in high school, the quarterback, the pitcher, the cowboy. Styles were different. Almost everyone wore Wranglers. There were fistfights, not knives—no knives really until Lennerd. And Max was a different person from James. He wasn't half white, for starters. But he was kind of a middle-class kid for the reservation, similar to James, since his parents both worked at the boarding school. They sent him to the public school every day on the bus. They must have believed the boarding school wasn't good enough for their own kids, just for kids from families living farther out, away from the bus routes, maybe poorer.

Back in James's day, the cowboy types were dwindling and the slackers and headbangers were on the way in. Music got better.

Max was again in the lead, and had stopped and dismounted at the top of a low rise. From here to the west only two ranches remained in the valley before the emptiness of the desert. Max looked toward them with the binoculars. The first was Beebee's ranch, the last of a well-known family. The ranch farthest down the road was Chester's.

"Anything going on down there?" James asked.

"I'm looking for the bull. But somebody's sort of jumping around down at Beebee's."

"We could go by and ask."

"Yeah, we could. And they might tell the truth. I think it's Beebee."

A large man gesticulated in front of the gate.

Beebee's place was a quarter mile off the road, almost surrounded by elms and ailanthus shoots planted eighty years ago by his grandfather. As they rode up the drive, James felt the old resentments of his mother's family, which went all the way back to Beebee's grandfather, stealer of land, his house built with thick timbers hauled from the railroad by oxen. Beebee waved his hands in front of the gate. Max told James quietly, "Watch out for this guy." He needn't have said anything: James had heard the stories.

The man, Beebee, was easily six three and three hundred and fifty pounds, wearing two long braids Plains-style, and blue overalls. It did not seem possible that he could hop around so quickly and wave his arms so frantically. Was he signaling for their attention? Or was he trying to warn them off? Drunk or crazy?

Max and James stopped and waited as he whooped and shouted, "Hey! Hey!" making his way down to them, arms waving like blades on a windmill.

His nose was bleeding and his upper lip was cut through the middle, making him look like a giant rodent. James thought he heard him say, "It's in the tub!" Then he would jump and say "Hey!" again. One moment he seemed threatening, and the next he was simpering, as if begging something from them. He sat heavily on the ground and flung off his boots, exposing socks full of holes. He hopped up again and back into his boots, pointed toward the house, then ran over the hill still whooping and stomping.

James and Max looked at each other and laughed. They rode up the hill, but when they saw him cavorting in the direction of the wash, away from the house, Max said, "I'm not going after him." They laughed again.

They rode around the solid old ranch house, peeked in the windows, and saw nothing. Beebee's truck, which Max recognized, was parked under an elm with its door wide open, but there was no sign of anyone else.

"One of my friends in Ganado was an EMT," James said. "And he swears one night these guys showed up in a pickup, coming in the ER yelling about how the baby was just about to be born. They were laughing and drunk, but the emergency guys took them seriously and carried Beebee into the hospital—they had to use an extra-big stretcher. He was just about passed out, but groaning with all the jostling, and they had put him in a dress. With his braids and his shape, the doctors thought the delivery was going to happen right then. My friend said the doctor reached under the sheet and said, 'It's a boy!'"

They laughed. "I don't believe that," said Max.

"Me neither."

They rode back down the driveway and Max suggested they go to Chester's place and then if they didn't see anything, ride back. It was too hot, and the gnats buzzed around their eyes.

They were joking about Beebee all the way to Chester's. Max said he thought he had become a Christian and was speaking in tongues. "No, he's pregnant again," said James, "and in labor."

Chester was out beside one of his sheds, picking through a pile of old lumber and posts. James could see the pond below, the result of an earthen dam blocking several of the constantly flowing springs. Chester was older than both of them, a generation older than James, a small wiry man who spoke in a soft voice—nothing seemed to disturb his calm. He was his mother's cousin of some sort. He looked amused to see them.

Max jumped off his horse. He shook Chester's hand and called him uncle. James stayed on his horse and nodded at Chester, whom he had met only once or twice.

Max and Chester spoke for a while in Navajo and James drifted in and out, listening to their conversation. He kind of got the gist of it. His Navajo was never good, and he had heard much less of it these past six years. Eventually he heard Max asking about the bull, dóola, who hadn't been around for weeks, that maybe he had wandered over here.

"Hóla. Dóola doo kodi níyáada . . . Ákondi damóo yę́ędą́ą́' shį́į́ . . ."

Chester said that the bull hadn't been around, but a week ago . . . something about Beebee, but James didn't catch the verb, and his concentration faded. This was what usually happened in these Navajo situations: he just kind of turned invisible. After a while Max saddled up again and they said their good-byes. "*Hágoónee'.*"

"He said he thought he might have seen Beebee and two others up the road a little ways," Max told James, "loading up a bull. He said he wondered about it at the time, but hadn't seen the brand."

They were headed over the mesa on a slightly different route back home. In the east a thin line of clouds had gathered somewhere over New Mexico, without a hint of rain. Max was frowning.

"What are you going to do about that?" James asked. He didn't say *we.*

"I don't know. I'm thinking."

James's horse knew they were on the way home and picked up his pace. Before long they found themselves among a scattered herd of cattle. Two cow-calf pairs had James's aunt's brand. Max said, "I ought to come out here and get them. What the hell, I've got you here, let's do it now." He yelled orders as he rode, and the two of them cut the two pairs from the herd and headed with them back over the mesa.

CHAPTER FOUR

MAX HAD TO be at work at the refinery at six, and well before first light James heard him drive out, and then he fell back asleep. He got up around seven and made a cup of coffee, which he drank on the doorstep, facing the yellow sun just above the hills. The evening primroses were blooming over the ground like litter, still smelling sweet. A moment earlier he had not known what he would do today; now, because of some quiet change in his head, he knew he could not spend another day out here alone.

He needed to make music. He lifted his guitar from the cradle of its case and picked out the beginning of his old band's best song, and felt himself become calm and focused, like when he watched a flame or the flow of a stream. He gave the song a new flourish, perfecting it, and felt that he had done something worthwhile. It was ridiculous to believe that he had made the world better by a chord change. But it sure felt that way.

Often when James was in high school he would hide out in his room, Metallica and Megadeth glaring from the walls, making up songs on his black Ibanez. It was the only cure for a bad day: assholes messing with him or his friends, teachers scolding on and on. There was enough in his life, any day of the year, to make him want to shut it out—not with oblivion, but with the kind of transformation music makes: electrifying, then calming, soothing. Not that these words were on any of his favorite disc covers, or would ever be used to describe his own music, but there was the truth: even savage music charmed the beast.

He could fool around alone with his guitar and feel better, but to really make music he needed other musicians. And Nolan was the closest musician.

He ate a couple bowls of cereal with canned milk, which didn't taste as sticky sweet as he remembered, and had another cup of coffee. He washed up and noticed his hand eczema was worse after their ride the day before. He slathered on the only salve he could find, his father's Icy Hot, and was soon sorry he had, as his hands swelled with pain. He wiped it off with a rag, put on semiclean clothes, and drove back out to the highway.

He stopped first at the post office in Ganado, where he saw spray-painted in red on the cinder blocks of the building:

Minnie is a Whore

A couple of men were slouched nearby, smiling at the words and shaking their heads. He took out the mail from the box his parents kept there: smudgy colored flyers advertising sales in Gallup, campaign post-cards, missionary stuff. All junk.

Nolan was leaving his house. "Hey, James. I was just going to cruise over to Chris's. Let's take your ride. I can give Mom back hers." James stuck his head in the house and said hi to Nolan's mother, who was feed-ing the baby something yellow in a bowl. "So who's Chris?"

"Wasn't he your brother's kindergarten teacher?"

"Chris Soros? Is that guy still here?"

"He's renting my uncle's old hogan out by the lake."

The lake was actually a small reservoir with an earthen dam, once used for irrigation but now silting in, with a few good spots near the dam for catching bass. A light breeze ruffled the water and made it sil-ver. Above the far shore a gentle slope climbed to the base of the mesa. Here, in a little grove of cottonwoods strung with Tibetan prayer flags, huddled an old timbered hogan, and on a chair in front of it sat a guy in a dashiki and a blond sort of afro, scrubbing a length of pipe with steel wool.

Nolan introduced them and they shook hands. "I remember you," Chris said. "And your brother."

"I remember you, too," James said. "As Mr. Soros." He'd once asked him for two eggs his mother needed: calling into the house, smelling incense, hearing the rustle of things, seeing his girlfriend pull a sheet around her. "I didn't expect you to still be here. Actually, I heard you were driving around the country chasing Jerry Garcia."

"That was a great sabbatical year," Chris said. "But ever since then I've been here."

"Well, for a white guy you've stuck it out longer than most."

"This is the best job in the world. Sweetest company you could want." He meant his kindergarten students. James's brother Ben had loved Mr. Soros, and Mr. Soros was the reason Ben had loved school. He encouraged the kids to sing, draw, and tell their stories, and was always delighted. Ben had visited him in his classroom for years. James never had a teacher like that: all of his seemed to hate their students. So what if Chris Soros looked a little pathetic now, still teaching kindergarten, living alone out beyond the lake?

Chris put down his work and went into the hogan. "Come on in, I'll make some coffee." James followed Nolan in, and his eyes adjusted slowly to the dark. In many ways it resembled an old hogan occupied by Navajos: the small cloudy window, the dusted-over look to everything—the oil-barrel woodstove, the single bed, neatly made, with piles of blankets against the walls, the crooked dresser. On the other side of the stove stood a set of African drums. The bookshelf was loaded with paperbacks, and a string of exotic beads hung on the wall. He could hear his aunt say *yíiyá* because they were foreign and might mean witchcraft. Chris opened the little drawer in the dresser and said, "You guys for firing one up?"

He passed the joint to James. The smoke was strong and spicy, almost like hash. He felt his windpipe burning and knew he'd be wheezing soon.

Nolan sucked away as if there weren't enough smoke in the world for his lungs. He always did that, James remembered, like some Cheech and Chong parody.

James's question came out of the blue. "Hey, who's Minnie?"

"Minnie?" Nolan said.

"On the post office someone wrote, 'Minnie is a Whore.'"

Nolan laughed, and Chris said, "Again?"

They said it must have been Robert Tsinnajinnie, who had once before proclaimed his wife a whore in spray paint, the last time on the front of the hospital, where she worked.

Nolan laughed and said old Robert must have gotten drunk again. "He goes *off*."

Chris took them on a tour of his place, showing them the spot under the big cottonwood where he played his drums. He pointed out the sweathouse a little ways off and said he was thinking about fixing it up and using it. Most of the timbers were still there, silvery from decades of sun.

"My great-grandpa probably built that," Nolan said. "You don't want to use some old dead guy's sweathouse, man."

Back in front of his hogan, Chris asked James if he was still playing guitar.

"I play it, but I don't have a band anymore."

Chris looked at Nolan and Nolan looked at his feet. Chris said to James, "Why don't you play with these guys, with Putrefaction? They can always use another guitar."

"Hóla. Don't ask me."

"Of course, on the other hand," Chris said, "they suck."

"Hey," said Nolan.

"All that growling, all those constipated chords," Chris went on.

"Right, Chris," said Nolan, grinning. They had obviously covered this ground before.

James would have argued about music with Chris—what the hell did he mean by constipated chords?—but he was too stoned to make sense. He sat in his truck and waited for Nolan, who had gone into the hogan with Chris. Why hadn't Nolan already invited James into the band? Just so James could reply, "Nah, Putrefaction isn't that good." Or he might say, "Sure." Nolan should really ask him.

When Nolan came out of the hogan he was carrying a brown paper grocery bag folded over at the top, which he put at his feet in James's truck. Nothing clandestine about this deal.

"Peace," said Chris from the chair in front of his hogan. "Say hi to your brother."

"If I see him," said James. "He's in California." *A law student, going to be somebody, way beyond us losers.*

His little Nissan truck wasn't bad on gas, but unless he got some money he wasn't going to be able to drive from the ranch to Ganado whenever he felt like it. And since he had no place to stay in Ganado now that his parents were in Flagstaff, he would be stuck out at the ranch.

Luckily, Nolan had an idea how they could help each other out. Graduation was coming up and there was always a big demand. James had some time and could fit a lot of beer into the back of his truck. Nolan asked him to make a couple of runs and would give him two hundred bucks in appreciation.

Each time he visited Nolan he thought of dropping by Angie's, but he had told himself to avoid women, to protect himself from torment and misery. But what was the concern here? She was married and he probably wasn't her type anyway. So he dared a visit, rapping on the screen door. He found her ten-year-old niece Evangeline at the kitchen table working on a poster. A teenager was being flung high from a pickup, and the driver, with pointed ears and a grin like the devil, had a bottle in his hand.

"The school has a poster contest against drunk driving," Angie said with a smile. The baby was sitting on the floor below the sink, poking an unidentifiable plastic toy, or a piece of one.

The year that James and Nolan graduated from high school, one boy got killed and his girlfriend lost an arm. A classmate who had seen the accident said sparks flew from her severed humerus as she flew across the pavement. Some years there weren't any accidents, and some years several students suffered and died by the side of the highway. That's just the way it was. Kids always drank.

"Whoa," said James, looking over Evangeline's shoulder. "That's going to hurt."

"Of course that's going to hurt," Evangeline told him. "That's the point. He might even die."

"I guess if you're going to ride with someone who is drinking, you should wear a helmet. You could use that as the caption. 'Don't drink without a helmet.'"

She raised her eyes from her poster and stared at him with a puzzled frown. "You shouldn't."

James laughed. Angie, back to washing dishes with the baby clutching her legs, smiled and said to Evangeline, "He's just joking."

Evangeline frowned harder. "I bet you win first prize," James said.

"Nah," said Evangeline. "Mercy always wins. Her mom's a judge."

Angie dried her hands and turned to face him. "What have you been up to? You moving back here?" The baby let go of her mother's legs and sat down hard on the floor. This time she had two horizontal ponytails, both a couple of inches above her ears, each tied tightly with a pair of pink beads on an elastic band.

"Uh . . . temporarily." He felt his face getting hot, as it always did when he had to explain himself. "If I stay I'm going to have to find something to do."

"If you're here for graduation, why don't you help us out with the Fun Night? We have movies and games and we keep it open all night."

"I think I'm still too young to be a chaperone."

"No, you're not."

"Nolan was talking about needing me for something."

Angie gave him a hard look, and the vertical wrinkle between her brows pulled in a little brown mole that James had been noticing, and completely engulfed it.

"I can bet what that is. Did he say what he wanted help with?"

"Not really." He hated how hot his face felt.

Evangeline had capped all her markers and folded her hands. "He's a bootliquor," she said, staring straight at James.

Boy, they learn early to be bitches. They teach each other to be self-righteous bitches.

James didn't want to be anywhere near Ganado High School during graduation; it reminded him too much of his own, six years earlier. Why celebrate the culmination of four years of ditching and near-flunking? If he hadn't been forced by his parents to go, he would have skipped the whole ceremony. They said it might be the last graduation of his they would attend, meaning that they didn't really expect him to go to college. In fact, his grade-point average was too low for anything but community college, which sucked from what he had heard. Graduation was all bullshit. A couple of boring speeches by a couple of corrupt politicians, those idiotic gowns and hats, the gymnasium in late spring that made you gasp for air.

So on this graduation day James stayed out at the ranch, repiling dozens of old juniper fence posts and pacing off where he wanted the new horse corral to go, until the hills in the east turned magenta. Then, as promised, he drove out to Nolan's house.

Nolan intended to sell the booze out at the lake where the seniors held an unofficial bonfire. The officers of the Ganado Chapter had in the past tolerated this, even though there was always drinking, but this year they refused to sanction the event or contribute logs due to the pressure from the community. Nolan told him this as they drove out to the lake. "I don't know how it's going to be, cop-wise. We're going to have to look out."

"Nolan, if there's cops there, we don't sell," James said.

"It should be fine if we park a ways back." They found a place down the shore of the lake where they could see the glow of the fire, but the fire itself was hidden by the sandy hillside. No sooner had they stopped the truck than they had customers, three boys walking close together, laughing wickedly at some crude joke.

"You selling beer?" the smallest one asked in a loud voice. He looked about twelve.

"Not to you, tater," said Nolan. "If one of your older buddies here wants to buy, it's ten a six-pack."

"Tallboys?" asked the taller one.

"Just regular."

"Shi . . ." He never said the "t." What he meant was, *That's too much, but what choice do I have?* He dug a five out of his jeans pocket, and his brother brought out another. Nolan opened one of the two big coolers and handed them the six-pack of Lucky Lager.

"Shi . . ." he said again, looking at the label. "Don't you have Bud? Fucking rip-off."

"Look, you don't have to buy it."

In the next hour or so they made a dozen sales. Then the three boys who were their first customers came back for more. They were a bit wobbly and louder, especially the little one. "Fucking rip-off!" he said, but again they put together two fives and James handed them their second six.

The moon was just a bit fuller than half, and rode high in the sky.

The lake, a shallow reservoir ringed with reeds and cow pies, now looked magical, reflecting the silver light. The voices from the bonfire rose and fell, but they could make out no words. From someone's boom box came the uncomplicated bass of some country-western song.

"Have one," Nolan said, handing him a beer.

"I thought you didn't drink the merchandise."

"One won't hurt."

It bubbled down his throat and warmed his stomach. "It's beautiful," James said, and immediately thought that was probably the only time he had said something so gay to Nolan.

"Yeah, I love the moonlight," Nolan said, and James felt relieved.

They'd sold all the beer before eleven, so they headed home, driving by the bonfire and the roving teenagers, around the curve by the sandpit where a white Navajo Police van sat waiting.

"Whoa, just in time," James said, driving slowly.

Nolan laughed and slunk down in his seat. "You're almost always okay if you can finish your business by eleven. And there's going to be plenty of chances to do business."

James dropped off Nolan at his house. The house next door was dark and the curtains closed. Angie was at Fun Night. Nonalcoholic Fun Night.

After graduation, James did have plenty of chances to do business. He made bigger and more frequent runs to Gallup. People drank more in the summer.

James always went by himself, as Nolan was babysitting. He didn't mind the drive, but he hated Gallup, all run down, with big holes in the pavement. And look at this guy walking down the street, dirty pack on his back, in his thirties but with a scarred, greasy face peering around, a wise fool kind of grin, one side of his forehead lower than the other. White or Indian, his deformities made it hard to tell. What was James's true honest feeling about him? Contempt. White or Indian, contempt. He was supposed to feel compassion. Yeah, right.

It could be a tricky transaction at the liquor stores, to buy so many cases of beer and wine. There were ambiguous laws and occasional crackdowns. Not like Gallup didn't owe its existence to bootlegging.

The whole reservation had always been dry, and Gallup had always been wet. James knew to go to a smaller store run by a Mexican guy he and Nolan were acquainted with. He didn't ask any questions. They loaded it up together, put some lumber and a tarp over it. Then he was driving back past the huge piles of pulverized soil and rock and coal, across the pink reef at Window Rock, and then, when he began to feel his freedom, up the Defiance Plateau and into the big pines, back to thirsty Ganado.

There were big crowds at dances, ceremonies, and rodeos, and James stayed busy helping Nolan over several weekends. It was better entertainment than just sitting out at the ranch, trenching out the horse corral, doing little cleanup jobs around the place. Nolan said, "I appreciate having some muscle with me, because some of those guys will really get in your face."

They dealt the beer from James's truck, still with the tarp and lumber over it. Older guys bought wine and stood around in a circle downing it in a matter of minutes. James had to chase them away from the truck. Once in a while somebody would buy a pint of Jack. The twenties kept coming in, and they carefully folded them together. One after another—amazing.

Grandma sat at home with the baby. She never made a fuss about it, because she liked being with her only grandchild, but Nolan's father grumbled. "Shouldn't have had the kid if he couldn't take care of it."

James wasn't sure how much Nolan's parents knew about how he was making his money. He had his little dope business right there at home. "We just don't talk about it," Nolan said.

James spent some nights on Nolan's couch, but usually he drove back to the ranch when there wasn't anything going on, and tried to catch up on sleep.

On the Saturday morning after the bull was found dead, Max showed up with several rolls of roofing material. He balanced a roll on his shoulder and handed it off to James who stood on the edge of the roof. They rolled out each heavy one, then another, tarred them, and nailed them in.

"It's about time this got done," Max said.

It was hot, and they didn't do a lot of talking, but Max told him that two illegals had jackknifed the trailer they were hauling on I-40, spilling out Max's bull and several head of the neighbors' cattle, all killed in the accident. "They sent the guys back to Mexico. I wonder how much booze they gave Beebee for our bull. They found him asleep the other day on an ant pile near the chapter house."

James worked on the roofs for two days, even after Max left at noon on Sunday for the refinery. Now that he had satisfied for the time being the need for money, physical work seemed like the most purifying thing he could do. Even as a kid, he had liked joining his father and brother and cousins on various projects. He remembered the proud feeling of completing several miles of fencing. He always wanted to be the one who was the strongest, most enduring. His brother Ben did everything he could to get out of it. James swung the post driver when they made the fences, and Ben attached the wires to the posts with the triangular clips.

Now he was getting up early again, getting things done, feeling the sun on his back. He felt the power of the country, the solitude. Meadowlarks and horned larks sang their watery notes, doves gurgled and cooed, and the only mechanical sounds were the jets that crossed the sky high above, almost invisible except for the spiderwebs of contrails they left behind. From the roof he could see west toward the edge of the Petrified Forest, a maroon stain on the horizon.

Standing up and looking at the world from here made him feel strong.

Steve, the bass player in James's old band, Ataxia, had everything he needed, then decided he needed those drugs: tweaking out, raging at everyone, skinny and shaking. Was he dead yet, or had he found a way off that stuff? Mood was such a mystery.

Living near no one in the world, James was carried into loneliness and back out into another mental state, the lulled state of deeply rural people. He talked to the dogs, who had stopped barking and hardly noticed him. They too were hushed, country dogs, moving slowly from shade to sun and sun to shade. He moved the same way, his thoughts came more and more slowly, one day the same as another. He lost track. Was it Thursday or Friday?

What would happen if he were to spend the next several years out here? Slower and slower he'd be. He would look forward to trips to the store or to Gallup. He would reach the stage of subdued paranoia he recognized in his aunt, who told stories of *yee naaldlooshii* and their evil attempts, which made his skeptical hair stand on end despite itself.

His mother had said that no Navajo was free of the belief, deep down, in witchcraft. He had asked her if that was true of half-Navajos and she scolded him as she always did. "As if you don't have a clan. You're Navajo, boy, like it or not."

James told her he didn't believe in all that, but when he'd been walking around the school grounds with Nolan and remembered Rodney, he wondered again what had caused that little squabble to turn deadly. And wasn't there some trace of Rodney still?

The stories of witchcraft he had heard in a low but expressive voice, stories about evil that themselves suggested they should be left untold, but so fascinating they could not be resisted: these stories drew toward the hushed voices of their aunt and grandmother the heads of little James and little Ben as they sat at the kitchen table, propped up on elbows, silent but wide awake, their eyelids hardly blinking. Stealing babies, eating human flesh, powerful and evil prayers and songs, foul-smelling burned herbs fanned with raven and owl feathers. Skin-walkers with glowing yellow eyes, running at night alongside a person's pickup truck no matter how fast the person drove. Skin-walkers whose skins—wolf, coyote, fox, lion—took shape on their bodies almost perfectly down to the claws, with only an occasional flap of fur dangling. Skin-walkers who either died or killed you if you glanced into their eyes and recognized them. Skin-walkers exposed and defeated by the summer storms, when raging washes kept them from making their way home before morning.

It was as good a way as any to understand such things as what had happened to Rodney, who only wanted to go home, and to Steve, who had begun as a musician and ended an addict.

It was Friday, the end of the week, and the gray Chevy pickup coming down the road, pursued by a long line of dust, belonged to his father.

CHAPTER FIVE

▧ **HE STOOD ON** the doorstep, watching their truck draw close. His mother gave him a hug and he smelled her lavender soap. "How are you, dear? Are you getting enough to eat?"

His father laughed, and they shook hands.

"Yeah, I'm eating, but what have you got?"

At the table, James wolfed down two pieces of his mother's peach pie.

"Looks like you've been working around here," his father said. "I noticed all the junk piles seem a little neater."

"Mm. Max brought a whole bunch of roofing and I had to do something with it."

"Has your auntie been out here?" his mother asked, carrying James's plate to the sink and covering the pie with a piece of a flour sack. "Have some more if you get hungry. There's stew here, too."

"Nobody's been out here except Max. He says his old man has dialysis three times a week in Gallup, so she takes him there, sits in the waiting room while they run fluids through him. Max says he treats her worse than ever."

"I don't know what's wrong with her," his mother said, then laughed. "It must be true love. I brought a bunch of stuff that you probably need, things you said you didn't have room for when you left. You know I would have packed them for you then, if you'd given me a little more time."

"Did you bring any of my inhalers?"

"No. Don't you have any? Have you been wheezing?"

"Only when I run."

James hadn't told his parents he was leaving town until the day before he left, waiting that long, he told himself, to spare them worry, but he knew he also had in mind to spare himself the interrogations and lectures that his parents always thought were their duty to deliver, and that he was not spared anyway. At that point his mother had started packing boxes: towels, sheets, and cooking utensils.

His father, on the other hand, had seemed completely taken aback that he was leaving town to "hide out on the reservation." He wanted to know what had happened to his job, what had happened to his girl-friend—who, the last time he had heard, was thinking about moving in with him. He wanted to know how he planned on making a living, even in the short run. "And how come you never talked to us about any of this?"

"Dad, I'm not in the habit of discussing my private life with you." James still felt badly about the look on his father's face as he drank his coffee silently while James's mother scurried around loading boxes.

Now his father said, "We just thought we'd check up on you."

"Everything's fine."

"Just to see how you'd been in the last month. I'm glad to see you're doing your part to keep the place from ruin."

"Has it been that long?" James locked gazes with him with a direct, neutral look that he had learned sometime in high school. His father dropped his eyes and cut his pie into tiny pieces, then put them one by one into his mouth.

His mother said, "We heard from Ben the other day." Her face was skewed as if she had a toothache.

There was no point in trying to avoid what was coming. "Oh? What did he have to say?"

"He's in the *Law Review*," she said.

"What's that?" James asked. Like he would know what happened at law school.

"They publish articles on the law. I guess it's a big deal."

"It *is* a big deal," his father said. "Quite an accomplishment."

"Good for him." James didn't feel resentment toward his brother, who tried hard not to brag to him about his successes. Ben wasn't doing what he was doing because he wanted to be a big shot. What James disliked was his parents' tone, calculated to needle him, motivate him.

He also didn't like the tone of his own voice, because it sounded like he *was* resentful.

"He's working on an article on Native water rights," his father said. "What are your plans?"

"I've got to help Nolan out this weekend."

"I mean more long-range."

"I don't know, Dad. You're the long-range one. I don't like to make plans because I hate being disappointed."

His mother said, "Even us Navajos have to plan ahead *some*."

"Whatever."

His father said, "How long do you expect to be here before you find a job or go back to school?"

"I'll be here a while yet. I'm enjoying not being in town."

His mother asked, "What are you doing for money, honey?"

"I saved some up. And I do little jobs for Nolan now and then."

"What kind of jobs?" asked his father. It wasn't possible he knew anything about the bootlegging.

"Errands. He's the only one taking care of his baby."

"That's too bad. He seemed like a smart kid."

His father went out to his pickup and started to unload the cans of paint and varnish and brushes and tools. James came out to help him, and soon they were scraping and sanding the doors and window frames. The sun had blasted the varnish in the last couple of years. It was hot and very dry, the sweat drying into a band of salt on the crown of his cap, and the hours of the afternoon dragged on.

In the evening his mother warmed up the stew and made fry bread, which made James happy. "I've tried to make it," he told her. "But it comes out horrible. Lumpy, chewy, raw."

After supper his mother sat in front of her loom, strummed the warp to loosen it up, and started weaving. "Seems like every time I get a chance to weave, I end up undoing more than I do. I need to be here all the time. Or take the loom back with me. It doesn't make sense to weave a little every few weeks." She slid the yarn through the warp, flipped the batten, and he heard again the comforting *thunk thunk . . . thunk thunk* of the comb as she pounded it down.

As a child he had listened to her weave, and he remembered the peace that gave him, sometimes a kind of lullaby that would follow him in and out of sleep. He felt that pain in his heart, that sadness he tried to steer away from. But this time it had caught him. It said: *You will never again have a mother the way a child has a mother; you will never again know the peace of napping to the sound of her weaving; you will never be happy again.*

His parents went to bed soon after dark, but James read his piles of old guitar magazines in bed for hours into the night. It was interesting to look at these magazines from the early nineties, how styles had changed. It was mostly metal then, also, but the glam stuff, makeup and costumes, was more popular. Guitar solos were still allowed.

In the more eclectic *Guitar World* there was a retrospective issue on the sixties, with a photograph of one of the most ridiculous trios in history: Peter, Paul and Mary. The picture was from back then, when they were all thin and Mary's famous pathetic bangs were still blonde. Still, according to the article, performing! Performing where? Who bought tickets? Even his father wouldn't pay money to see these guys. James laughed at the thought of some dorky kid in this, the year 2000, with a taste for Peter, Paul and Mary. His father would probably be happier if James listened to that kind of stuff than to his own music on the edge of civilization. That possibility was long gone. James couldn't remember a time when his music was not different from his parents'.

By high school, headbangers outnumbered stompers, and concerts in Gallup and Albuquerque and Phoenix were packed. James had shrieked along with Napalm Death that he was an enemy of the music business, "You corporate fucks!" Cultural slime, that was his tribe, a paradoxical way of remaining pure. Since then, Napalm Death had turned pussy, but at least they wouldn't be invited to the White House.

Back in the days of James's first band, Ataxia, they were developing a sound that was starting to come together: fast, short songs with open chords but not tuned down, guitars playing percussion along with the drums. Their models were bands like Regurgitate, but toward the end they started adding layers to the rhythm, and it got almost Afro-Latin in complexity. Along with the grind-core kind of high-pitched, scratchy staccato vocals, it was a unique sound. James was just figuring out how to break out and solo a bit when Steve, the bassist, spun out into the tweaker universe.

Lying awake in the reservation night, quiet except for the occasional coyote yipping and howling as if he were a dozen, he could remember the exact feeling of making the music, of playing together. James played the primary rhythm in perfect synchrony with their drummer, then looked over at Steve while he echoed it. Steve, when he could still play at human speed and still looked like a human being. Not straying more than a third, so the chords didn't really matter, they did it again, perfectly together, then made the transition to double time. The quickness of his fingers, the intense concentration it required. The bubbling out of hell. The immeasurable injustice and violence by the masters of the corrupt world. The revenge on these masters, their bloody doom. They played until their fingers bled. Urgent, onrushing, unending crescendo.

On Saturday morning, near sunrise, James woke to the sounds of his parents working around the house. His room was just off the big living area, which included the kitchen. He heard his father scraping the paint from the door not far from his bedroom window, and his mother sweeping, the broom knocking on the sides of the walls. Boy, these guys were busy.

"I guess it's time for me to get up," he said to neither of his parents in particular. His hair was sticking up from his head.

"I'll make breakfast," said his mother, and put the bacon in the pan.

"I've got to get to Ganado."

"What?"

"I told you yesterday, I have to help Nolan run some errands in Gallup."

"You did?"

"You just weren't listening."

"Well, just wait a minute, I'll have this done soon."

James sat at the table.

His father looked like he was sulking. "I guess I can get this done myself."

"Well, gosh, we just got here, and we barely saw you," his mother said, putting orange juice and a slice of cantaloupe in front of him.

"I'll be back tonight, you guys. I can help you tomorrow, Dad. I'm going to get some screen doors, too, and we can put them up."

"That's fine."

"Oh, good, dear. Then we won't have to worry about the flies."

The cantaloupe was sweet, the bacon crisp and salty. Wonderful to eat his mother's food, if only it didn't come with the guilt.

"Bye, Mom."

James had driven past the windmill and the corrals before he remembered his guitar. There was a chord sequence he was working on that used a lot of open strings, much richer than the original, and if he ended up waiting around in Ganado or Gallup, he wanted to be able to work on it. So he turned his truck around. His father was already taking a walk on the hill behind the house, and he waved. His mother was still standing with her broom.

"Forgot my guitar."

"You ought to just leave it hanging around your neck," she said.

Back out on the road, past the corrals, the far fence, and up into the hills, he was alternately feeling angry at his parents and relieved to be out of there.

It was harder to stay mad at his mother. He could stay mad at his father for days, weeks, years.

When he and his brother were growing up and there was some disciplinary matter (cigarettes, beer, sneaking out at night), their parents acted completely differently. His mother would lecture James the way she had been lectured when she was young. After she was through with one lecture she would give it again at a slightly higher pitch. She worried so much that she sometimes hyperventilated and had to use a paper bag. She worried about the trouble she assumed the boys were in, worried that they did not have everything they needed, that they hadn't eaten enough. She worried about witchcraft. She sometimes enlisted her older sister to reinforce her messages.

His father, on the other hand, would keep asking questions no matter how surly, evasive, or untrue James's answers were. "What did you think you were doing? Did you think we wouldn't find out? Who were you with?"

When the boys were in high school their father hammered at them about going to college. Ben liked school, did well, spent summers in special academic programs, and said all along he was going to college and beyond, maybe to be a scientist or a lawyer. All James had tried to do in school was to get through it in one piece. His father hammered away at him even more when it was clear he didn't have to hammer away at Ben. "I'm not college material," James told him.

His father had asked angrily, "Why do you have such a low opinion of yourself?"

"I just have a low opinion of college," he said.

"What do you plan on doing, then?"

"Maybe trade school."

"What, you want to be a welder or a plumber on the reservation? Where everyone is a welder and a plumber?"

It still made James mad to think about it. And who asked them to come out to the reservation and interrupt his life here? It may be their house, but he was the one living in it. He thought they should respect his privacy. But that wasn't like his parents to do; they never considered it. He tried to think about what he had wanted six years ago when he'd moved from here, finished with high school, not sure how to live on his own. He remembered when, a few weeks after he had found a place in the Sunnyside neighborhood, his father knocked at the door. He almost banged his head on the door frame coming in; the house had been built in the fifties, with many violations of code, like the six-and-a-half-foot ceilings, and it crouched between a taxidermist and a body shop. "I just wanted to see your place. It looks like a chicken coop." From two doors down, babies cried and toddlers yelled. They sat in the backyard on upside-down paint buckets under a huge unpruned elm and caught the smells of masa and menudo and the eager sounds of kids shooting baskets and learning to rollerblade. A car crept down the street, its superwoofer rattling the back window. They heard odd whistles, like birds or chipmunks.

"It's a code," James explained. "I don't know if it means 'cop on the block,' or 'meth for sale,' that kind of thing."

"You can hear just about everything from here."

"In the afternoons, if I get off early, I can hear the kids on their way home from school, letting out their stress. On the weekends, there's a big party house just down the street: loud music, I mean rowdy. Firecrackers, sirens . . ."

"At least it's lively," his father said.

"More than lively. Right across the street the couple is always yelling threats at each other, every day, worse on the weekends. Sometimes the cops show up. It's a regular routine. I swear one day they're going to kill each other."

"Jeez, James, maybe you should move back in with us."

"Nah. The neighbors don't scare me. They look like me. It's the cops I don't like. See, I 'fit the description.'"

That had always been a big part of the problem with his father: he was white. He looked at certain things with those blue eyes and saw something James didn't see. Or, he thought more likely, did not see what James could.

At Repent or Perish the retarded guy with Coke-bottle glasses was chopping wood, and he waved back at James. This made him feel better.

CHAPTER SIX

▨ **AS RAY WALKED** down the hill to the house where his wife was sweeping, the day already hot and dry, he was thinking that he had been living in northern Arizona a long time. You get tired of the place this time of year, before the rains come, when the cheatgrass is dry and spiny, and you think about moister places like the Oregon coast. When he first came out to the reservation after getting his teaching certificate, he thought the job in Ganado would last a year or two. He had wanted to do something exotic before going back to Tucson or some other normal city. After a youthful adventure, back to a regular job, a regular life, where he wasn't an Anglo, a *bilagáana*, but just a regular person. It wasn't his plan to stay on the reservation for so long, to fall in love with Rosina, to become a part of the place, or almost a part of the place.

The cloud of dust from James's truck still lingered in the air over the road after he had disappeared across the hills. His son was gone again.

It wasn't something he had really intended, staying here, then having the boys and watching them grow year after year. They were from the start really a part of the place, he believed. Maybe if he had sat down and thought hard about it beforehand he could have predicted the kind of grief he would later feel, and this might have changed everything, but perhaps not. Nobody's life goes completely according to plan, and everyone knows better after they've been through it.

It took him a long time to begin to realize what he had set his kids up for.

Ben was seven, probably. Ray had seen them walking his way a few yards from the house late one afternoon on a school day. James had his arm around his younger brother, his head leaning into him, talking softly. Ray thought maybe James had made him cry, the way it happened sometimes when James pushed too hard, but Ben was walking along compliantly, with tears down both cheeks but an expression indicating that he was listening.

"What's wrong?"

Sniffling, Ben said, "They think I'm a bilagáana."

"I'm gonna beat his ass," said James, slamming his fist into his left hand.

"Who?"

"Lennerd," said Ben, the tears falling quietly but more rapidly.

"Ben, did he hurt you?"

"He hurt my feelings."

"I'm going to beat his ass," James said.

"No you're not," said Ray, his hand on James's shoulder. "No fighting."

"Yes I am. Or they won't stop."

The schoolkids had all kinds of stupid taunts, like *bilagáana bilasáana bił łikan*, which only meant *white people like apples*, but it was cruel and poetic. When they all talked about it later Ben explained that he wanted the kids to understand that he was Navajo, and Ray didn't know what to say.

The kids don't leave once; they leave again and again. Ray had watched from the hill as James walked back into the house and out again with his guitar. There was some self-consciousness in his gait, some slight stiffness as his upper body swayed from side to side that presented him as a challenge, a dare, even among his own family. Then he was gone again. Ray walked down the hill back to the house to resume scraping the old paint from the door. "I guess I have to do this by myself," he told Rosina, who was mopping the floor.

"Oh, he'll help you when he comes back tomorrow. And it'll be nice to finally have screen doors."

"Yeah." James did contribute. Hadn't yet made up for Ray's changing all those wet and dirty diapers, but slowly he was repaying them. He was smiling at Rosina and she was smiling back, knowing more or less what he was thinking.

"Well, he's got his own life," she said.

"Out looking for a girlfriend, no doubt."

"Well . . ."

James didn't know what he was looking for any more than Ray had. Ray had just known what he liked, which was the way Rosina looked, the way her skin felt, her sweetness and easy laugh. James would probably fall the same kind of way, and who could say if it would be a good thing or not? Would his own bizarro kids have been happier 100 percent white in some white town?

You could only take that guilt and regret so far, because to undo it you would have to sacrifice a person, two people. Wrongful life, they said, was a claim unrecognized under the law.

He had done everything he could to make them comfortable in both worlds. First-laugh ceremonies, salt in their little hands from the Great Salt Lake. Language classes after school. And they were proud, never ashamed. Both of them stood there and said my mother is Navajo and my father is white. Said their mother's clan in Navajo and that they were born for a white man: *bilagáana bá shíshchíín*.

A year or two later Ben was laughing about how one of his friends asked him which half of him was Navajo. Couldn't stop laughing.

Yet it was never easy. That day when Ben was in the second grade, James in the fifth, his face no longer the face of a little boy, now holding a new kind of toughness that he would never lose. Pain and toughness. Ray wanted desperately for his son to be that boy again whose default expression was a smile, who loved to laugh.

But that boy was gone, just as James the young man was gone now, leaving his father to repaint the woodwork in his house. Little splinters of the off-white paint stuck under his nails as he peeled it with a scraper, and it stung a little. Rosina walked out on the doorstep and swept the paint flecks into the dustpan.

"I should weave him a belt so he can keep his guitar strapped to him."

"He'd sleep with it if he could."

If they weren't talking about their children they rarely talked. After Rosina was done with the floors she banged around some in the kitchen then settled down at her loom. That was a noise Ray didn't mind.

He liked his house. They had it built fifteen years ago, when the kids were in school. It was one of the first passive solar houses on the reservation, and it worked: warm in the winter, cool in the summer, lots of light. It taught you how the sun moves. You thought you knew, but this made it clear. It was kind of a dream of theirs to live there full time someday, but of course that was impossible. Too far from everything. The family had used it on weekends when they lived in Ganado, and now James was living there; Ray hated that it had been empty so much of the last six years since they had moved to Flagstaff, but it wasn't the only empty house. All over the reservation the land was being abandoned. People left the beautiful country for rented cinder-block houses in the population centers, all alike in double semicircles, and let their sheep camps decay. At least they were out there now, trying to keep it together, scraping the paint, assembling the pipes of the scaffold.

Fifteen feet above the ground, he sat on the plank in the scaffolding and sanded the skirting and repaired the disjointed gutters. It was hot and dry, but a little breeze dried the sweat from his forehead and temples and it was nice sitting up there looking out over the valley, daydreaming. By the afternoon there was only the slightest buildup of clouds in the east, and far to the end of the valley in the south he caught a sense of movement, then a momentary glitter of metal or glass, then the rise of dust above the road.

"Thelma's here," Rosina said. As she neared the house in her pickup he climbed down from the scaffolding and washed his face and hands. He shook hands with his sister-in-law and sat down to coffee with the two women. Thelma was at least five years older than Rosina, almost a different generation. Bigger, grayer, less comfortable in English.

"Did you come from far?" Rosina asked Thelma in Navajo. It was a formal question, almost a joke. Rosina knew where she had come from.

"From far," she answered, smiling. She used the locative that meant out of sight, and then said in accented English, "Way over there, the Gallup."

"How's Merwin?" Rosina asked, actually saying *hastiinshą́*, meaning, *How's mister?*

"*Haa shį́į́ yit'é hóla.* I don't know how he is, or, however is he, or . . ."

"He still going to the hospital all the time?"

"Monday, Wednesday, Friday. It's supposed to be four hours, but you got to sign in, and get blood drawn, and something always goes wrong. It's always three in the afternoon when we get out, and I'm too tired to do anything else. And he's all woozy and weird and sleeps the rest of the day if he isn't talking crazy or cussing me out. Then the next day I'm so tired I don't want to do anything."

Ray got up from the table and took his cup to the sink. He wanted to hear about Merwin, but he wanted to be doing something. In-laws really weren't supposed to be lazy. White in-laws, especially. So he sat on the floor of the kitchen and sanded the baseboards while they talked.

"Is he any nicer than he used to be?"

"Oh, he's still a grouch." Thelma used the word for coyote. "He's worse. The days between dialysis he's really mean. You'd think he would be grateful for me driving him around and sitting with him reading torn-up magazines in the waiting room while they wash out his blood."

"Merwin . . . not grateful, no."

Ray sanded, losing himself somewhat in thoughts of Merwin, who was a bastard, always. Years ago he would tease James to the point of crying. Ben wouldn't even talk to him. Ray had wanted to fight Merwin for that but held back his fists and his tongue because he wanted to teach his kids nonviolence or at least control of anger. But it was hard; it wasn't even clear to him that this was the correct thing to do. Even considering it now, it seemed right to challenge Merwin rather than let him get away with it. Calling the boys "little white men," telling James his brother was a baby for wetting the bed—when Ben was three!

Ray had to cut out another strip of sandpaper and attach it to his block, and by the time he got back to work they were talking about Thelma's son Max.

"I told him to get a job somewhere safer. He said all refineries are the same. There's no safe place to do what he does."

"Did he actually see those five guys get burned up?"

"I don't know. I don't think so. He talked about manhole covers being blown way up in the air, and being scared, but he didn't say he saw anyone die." She used the word *manhole* in English.

The English words were important to Ray; they flagged the conversation for him, brought him back at least to the general subject. Ray wanted to make sure he understood, so he asked Thelma, "Somebody died where Max works?"

Rosina answered, "I read about it in the *Navajo Times*. One of them was a Navajo. It didn't get into the paper in Flagstaff."

"James was talking about going to work over there."

"He better not," said Rosina, as if that put an end to that.

"That's what I tell Max, too, but he won't listen. Seems like anywhere there's danger, that's where he wants to be. Now he's messing around trying to find cattle rustlers."

"People are always stealing cattle," Rosina said.

"It's different now. Did you hear about that wreck they had on the interstate?"

"We never hear anything."

"I don't know if they know who's behind it. There were dead cattle everywhere. Lots of brands from around here."

"Someone hit a cow?" Ray asked.

His wife clucked at him. She meant, *Don't you hear Navajo anymore?* "A big truck full of stolen cattle turned over."

"Who?"

"Some Mexicans," Thelma said in English.

"She said they don't know who's behind it," said Rosina. "*Yáadilá.*"

Ray no longer felt excluded in these conversations: he understood enough Navajo to follow along in a general way, and Rosina would translate as needed. Thelma usually wasn't actively trying to hide anything from him. But his concentration would also fall away from time to time and he often found himself following his own thoughts instead of the conversation. He had noticed his sons doing the same; as much as they had wanted to give them the language, the boys didn't have much more than Ray did.

He stirred the brown paint and climbed the scaffold again. It brushed on smoothly, like thin melted chocolate. He saw Rosina and Thelma walk down to Thelma's house.

Merwin. Baby Merwin.

Ray remembered his own babies, James and Ben, how he would have killed anyone who tried to harm them. When they had grown some it was still his job to defend them. He told the idiot Christian teacher who warned them James might be susceptible to Satanism to back off. Then when James got into his teenage trouble, when he was wrong and even dangerous, and even now when he was an adult and had to answer for his own mistakes, James was still his son, and if Ray weren't there on his side, who would be?

Yet there was a limit to how long you had to remember that a person had been a child. Like Merwin, Thelma's sick husband. The first time Ray had met him he was already a hairy-bodied, bald-headed, sarcastic, selfish middle-aged man, decades past the time when he was a child anyone felt tender toward. It no longer mattered that he had had no mother to love him in spite of himself, to shield him from the teasing, the beating, the insults of his aunts and in-laws. At some age—was it seven, or twelve, or twenty?—the guy had to stand on his own, not as a child to be pitied but as a man who had earned respect, or not.

Not Merwin. He would never get over being motherless, feeling that he deserved every tiny bit of sympathy, every gesture of esteem he got and more. Never enough. So he became a tyrant, ordering around his wife, bullying Max and his other children.

The only pity Ray could feel around Merwin was for his victims. No longer for him. What they called the cycle of abuse was actually a seesaw: victim became perpetrator, the pitied became despised. Now he was dying, hooked up to his dialysis unit, and Ray wasn't sorry.

He didn't think Thelma was sorry, either, and he didn't know why she put up with him at all, let alone sat with him three days a week, hauled him around, fed him. It was good that she was here visiting with Rosina, free of Merwin for a few hours at least.

By sundown Ray had put the lids back on the paint cans and washed the brushes. Rosina walked up the hill as Thelma drove back down the road. Still James had not come home.

"Should I cook for him?"

"I don't know. It's kind of late. He might come home tonight."

"I hope he doesn't," Rosina said.

"I hope he does."

"I don't want him driving at night. There are all those drunkards. And horses."

"And yee naaldlooshii." Ray was always teasing Rosina about skin-walkers because, despite what she said, he knew she believed in them.

"I'm not worried about anything stupid. I'm just worried about all the real things I ought to be worried about."

"What good does it do to worry?"

"I *am* worried. He's my baby."

It was late. The stars were turning. He switched off the light and fell asleep, or very close to it, then woke up fully as Rosina tossed her weight violently from side to side.

"What *is* it."

"Can't sleep. They say that happens when you get old."

"I thought you were supposed to worry less about your children when you got old, when they got older and wiser."

She flipped loudly onto her side facing him. "I *wish* they got wiser."

He kissed her forehead and laid his hand on her thigh. Older, but still with skin like silk.

"What can you do," he said in a mock Navajo accent. This was old with them: one of the old-timers at the school had said this. "Tell 'em once, they don't listen."

"Tell 'em once, they don't listen, *t'áá 'aaníí*. There might not be a thing I can do, but I still worry."

"He'll be okay." The moonlight was bright, not shining directly on them, but it had risen, two or three days after full, and they could see the whole valley from their bed.

"Why does he always make life so hard for himself? Why can't he be like Ben? Maybe then I would drift off as soon as my head hit the pillow." She was sitting up now, looking out the window.

"He's a test for you," he said.

"Yes he is. He's nice looking, he's strong, he can fix things, he can be really sweet . . . but his temper! Where did that come from?"

"Not me."

"That girlfriend of his, Terri, not that she was the right kind of girl. Turning over a table, throwing things, breaking dishes."

"He didn't hit her."

"Thank God."

"He wouldn't have hit her. He probably broke all those things so he *wouldn't* hit her."

"Who said it was okay to break things?" She turned her back to him. He thought he might try sleeping again, but just as he drifted off she laid back down, facing him. "Why is it always me losing sleep? Why can't you do your job of half the worry about our son?"

"Lord have mercy."

They waited all day on Sunday.

James was always leaving. The way he left town six weeks ago without telling anyone, without giving anyone a chance to talk him out of it, to tell him he was trying to run away from his troubles, hiding out on the reservation. But Ray had already told him that.

Maybe he had angered James. Maybe that's why he wasn't coming back. Rosina suggested that.

They had mentioned Ben. James always said he wasn't envious of Ben, but they had to be careful.

Rosina showed Ray the photograph that was among the old stuff she had sorted through at Thelma's the day before. James was five, his arm around his little brother, facing each other, their heads close, both smiling. James must have been giving him some sage advice, and Ben was listening, trusting and curious.

Rosina cried. "I have all this food."

It should have been a long weekend with the Fourth on Tuesday, but Ray had scheduled a meeting with the superintendent on Monday.

He had brought two more Library of America books he thought might interest James: Henry David Thoreau and Thomas Jefferson. He left them on the shelf.

They waited until sundown on Sunday, and then they left.

CHAPTER SEVEN

 NOLAN WAS GIVING his little girl a bath, and through the open door James heard the happy splashes and wheezy squeaks of a rubber ducky. He waited on the living room couch looking at someone's *American Horseman*. Bored with ads for boots and dewormer, he got a *Guitar* from Nolan's room and checked out pictures from the latest Ozzfest.

"Hey, Nolan!" The baby was screeching happily and slapping the water. "One thing I noticed about your band: nobody's got a single piercing or tattoo."

"Our moms won't let us!" He carried the chubby girl into the living room wrapped in a towel, beaming, and for a few moments, clean. "Muzz got a temporary tat for this one concert."

"You mean like those ones we used to get with bubble gum?"

"Oh, man, they're way better than that. Covered his whole shoulder. He looked like James Hetfield. I don't know, I thought it sort of messed with our image." He carried the baby into the bedroom to dress her. "I mean, we're Indians. It's not like we should *aspire* to be redneck bikers, you know."

"So what's the plan, exactly?" James asked. He grabbed the baby's cheek with his thumb and first finger and she smiled broadly at him. Babies, such an easy shot of love. "The Beast!"

"Well, just the usual run. Here's a list. And I've got an amp waiting for me at the music store. I'm going to give you the cash for that, too. And Chris Soros wanted to know if you could pick something up for him. A guy has a pound for him."

"Why doesn't he pick it up himself?"

"His car won't run. You don't have to if you don't want to."

Nolan was daring him to back out. "I guess I don't mind. But I don't know this guy. How's he going to trust me?"

"Actually, it's the guy that works at the music store. I'll just let him know you'll pick it up with my amp. Just watch the baby and I'll be back in a few minutes."

Nolan took off in his mother's car, and James walked the Beast over to Angie's house. As long as she clutched his finger firmly she was steady on her feet. She had a strong grip.

Angie was sitting on the couch with her own baby, struggling to cut her nails, while a kid's wordless video played, some boxy little robots that tooted and whistled and sighed.

"Hi," Angie said, bunching up the Kleenex where she'd put the little nail clippings, and carefully took that and the scissors to another room. The two babies started to squawk at each other.

"What are you up to?" she asked, sitting back down on the couch next to him. She was wearing a sleeveless top. On the top of her right breast was a little brown mole like the one on her forehead.

"Just about to drive to town."

"Flagstaff?"

"No, *town*, Gallup. That's funny, isn't it, that town is always Gallup."

"Like that kitty-cat joke. A guy drives up to a hogan and no one's there so he asks the cat where they are. '*Toowwn*,'" she purred.

"'What for?' '*Wiiine*,'" he finished for her. It was an old joke.

"That's probably what you're going in for—more bootleg supplies."

"No, not just that," he said, trying not to sound defensive. "Got a bunch of errands. Some doors for my mom's house, over to the music store . . ."

"And the booze. You know, I was thinking what Gallup would ever have been if there wasn't such a thing as alcohol."

"Wouldn't be there," he agreed. "Look, I know you don't like drinking and bootlegging, and I'm sure you're right . . ."

"I just can't stand it. My husband . . ."

James felt a wave of pity, or protectiveness. He waited for her to continue, then realized she wouldn't on her own. "What about him?"

"I just hate him when he's drinking. I dread when he's on leave."

James waited a while more, then said carefully, "I don't know him. Is he from here?"

"Fort Defiance." Nolan's baby had found a string of plastic beads and Angie's baby was trying to take it away from her. "No, it got to where I really couldn't stand him. When he's at home all he does is pick fights with me and everybody else."

"Where is he now?"

"Korea."

"Nolan says you have an older kid. Where is that one?"

"She's with my sister in Shiprock. Evangeline's mom."

She wasn't crying, but she was quiet and looking hurt, and that was why he put his hand on her shoulder and patted her. It felt like a dangerous moment to him: she might have shrugged off his hand, or told him she wasn't interested, but what she did was smile. A little smile.

Across the room Angie's baby was swinging around the plastic beads, throwing drops of water all over the room. "What is she doing?"

Angie stormed up and took the beads away. "*T'óó diisha'*. You're bent," she scolded. "She's always dunking things in the toilet."

James laughed and, picking up the Beast, said, "I better go. So you think I should tell Nolan to shove it?"

"It's up to you."

"I promised him this time. Then I'm out." He realized he really meant it, didn't want to be in this shit anyway. Angie was watching him, and he wanted to look respectable.

Her baby was crying, angry at being scolded. "There are better things to do," she said.

"Well, I'm working on finding them."

Nolan handed James a fat envelope from Chris and asked if he wanted to fire one up for the road. "No, I don't like to drive when I'm stoned. I get too distracted." He already felt edgy.

"This is supposed to be some boss weed he's got coming in."

He wished he could back out of it. "So, is it the Mexican guy that works over at the music store? He knows I'm coming in for it?"

"Yeah, you kind of know him, right? Just tell him you're picking up the amp for me, and give him this cash, and you're out of there. Oh, hey, you want to borrow the Cephalic Carnage CD?"

"Sure. You know, you guys should try out their style of vocals." He imagined one guy doing Cookie Monster and the other some grind-core kind of voice.

"I'll tell Zella what you think."

"Zella. What a bitch. Well, guess I'm off."

After the long patch of sage-flat above Ganado he was back in the pinyons, and then the ponderosas. All around here were places he had gone with friends and family, picking pinyon nuts, cutting firewood, hiking into and out of those narrow canyons, little frog pools up and down the washes, ravens calling and squawking overhead. He should take a day or two off and come up here, just to walk. At the summit, his eye glanced down toward Manuelito, as it always did, and toward the huge-ass sandstone reef running thirty miles between Hunters Point in the south and the old sawmill in the north. Gray and black heaps of coal and earth and rock lay like giant turds the big cranes and earthmovers had left. In the beat-up semiurban stretch between Saint Michael's and Tse Bonito stood two huge man-made mesas of turned earth and rock. The mine was as proud as a toddler of his pot of shit.

Now he was off the reservation, and, as the traffic from the north joined his route, was pulled into the core of Gallup toward the banks and the courthouses and the bars of the stone-front downtown, as if caught in a spiderweb and tugged toward the center. The outcroppings here were a pale yellow sandstone, with streams and dribblings stained deeper, like piss. Ever since first grade he had thought for some reason that these rocks were radioactive. As he drove toward the center of town, the pawnshops and trading posts and gas stations became less isolated, and pedestrians walked on the broken sidewalks and footpaths through the weeds. Cars, pickups, trailers, and semis all competed on the highway. There was energy here, plenty of human movement, and plenty of money, often as crumpled small bills in dirty pockets, but these were eventually stacked in the vaults of the pawnshops and supermarkets and sent in armored cars several times a day to banks in Albuquerque. Angie's question: was Gallup even possible without alcohol?

He pulled into the Fina station to fill up. There was a "trading post" attached to the station, really a gallery of rugs and jewelry and other crafts. James saw a couple get out of a long gray Lincoln with California plates. It looked like they didn't really need anything from inside: his shining white hair bulged out from under a big hat with a sterling band, and the turquoise in his belt buckle and bolo tie were as big as Frisbees. She was thin and long, with the same sheen of silver hair down to her shoulders, and her face seemed to have been stretched tightly from ear to ear, making her pores oval. She seemed too skinny to be able to stand beneath the weight of her squash-blossom necklace and massive turquoise bracelets. All hat and no cattle, but they didn't seem to care if anyone knew that; they certainly weren't shrinking from view. Yet as they blinked in the light and looked around, James could imagine them thinking, *There's nothing here but dirt.*

His first stop was the lumberyard. He had a scrap of paper in his pocket with the dimensions of the doors for his mother's house. Now that the weather was hot, he wanted to be able to open the doors without letting flies in: flies that started out fat and slow but would gradually get cagey and even fatter, and would learn to avoid flypaper and flyswatters, and might some quiet day actually drive him crazy. He knew from living deep in the country that flies can put a person over the edge.

On the side of the warehouse two white boys, about twelve years old, were throwing rocks into the weeds of the neighboring vacant lot. From behind the warehouse a middle-aged Indian man walked, somewhat unsteadily, in the boys' direction. One of them, stones in hand, stood on top of a low stack of railroad ties, his strawberry hair sticking up in whiffs around his freckled face. "Ya-ta-hey!" he screamed, mispronouncing the Navajo greeting. The man kept walking, determined but staggering, and muttered to the boys, "*T'áadoo biniiyéhígóó doo jidilwosh da,*" don't shout for no reason. This sent the boy into a fury of mockery as he shouted nonsense syllables at the man. His friend also tried his tongue at imitating the language. It seemed strange somehow that they didn't even understand the man's simple words. They were ignorant and should be walloped.

After loading the doors from the warehouse he noticed a black cat slinking around, reminding him of Terri, ass up against the post holding up the second-floor balcony. He hissed at her and she slithered away resentfully. For a moment James was troubled again with the thought of Angie. He would be better off staying away, unless he was wrong and she was worth cultivating. She had brought up the subject of her husband for a reason, he knew. When he was younger he never knew why girls said anything. He didn't believe they had any interest in him. All through high school he had thought that girls would talk to him only to make fun of him. After he started fucking he realized he had something they wanted, something of value. He thought of the mole on her breast, kissing it, then sucking on her breast.

"Jesus, get a hold of yourself," he said out loud.

He drove to the music store. He was a little nervous to go up to the salesman behind the counter, so he spent some time trying out guitars. There was a guy about his age looking at bass guitars. "Do you play?" James asked him.

"A little. I'm in a blues band."

"Where, in Gallup? Blues?"

"Yeah, man," the guy laughed.

"Play any metal?"

"Used to do a little." The man tried out "Black Dog" on the Hartke, but he just couldn't get it right, kept starting and four bars into it screwing up exactly the same way every single time. After the third time, James grabbed at it, saying, "Gimme that sucker. It goes like this." He played it for him twice one way, then did a variation and gave it back.

The man was grinning when he said, "Okay, asshole."

James told the guy behind the counter that he was here to pick up Nolan's amp.

"I thought it was you. Let me go get it from the back. Is that your truck? I already got the special modification installed." He gave him this sly look that James didn't really like, even though he understood it. James followed him into the storeroom and handed him the envelope of cash.

The last stop was for the liquor, and then he stretched the tarp over the back. He felt rich somehow, taking back things from town, and rich, for a moment as he thought of Angie, with something deeper, smoother and warmer, more important.

CHAPTER EIGHT

▧ **THE BEER AND** the alcohol were well covered in the back of the truck, and this part of his cargo was actually legal until he reached the reservation line. He realized he had no reason to feel relaxed or reassured on this account, especially since he also had Nolan's package of marijuana taped inside the amp that rested against the cab.

He took the interstate to avoid the roadblocks the tribal police often put up near Window Rock. The sun had not yet set, but it blared just above the edge of his visor, warming the western walls of the mesas with a golden light. He felt calm. If he hadn't had his illegal load he would have pulled off on the shoulder and watched the violet shadows lengthen across the flats.

Tomorrow he would hang his parents' screen doors, visit with them before they went back to Flagstaff. Restore the old family feeling.

Then he would visit Angie. Just knock on the door. But what was the right way to ask the questions? *Are you planning on staying married? Just exactly where do I fit in?*

Whoa, boy. Might as well say *Let's do it.*

It was always a mistake to plan too much ahead. Something always happened to mess it up and disappoint him. A wise man doesn't expect anything good.

He drove along the foot of the huge orange cliffs and by the run-down tourist trap of Chief Yellowhorse. Yellowhorse, too, was just trying to make a buck.

This business of selling alcohol was not something he ever wanted to do, and he felt better that he had decided to give it up. Not just for Angie. He had to be doing something he was proud of, even if it was some dumb job to support his music. When Aunt Thelma prayed, she would mention the holy people, then the family, then our livelihoods. Bootlegging didn't count. In fact, what the hell had he been thinking, selling beer out of his truck with Nolan? It was money, yes, but shit . . . There must be another job for him.

He could see himself, hear himself, on his guitar, playing his songs. He could turn Nolan's band around; they'd be crazy not to ask him in. Even now in the silence, music was working its magic on his mind and mood, draining him of frustration and anger, calming him, making him think. Death metal harmony.

At Chambers he drove north toward Ganado. The road was uphill until the reservation line, when it curved down and up again in the sand hills, not far from the ranch. The sun had just dipped below the distant rim of the Painted Desert when he saw the oh-no lights in his rearview mirror, and heard a couple of ostentatious whoops from the siren. He pulled over and told himself to act natural. It was still hard for him to deal with cops, to find that right balance between being bullied and provoking them.

"Good evening, sir," the cop said, standing at James's window, his face unseen above the roof. He was wearing a tribal uniform, looking like the kid in middle school who got the Principal's Patriotism Award.

"Good evening." James tried to sound all innocent.

"License and registration, proof of insurance, please?"

James provided them.

"Please wait in the car, sir."

The cop sat in his cruiser with the dome light on, talking on his radio. He was back there a long time and James tried to keep calm and measure his breathing. He didn't think he'd been speeding, at least not by much. It would just be a warning, or maybe an insignificant ticket. Still, he found himself fighting a rising panic. What if something showed up on the computer, some warrant he didn't know anything about? He tried to remind himself that everything was getting better for him, that he had plans that might soon be fulfilled. If this goddamned cop didn't mess with his destiny. His chance for love and music and a better life. Why would anyone want to be a cop?

At last he was at the window, this time leaning down, handing James back his papers. He looked toward the back of the pickup, the tarp still snug, and said, "What have you got back here?"

"Oh, nothing . . . some screen doors for my mom, groceries, some music equipment."

"Mind if I look?"

"What the hell for, when I just told you?"

"Are you refusing permission?"

"There's nothing there you need to see."

"If you're refusing to let me look, sir, I may need to call the canine unit."

"Fuck."

"And you'll be a lot better off cooperating now."

"Shit."

"So you consent." The cop peeled back the tarp, glanced at the liquor, and went straight for the amp. He tilted it away from the cab, and in an uncannily graceful maneuver, pulled the marijuana away from its inner wall, as if he knew just where to look.

When the police wrecker finally came to impound his truck, it was pitch black, and from time to time the lights from a single car or pickup shone in his face and blinded him. After the truck was in chains, James signed a paper in the back seat of the cruiser.

"This is stupid, having me in handcuffs. How am I supposed to sign it?"

"Plenty of people have signed in cuffs." The cop sounded to James like he was taking this whole business personally, as if James had committed some offense against him or his family.

They drove to the jail in Fort Defiance, a low block building near the hospital with one floodlight out front that was working but aimed at the street, and one that was shattered like a broken mouth. There was a lawn, mostly dirt, decorated here and there with coils of dog shit.

Beyond the second set of doors, the cop removed the handcuffs, and a fat woman in a uniform, chewing gum loudly, asked him questions and filled in a form on a clipboard: "Name?"

"James Claw."

"Birth date?"

"August 5, 1975."

She popped her gum. "Census number?"

"I don't know. I never remember it."

"Address?"

"P.O. Box 778, Ganado . . ." His face was hot: he was having to explain himself again.

"No P.O. Box," she said, and popped her gum. "Physical address only."

The ranch didn't have a physical address, no place out in the sticks had a physical address, and this bitch knew that as well as he did. A few years back there had been a rural address program, and someone had brought out some numbers to stick on the gatepost, but these had fallen off after a couple of years. He gave the address for Angie's house in the public school compound in Ganado, thinking she would never find out.

She made him empty his pockets—his wallet, change, a tiny knife on his keys, his scrap of a "to do" list for Gallup—and slid it all in a brown envelope that she made him sign. Then she fingerprinted him, spoiling a card because he smudged his thumb.

"Just let me roll them for you! Don't fight me."

A jail guard, a grim Navajo with a Cantinflas mustache, led him into the cellblock. "Don't I get a phone call?"

"Maybe," said the guard.

"Depending on what?" He wondered if they weeded out all the decent potential guards in the application process.

Unsmiling, the man led him through two locked doors to a room with a telephone sitting on a small table. "Local calls only."

"Can't I call collect?" He was not yet sure who he might call, since his parents were out of reach at the ranch, but all the people who he thought might be able to help him were outside of Window Rock. Nolan? Couldn't be trusted. He thought it would be good to talk to his brother, sitting in some room at Stanford. But what could Ben do? Then he remembered that his old classmate Larsen lived here. It would be embarrassing, but if it helped get him out of here, it was worth it.

The phone rang several times before someone picked it up, someone with the voice of a little kid, who said, "What?"

"Is your dad there?"

"What?"

"Is your father there? Let me talk to your papa."

"Wait," said the little voice, and then there was the sound of the receiver being dropped somewhere hard.

"Hello?" James said, and waited, hearing voices in that distant house without being able to discern the words. "*Hello?*" James held for as long as the guard would let him. Then the guard took the receiver and hung it up.

"That's *it*? What am I supposed to do now?"

They went through two sets of locked doors and James found himself in a large room. The first thing he noticed was the really bad acoustics. Just the opening of the doors and the footsteps on the cement floor clanged and echoed in his ears, the same ears that took heavy metal at full volume. From the hall he had seen another large cell, and from that direction came the magnified sound of someone vomiting.

Two other human forms loomed in the shadows of the cell, one standing at the opposite wall, back to him, and the other sitting on the floor with his head between his knees, rocking, then occasionally headbanging, as if he were at a concert. His matted hair shone like an oil slick.

At first all he could smell was Lysol, very strong, but after a while he smelled another, deeper, stronger smell, a combination of sewage and vomit and some other sweetish reek. The toilet, plain and ugly, crouched behind a cinder-block wall, open on one end. The portable, stackable beds, made of molded plastic, were the only other features in the cell. James's choices were to sit down or lie down or use the toilet. There was enough room to walk eight or ten paces and turn. How much could they take from a person? Wasn't this against the law, wasn't it cruel and unusual?

As he paced, he caught the smell of alcohol first from the headbanger on the floor, then from the older guy leaning against the wall. The drunk tank, though James hadn't been drinking.

He had learned from movies and television that you never asked your jail mates what they were in for. The fortyish guy leaning against the wall, who had new scratches over his face and a bandage over one eye, looked like hell, like he could use a day or two of rest and vitamins and lots of fluids. His arms had good muscles and his body was trim, but he was dirty, and the alcohol fumes still rose from his pores. His face was greasy and red, and a blotch of dried blood spread down from his nostrils into the sparse stubble on his chin. "What the hell you looking at?" he asked James.

"Nothing." James gave him a level gaze and the guy laughed.

"I'd smack you down, punk, if I didn't feel like shit."

Before long he was telling James about the time he was trying to take a shit and he was really bearing down—he mimicked the process, and his face flushed deeper red with the effort. "But all that was coming out was like these little deer turds. And when I looked down the whole fucking bowl was fucking red."

"Ugh."

"Fucking pure red, man, just totally . . . *blood.*"

"So what did you do?"

"What the fuck was I supposed to do? I wiped my ass."

James hadn't asked any questions, but the man said, "Yeah, I got to get into some alcohol treatment, I know I do. You don't have to tell me that. I did have this restaurant job with insurance that would pay for it, but they fucking fired me, so fuck them. Sexual harassment! I had to move some trays, so I told this little chick, this fat round four-and-a-half-foot girl to stay right there and watch the food line. I said, 'Just watch this, Babe,' and when I got back I said, 'Thanks, Babe, you're a sweetheart.' That's all I said! Sexual harassment. A little fat ugly girl. I bet nobody ever called her sweetheart, must have confused her. They told me I had to get counseling. I said, 'If that's what you fucking think of me,' and I threw off my gloves and fucking walked out."

At last, he volunteered the story of how his wife had turned into this bitch and how much he loved his little kid and how she was trying to keep him from seeing him. The crazy bitch was accusing him of domestic abuse "against her *and my son*—I never raised a hand to them, especially my son."

Before long the man had stretched out on the plastic bunk and was snoring. James was thankful for that, but he paced around, wanting to talk to somebody and find out how things worked here, when he was likely to get out. The teenager sat on the floor, bobbing his head from time to time. "You making up your own music?" He kept banging. "Or maybe I'm deaf. Or you got hidden earphones." The kid didn't stop banging, didn't say anything, but held up his hands briefly in the "Hail Satan" gesture.

That night James's mind also created its own music in that strange way he'd learned as a child on long trips in the family car. As he hovered in and out of sleep, the sounds around him would somehow become ordered: the hum of the highway, the wail of the wind. The music wasn't just a simple tune or a rhythm, but was complex, with themes playing off each other, harmony, orchestration. If he started to wake up more fully, the music would start to fade or skip in and out like a damaged CD. One of these days, he hoped he would figure out how to transcribe it or remember it, to hold it in his head, but so far all he could do was return to it by returning toward sleep. It was the only way he knew to do nothing and yet be creative, actually dwelling inside music itself.

Now, with his cheek against the plastic bed, in this place where nothing was provided except snores and headbanging, he pulled the notes and patterns from the air around him.

All night long the fluorescent lights shone, and James blocked them as best he could with the frayed and torn black blanket they had given him. Finally he gave up and sat on the bunk, his elbows digging into his thighs, his head in his hands. A new metallic smell joined the others as his cell mates slept, something from their open mouths. Nobody knew he was here. His parents would be leaving the ranch soon and returning to Flagstaff, disappointed and tired of waiting for him to return as he'd promised. Every thought increased his misery, and he expected to feel miserable for a long time.

Then the last set of fluorescent lights came on and a guard clanged in with breakfast. "You're lucky, it's Sunday," she said, the same gum-chewing woman who had fingerprinted him. "Pancakes." Two small pancakes were clumped in the middle of a Styrofoam plate, covered with thin syrup. Beside it stood a little carton of milk smelling like damp clothes. Trying to cut the first bite, his white plastic utensil, something between a spoon and a fork, snapped in half. He ate with his hands.

Neither cell mate wanted to talk. "Couldn't sleep," was all that came from the wife beater, who had been snoring all night. The teenager ate his breakfast quickly with his hands and was already seated on the floor, bobbing his head, swinging his knotty hair.

For hours it was quiet and would have been boring without his worries. It was Nolan who had gotten him in this mess, arranged for him to pick up the weed, and he deserved to suffer somehow. Beat him up? Snub him? But James knew it was his own damn fault and flared up in anger again. He'd been an idiot to go along with Nolan's plan in which James was a dumb mule.

Who was going to help him face judges and jails? How would this change the rest of his life? The view forward had never been clear, but now he felt that nothing good would ever happen to him again.

In midafternoon, half a dozen detainees stepped off a white van from Shiprock and into the holding cells, and there was no more quiet. Most of them were hung over, and one of them, who had a huge urine stain on the front of his pants, was clearly crazy, screaming in terror about things at his feet and around the toilet. Another man, slurring his words and ready for a fight, screamed back at the madman, "Shut the fuck up."

All speech was berserk. The kid was bobbing his head silently, and, it seemed now, wisely.

On Monday morning he and his two original cell mates were led out, one by one, to court. James was the last. The tribal courtroom had better acoustics than the jail, but the number of people in it made it loud, and it smelled of their sweat. This was the majesty of the law. The judge was a fat Navajo man with white temples and wavy Mexican hair. He seemed to enjoy himself most when scolding someone or pounding his gavel, telling people to "come to order, come to order," saying it again in Navajo: "Ałch'e' ádadohnééh." In English he sounded like he was trying to be a big shot, and in Navajo it sounded like he knew he was a big shot. He called two men in suits to the bench, and they talked in voices too low for James to hear. The judge asked James if he understood and he said no and then the men conferred in whispers again. No one asked him anything else, and he wondered if anyone knew he was here. Just as he considered walking out the door, a guard had him by the elbow, and he was led with four others to a van parked behind the courthouse.

Two of them were guys in their early twenties, maybe brothers, who kept giggling and hitting each other on the shoulder not quite hard enough for the driver to consider it fighting. "There'll be none of that once we get on the road."

"What the hell is going on?" James asked the guy next to him, a Plains-looking Indian with balding long hair who smelled of cigarettes.

"We're going to Flagstaff. Federal magistrate."

Flagstaff. Federal. Fucked. "Oh boy. A field trip."

CHAPTER NINE

◈ **"FELONY?" THE PLAINS** guy asked him.

"What?"

"You facing a felony?"

"I don't know."

"New at this?"

"Very."

"First of all, let me give you some advice: don't tell anybody, including me, anything about what you done or didn't do. You'll get a lawyer in Flagstaff, probably tomorrow, at the initial hearing, they call it. And second, don't get in any fights when you're locked up, not with the guards, not with the other guys."

"You seem to know your way around."

"Yeah, well. Maybe when this is all over I'll become a lawyer. Hey, driver, you got a smoke?"

"There's no smoking."

They left Window Rock straight south past Hunters Point to the interstate, then west across the flat land, *ch'ilzhóó'* or sand sage waving its blue-green brushes, fading in the blinding light of midday. Trains passed miles farther down the Puerco and Little Colorado valleys, also going west. The countryside seemed dreary, entirely unlike when he was driving around it in his own truck. High in the middle of the sky there was a strange brown band stretching from west to east, somehow dimming and flattening the light, and he wondered if there were forest fires in California.

Once they got to Flagstaff, the Plains guy was immediately transferred to Florence. "I'm too big for this sorry place," he explained. "Remember what I told you."

They gave him jailhouse clothes and flip-flops and a blanket just like the one he had in Fort Defiance. Before they would let him get into the clothes they had a routine that ended with his mooning the guard and coughing. One of the brothers he came in with asked the guard, "Do you hate your job yet?"

The cell in the Flagstaff jail—the pod, they called it—was much larger than the one in Fort Defiance, with a couple dozen metal bunk beds lined along two walls. The white-tiled bathroom and shower were separated by a white curtain; he eventually learned that inmates—that's what he was, he learned that, too—put a plastic pail upside-down in front of the curtain when they were using the shitter. *About as civilized as you could be under the circumstances,* he thought. A television was bolted to the ceiling and picnic-type tables sat below it. Bodies were lying on the bunks, most of them with blankets over their faces, and two were watching a NASCAR event on the TV. James lay on the top bunk that he had been assigned and ignored them all.

In the evening the jailer came by with long-sleeved shirts that were probably supposed to keep them warm but didn't. They were trying to make him mad with these stupid, petty insults and inconveniences. And they did, but he wasn't going to let it show.

That night he drifted in and out of sleep, but this time he did not experience the dream-music. The clangs and cries remained clangs and cries and never made any more sense than that. He conjured up Terri's body until he became enraged. Then he thought of Angie and heard her asking him, "Where were you?" and his reply, "In jail for bootlegging." Or maybe she might not talk to him at all. Then he could forget about doing what he wanted to do with her.

His jail-bunk erection was secret enough, but he was afraid he would make noise if he masturbated. What happened instead, while he was lying on his back asleep, was a dream of a dark place, her face obscured. His penis was pushing against a furry mound, which was pushing against him, then something gave way. One of those sudden orgasms that must take five seconds from start to finish, and all from deep in his head. Was it Terri, or Angie?

In the morning James was in court again, a cleaner and quieter place than in Fort Defiance, with a white judge who looked at him from time to time over small eyeglasses. He appointed him a lawyer, and they met in a wood-paneled office in the courthouse.

He looked no more than ten years older than James. How did a guy that young end up with a job that made him look so tired, made him lose his hair?

"We're in luck if the prosecutor offers you a misdemeanor, which is usual for bootlegging. But the pot... if it's over a pound he'll press felony charges, and it's a whole different thing. I asked him to release you, but he said no, so you'll have to stay until Friday."

"Does he know my father is a school principal in town?" He didn't want to mention it, but he was feeling desperate.

The lawyer sighed. "No, neither did I. Too late." They shook hands, that vigorous and phony way of men in this kind of world.

When he was returned to jail, after the bend-over-and-cough, something dark settled in on him that until now he had kept away: a feeling of utter emptiness, as if his life were already over. There would be no music, no woman, no babies, no horses or sheep, no beauty, no purpose, no meaning. He was now where so many people had told him he would end up one day: teachers, principals, cops, employers. Even his father, though he never put it into words.

There was a big kid in the cell. He looked about eighteen with a face full of acne and a lineman's kind of fat, and he started by bothering the brothers who had come in from Window Rock with James, shuffling up too close to them. James saw this happen several times, until one of the brothers yelled at him and pushed him away. The big guy didn't move very far, but the commotion was enough to bring the frightened guards with pepper spray. The brother was down on the floor, howling with his eyes closed, and then the guards dragged him out of the cell.

Soon after, the kid shuffled up to James, who was trying not to think of anything. He had a sort of imploring look on his face that reminded James of a country dog. He mumbled his words, and James asked, "What?"

"What's your name?"

"James." James noticed the dot tattoos on his knuckles, and the unpleasant, sweet odor he had identified when he was first in jail.

"I'm Ronnie." He leaned in closer yet, and his voice lowered. "Let me see your dick."

James jumped back as if he'd been burned, and yelled, "What?" Then quickly, "No, don't say it again. Stay away from me."

It felt like a reprieve from the insanity around him when, on Tuesday afternoon, Greenstone was brought to the cell. "Could you bring the chessboard, please?" he asked the guard. One leg was a stump below the knee where it peeked out from the shortened right pant leg like one of those hairless laboratory rodents. He had to lean on the guard to walk, who sat him down in the dayroom section. "What else can I do for you?" he grinned.

James had looked at all the old and torn magazines and was sick of TV, so when Greenstone invited him to play, he agreed.

"You're going to more or less have to teach me."

"Okay, well. You'll learn while you're losing, then."

He was a white guy in his late forties, James guessed, small and lean in his jailhouse blues. His eyes were bloodshot but he was stone-cold sober. When he set up the board and they faced each other over the small table he began the conversation with, "What brings you onto the wrong side of the law? I already assume the charges are trumped up."

"I can't say anything about that. The lawyer tells me I shouldn't admit anything to anybody."

"Aha. Good advice."

"How about you? Since you asked."

"I can talk. I have nothing to be ashamed of at the moment."

"I wish I could say that." James was surprised to hear himself say it: shame was not a word he would have purposefully chosen.

"In fact, I seem to be something of a local celebrity. So . . . you know the moves, right? You want to save time and have me set it up as if we've made some opening?"

"Next time. I need to practice my openings. Celebrity, huh?"

"I don't suppose you read the local papers."

James thought he should be careful. Was this guy some kind of serial killer? Was he playing chess with Hannibal Lecter? "I've been out on the reservation." James put out his king's pawn.

"Oh, really? Navajo?"

"Yeah, out by Ganado. We don't have the paperboy coming by every morning, if you know what I mean."

"Lucky you," he said. "What do you do there?"

James moved his knight out. "I'm a musician. Guitar. Metal."

Greenstone grunted, mirrored James's move, and said, "The Forest Service, in its infinite wisdom, has removed me from public land, apparently not regarding me as part of the public."

James laughed at his fancy language. Was this guy another crazy bum? "So, they had one of their homeless roundups?"

"So they must consider it. But they singled me out for their high-visibility publicity campaign, front-page treatment, claiming that I *negatively impacted forest values*. They first started picking on me after the mountain lion got me a couple of years ago, and I had quite a lot of support in the letters to the editor and so forth. They're getting nasty, lately."

"Maybe I did hear about the mountain lion. That's when they shot several of them, wasn't it? They said they'd lost their fear of humans." James's bishop came out to attack the knight.

"Alas, they did destroy two lions, but it was through no fault of mine. I was a staunch defender of the beasts. That's one reason they despise me."

"Who?"

"Ah, that is the question, my friend. Certain higher-ups in the Forest Service. But how deep and how far up this goes . . . that is the question."

"So is that what happened to your leg?"

"A series of complications. Certain poor medical decisions. Started with the mountain lion, yes. I've got a prosthesis that works pretty well, but the rules are I can't wear it in here. Can't you see me swinging that thing around over my head, knocking out guards with it? And they won't give me a crutch, which I could at least get around with, for the same reason. And they know I'm not dangerous."

James watched as Greenstone kept control of the center and attacked in one tricky maneuver after another. "You need to work on your middlegame. Let me just set it up. Let's say we start again with the Spanish game . . ."

James found the time going by quickly as they played and talked. The game seemed to give their conversation a kind of order of manners and rhythm. Greenstone said he had been living in the forest for seven years, in some caves not too far above James's parents' house. He called it his "redoubt."

"I doubt it, too. You mean up in the boulders at the base of Mount Elden? I've been in those caves lots of times, and nobody was living in them then."

"Off and on for seven years. And in the hot weather I would go to my summer retreat farther up the mountain. I would rather be there than inside somewhere like all the other fools." He said he had the opportunity to observe the deterioration of the environment from there, while a person in town might not notice it: the line of dead trees across the mountain in the path of the microwaves, and the warblers returning earlier every spring. "Just a couple of days ago there was a huge plume of polluted air and dust up in the jet stream, blowing from Asia."

"Is that what that was?"

"All the way from the Gobi desert and the industrial heart of China."

"I wondered. It made a very weird light."

Now he had Greenstone's attention. "It's amazing how many people won't notice a thing like that. Observation is very much in decline. You would think that the Forest Service would appreciate all the pro bono work I did for them: I rescued lost kids, I counseled teenagers, I kept the yuppie bicyclist zealots from tearing up the forest for their trails. But no, they evict me from my rightful home, claiming they had to clean up half a ton of junk, which is a lie. I didn't have anywhere near that much stuff."

"What do you mean you counseled teenagers?" Greenstone's language was so inflated, it could have meant anything.

"Oh, some kids used to like to ditch high school and come talk to me. When I was in the mood I'd put up a string of white and yellow Tibetan prayer flags. Several of them were Native kids, too. I always encouraged them to respect their culture, their elders, especially if they were Hopi, no offense intended."

Greenstone also claimed he had once taught philosophy in a seminary, used to play bassoon in the Louisville symphony. "I turned my back on it all and have never regretted it."

James smiled. Greenstone's language was meant to entertain, meant to make fun of himself. At first James thought he was full of himself; now he saw that it was just the opposite.

On Thursday morning the guards called Ronnie's name and told him to "roll up." He carried his mattress and plastic tray of stuff to the door and never came back, and two of the white guys claimed the chessboard. They played checkers until they argued about the outcome and one kid threw a piece at the other. On his one leg Greenstone hopped over to grab the game back from them, and called the guard through the voice grill to take it away. "You knuckleheads," he told the kids. "I want it to be here next time."

On Friday morning James met again with his lawyer, whose hairline seemed to have further receded since he had seen him last. "Things are looking up, James. It turns out the marijuana only weighed fourteen ounces."

"So they shorted me!"

The lawyer stared at him, a slight smile on his tired face, like a teacher explaining to a dumb student, "James, that's good. You should be glad. It's less than a pound. Because it's less than a pound, the prosecution has offered a misdemeanor."

"What the hell is offering a misdemeanor?"

"Well, it means that instead of holding a preliminary hearing, the judge will just sentence you."

Preliminary hearing sounded better than sentencing. Preliminary meant there was some chance in the future, and he fervently believed he needed that chance. "I don't get to defend myself?"

"Jeez, James, forget it. I'm telling you as your lawyer, this is good news. You'll probably get a year's probation."

"What's that mean?"

"You'll be assigned a probation officer, probably have to take drug tests. And the judge is going to tell you that you'll get jail if you screw up."

For the next few hours James sat in the cell waiting to be taken to court. Moment by moment his mood brightened, as each new fact became evident: He would soon be out of jail. His parents knew nothing of this grim episode. Sweet sex and music were still possibilities. In no time he felt happier than he had in months.

"Hey, Greenstone. I'm about to be a free man." James had to share it with someone.

"You always were."

"But now I'm going to be a free man, out of jail!"

"Congratulations. Use it wisely."

CHAPTER TEN

JAMES'S FRIEND ADRIAN had a job giving tours at the historic trading post, and he always came back from work with interesting stories like the wiggling wool bag. But then Adrian quit. Or got fired.

"Which was it, anyway?" James had asked Adrian.

"It's a matter of freedom of speech."

"Uh-oh, what did you say?"

"Just not their approved U.S. government Disneyland version of history, man."

"So they fired you?"

"They say I quit, so I couldn't get unemployment, but the superintendent made it impossible, barking shit at me after every tour I gave. Said some visitors were complaining."

One of Adrian's historical sources was John Littlesunday, a very old man with his hair tied back in a *tsiiyééł*, who was also a part-time employee of the Park Service, and who had worked for the old lecher Roman Hubbell, son of J. L., sixty years ago, before his trading post and land became a national historic monument. Littlesunday told the story in Navajo about coming across a wiggling wool bag, two people in the wool bag at shearing time. Roman Hubbell banging a woman woolstomper. Littlesunday just laughed, as he had told the story many times, but Adrian included an English version in his next tour, when he'd led the group of tourists to the barn and explained the sheep-ranching equipment.

"Of course Gabaldon wanted me to sing the praises of a sexual predator. Someone who was preying on *my* female ancestors," he told James.

"No shit. They got no taste for the truth. I should have taken your tour, got the straight scoop. Say, Adrian, would you mind if I applied for the job?"

"Suit yourself, if you want it. But I don't think you'll like Superintendent Gabaldon."

He woke at first light, his brain and his nostrils full of the beautiful wet smell that came in the window above his head, of the dirt he remembered eating as a young child. In the empty house—he was aware it was empty, somehow, even before he woke—he yawned and stirred, enjoying both the waking and the sleep that preceded it, while stretching against his erection.

He threw off the sheets and banged out the door. The best place to piss was in the fragrant outside with the cool moisture on his feet, and the light strings of fog in the valleys, already rising, exhilarated him.

He remembered the crashes of thunder during the night, the sound of a cosmic drum riff, the drama to his dreams, the mock terror in his safe dry house, the relief of the relative silence, the balm of the rain.

If only he could stay here all day, feeling and smelling, walking and running over the roads and paths nearby, but he was now a working man. Gabaldon—a chubby Chicano with an obvious shoe-brown hairpiece that often slipped—had stuck out his hand when James introduced himself and offered him the job without the slightest hesitation. James remembered making fun of Gabaldon's wig when he was in elementary school. It looked even odder now than it had then, the color was so wrong, so mismatched to the lines in his face.

"Had enough of the big city?" And after Gabaldon explained the job to James—the two daily tours, various labor and errands—he handed him the uniform and said, "Give my regards to your father. He helped my daughter a lot." James vaguely remembered that his daughter had gotten into some sort of trouble in school.

James missed the lingering in the morning, but he had been sincere when he told Gabaldon that he was very grateful for the job. He didn't know what else he would have done. When he had gotten out of jail in Flagstaff he felt like he was in the movie *Groundhog Day*, when things started over and over and over. Going by the storage unit again, waiting for the train again.

He snapped to in the National Park Service daily-wear uniform of a gray shirt and green pants and the fucking Smokey hat. Where was the cub-scout neckerchief, for Christ's sake? He had to use the mirror to make sure it was him, and as usual when he saw himself in the Park Service outfit, he felt like an asshole. *I see by your outfit that you are an asshole* . . .

But being an adult meant that you could put up with looking like an asshole for the sake of a job. Being an adult meant you needed one.

The road would be a struggle, and he needed to leave early. If he made the highway without getting stuck, he would be there ahead of time, but if he got stuck, depending on how stuck, he might show up caked with mud and find the boss glowering at him for being a reservation slacker.

He rinsed out the speckled coffeepot, the blue enamel classic made in Mexico, which seemed so much a part of life on the reservation—he had never seen a coffeepot like this in Flagstaff, and no coffeepot here looked much different. Even in the unofficial dumps scattered about, rusted, dented versions of it abounded. He filled it with water, threw in a handful of loose grounds, and set it to boil. On the table was a covered plate with the leftover *náneeskaadí* his aunt had brought up yesterday evening. He tore the bread in half and chewed it as he stood outside the door and looked east into the valley, where a foal ran with its mother and two other horses. The foal was pink and speckled, the mother was an almost-black roan. He had seen them before, but did not know whose they were; maybe they were unbranded. Everyone who lived in the country always complained about them, too many horses herding up, just running around eating the range, too wild to ride. But the sight of these animals in the rising mist made him happy.

From the nearby junipers, juncos and bluebirds flitted down to the puddles and back. The tops of the hills to the west turned gold with the first sunlight. He put the shovel in the back of his truck, along with his tall rubber boots. He also put in half a dozen cinder blocks to weigh down the back. One of these days he would have a real truck, heavy and fast, not one of these punky rice burners. "No offense," he told the Nissan, which had taken him through plenty of trouble, and in fact had recently languished in the Fort Defiance pound because of him.

He needed to be nice to what was his: the truck, his friends, who were headed down to a Cryptopsy concert in Phoenix this weekend, and maybe Angie, if that came together.

The slickest area was right below the house and in front of the windmill. In the middle of the puddle stood the sign that said the road was maintained only for the school bus, meaning that if you had trouble, tough shit. Then up into the little hills it was all sand, until the next valley and Repent or Perish. There had been a revival there while he was in jail—his aunt told him a white preacher and his family had come out from Kansas—and they had repainted the sign. These Christians knew how to play their cards: just when he was slipping around in the mud, there it told him, Repent or Perish. He hated himself for saying it, but there it was out loud, in the air above his mouth, "I repent." And sure enough, he got through the mud and was on the black highway, blessed. On the smooth highway, striped with muddy tire tracks coming off the dirt roads, early for work.

He was less anxious about the tour-guiding than he had been when he started. Gabaldon made it clear at the start that that was his most important task. "To represent Hubbell's and the Navajo Nation." James had grimaced inwardly. More than a grimace: screaming the vocals in a raging band. The last thing he wanted was to represent something to someone. James knew they really wanted to hire nice-looking full-blooded Navajos, who would tell coyote stories to the tourists and ease their guilt about the massacres. But being an adult meant needing a job.

What surprised him was how quickly he had come to enjoy it. By the time he cashed his first paycheck he had pretty much learned the routine, memorizing from a script Gabaldon had given him, and was only just beginning to deviate from it.

As he pulled into the employee parking area, old man Littlesunday was picking up trash in front of the trading post with a claw-ended stick. Three rounded hooks came together when the old man pressed a lever at the stick's upper end.

Walking by him into the store, James said, "Hi, Grandpa. Still pinching, are you?"

The ancient man laughed. "Always pinching," he said, using the Navajo verb with its other, suggestive meaning.

Gabaldon called James into the storeroom. "Here early, are you? Would you mind carrying this wool in to the weavers? I'd do it myself, but since you're here . . ."

It was a fifty-pound spool of roving, and James heaved it onto his shoulder. He liked visiting the weavers, who had their looms set up in a big room in another building. This morning only Mabel was at her loom, the weaving supervisor who would never speak to him in English, and lately insisted on hearing from him in Navajo.

"*Yá'át'ééh, shiyáázh.*"

"*Yá'át'ééh 'abíní, shimá.*"

She smiled at him triumphantly. All he'd said was "Good morning, Auntie," but he had learned over the years of speaking halting Navajo that when people smiled it was not because they were amused at his accent or mistakes, but because they were pleased at his effort.

"It's really heavy, is it?" she said.

"Yes, I should have let Grandpa bring it in."

She laughed. "Grandpa would have brought in two, one on each shoulder."

Back in the store Gabaldon had a book for him. "Take an hour and read some of this. It might give you some new material. You're doing the eleven o'clock tour, right?"

"If it doesn't rain." It was clear now, but lately the clouds had been building up early, and sometimes there was a cloudburst before noon.

He found a comfortable place on a tarp spread over some bales of hay and opened the yellowed book. He liked thinking about the way things were in his grandparents' day, and before that. This was a book about when J. L. Hubbell first came to Ganado. There were line drawings illustrating the text. Two men swam in a flood.

The Indians were notoriously poor swimmers in mid-river . . . the buck's horse had slipped and fallen, then floundered about on the rocks until he had broken his master's arm . . . Hubbell, on the bank, plunged in, swimming . . . to the Indian's side, and dragged him ashore.

James thought, *I hate this guy.* No wonder Adrian quit. Hubbell had been an asshole, and he taught asshole values to his sons. Somehow he got Teddy Roosevelt and the Park Service to declare him some kind of racial hero, and now they hired young Navajo men to parrot it.

Hubbell arrived mudcovered at an outlying post, shook hands all around, listened to Navajo troubles, opened a bag of silver (probably tokens), and handed out money while he pinched the Navajo women and children's cheeks.

James expected eventually to develop his own tour routine, as Adrian had done, but he didn't know enough yet, and he was anxious to keep his job. It wasn't easy. He had never really enjoyed this "interfacing" that Gabaldon talked about. James had always said he didn't want to work with the public. The public were morons.

Some of the tourists' questions baffled him. One lady wanted to know if she could get permission to build a little house on some of the "empty" land around here. Another wanted to know how closely related Navajos and Chinese were.

Today, as he wound up the morning tour in the jewelry room, a thin middle-aged man asked him if he had been abused in boarding school.

"I went to public school. There were some jackass teachers there, yes." He was learning to modify his language for the public. "Is that what you mean?"

"Not exactly."

"They didn't lock me in a dungeon, no. But some of these older people who went to boarding schools in the old days can tell you some stories."

"I hear there were some terrible pederasts."

A tourist wanted to take a picture of him; he told him he believed that would steal his soul, and the man got all serious. Maybe the soul stuff was true; he wasn't sure why he had always hated mugging for a camera, especially a stranger's. The man, a little white-haired guy in golf clothes with his even littler wife, turned to point the camera at a young Navajo woman walking across the parking lot in a long satin skirt and velveteen blouse. It was Angie.

"*Yá'át'ééh, shimá yázhí,*" James said when she was near. There really wasn't a better relationship term to use than the word for aunt, though he and she were the same age.

She laughed and shook his hand shyly, as if she really were his old auntie. "Yá'át'ééh, shiyáázh." He had made her call him son, as aunts are supposed to do, and it made her giggle.

James had only seen Angie once since he had gotten out of jail, and that was no more than a glance as she came out the post office door and he was sitting in his truck. He'd given her a little wave, which she returned, but he'd wanted to avoid her eyes altogether. Somehow he could tell by the little smile she gave him that she had heard all about the shit he had fallen into and she had *told him so*. It was an accusation, but maybe there was also a hint of forgiveness or understanding. Several evenings after work he considered paying her a visit, but he couldn't bring himself to do it. All week he had not been able to sleep, and thoughts of her criticizing him, or blowing him off, were among the swirling agonies and coyote choruses that kept him awake. Now enough time had gone by that he was feeling tough. If she didn't like him, that was her loss. Besides, she was married.

So he said, "You look like Miss Navajo." The velveteen somehow emphasized the softness of the breasts beneath it. He hoped he hadn't pushed his luck and sounded downright mean.

She laughed but he had made her blush, and it wasn't easy to make Angie blush. "I don't know. If I have two kids can I be Miss Anything? I'm here for an interview."

"You going to work here?" James didn't want to sound too eager or look too happy. "I mean, I didn't know you were looking for work, with your little girl and all."

"How would you know?" she said. "I haven't seen you in weeks."

James's face felt hot. Did she mean that she had wanted to see him and he had disappointed her, or that since they hardly saw each other, it was none of his business what she decided to do with her time? "I . . . I've been busy since I started working."

"Not too busy to see Nolan. I've seen your truck parked there plenty of times."

Something inside him was telling him, *Don't be mad, she likes you.* Yet his mouth seemed to open itself. "Well, I didn't want to bother you, since the last time I saw you all I got was a lecture about mending my ways." James tried to smile to lighten it up, but he felt like he was snarling.

"Oh, no, you remember it wrong. I might have given you a lecture, but you were the one who was talking about mending your ways."

"Okay." He was afraid the conversation was over forever.

"So did you?"

"What?"

"Mend your ways. Turn over a new leaf."

"Yeah, I guess. I'll tell you about it sometime." If he could explain what had happened with jail and probation in some private place, he thought she might understand and approve.

"Come over soon." She turned toward the store, but before she disappeared inside, he could see she was smiling.

A flatbed of hay arrived from Farmington, so James and the others spent over an hour unloading it. He tied a cloth over his nose and mouth, but before long he could feel the familiar burn in his chest. "Shit, now I'll be wheezing for a week." He'd be very attractive to Angie when he went to visit her: coughing and out of breath, snot spinning from his nose. "All for these goddamned picturesque livestock." The horses were rarely ridden, and there were only enough sheep to put on a show at shearing time. It was like a 4-H project.

At lunchtime he looked around for Angie but didn't see her. He ate crackers and a can of those funky Vienna sausages they called *awéé' bicho'* and gabbed a little in the store. He was thinking that the first thing he would talk to Angie about was that husband of hers. Mabel walked in and pretended to scold him for being lazy when she had a job for him. On the floor they had laid out the warp for the largest loom, and she needed him to help adjust and readjust the tension as they hung it. He couldn't stop coughing.

James waited awhile to start the afternoon tour, because by two o'clock only two people had gathered: a young Japanese couple who were now killing time looking at rugs and making surprised noises after reading price tags. "Is so expensive!" the girl said. She had short hair that was streaked magenta and both wore black sweaters with arms that extended well beyond their fingertips.

"Well, they're all handmade," James explained. "Someone figured it out; just considering the labor it comes out to a dollar twenty-five an hour."

"Dollar twenty-five?" the man asked. James was not sure he had understood, but he didn't say more. They went back to the stack of rugs, pulling one out from time to time and laying it on the floor. James noticed they seemed to like the ones with unusual colors: magenta, like the girl's hair, turquoise, yellow, and pink.

He was also hoping to run into Angie again, but he hadn't seen her come out from Gabaldon's office. She couldn't still be in there! Doing what, exchanging recipes? Did she run off on purpose without saying something to him? Maybe she hadn't got the job and was embarrassed. He wondered if his chances with her would be better if she worked there, so close to him for so many hours—he again remembered the story of the moving forms in the wool bag, and laughed. Or would it be worse, Angie tormenting him with sharp words and sarcasm?

Around quarter past two, two other couples joined them, and James walked them over to the Hubbell house, to the old apricot tree that had grown from seed planted in place in the courtyard. He led them through the dark, well-furnished rooms, pointing out the paintings and sketches by Maynard Dixon and E. A. Burbank, and Mary-Russell Ferrell Colton. He talked about Hubbell's friendship with Teddy Roosevelt, his Republican political aspirations . . .

The tourists were polite but bored. Before long the two American couples disclosed that they were parents of Mormon missionaries in Chinle. They were touring around, learning "so much," as one of the ladies said, "about Navajo culture." They asked more and more questions, until James thought it was useless to go on with the usual spiel. Before long they were relating the story of the former Mormon colony at Tuba City, and then somehow drifted into the archaeological evidence that supported the stories in the Book of Mormon. About the Lamanites, one of the men said to James, "You should be very interested in that. It's the history of your people." He had heard it before in general form: the tribe was kicked out of Israel, their skin "black and loathsome," and wandered their way to the Western Hemisphere, built temples, smelted steel, used horse-drawn chariots, and wrote in altered

Hebrew and Egyptian. Then they became primitive again. Their descendants' only hope was to convert to Mormonism, which would make them "white and delightsome."

James didn't really care where anybody thought American Indians came from, whether it was this Mormon fantasy, or professors talking about the Bering Strait, or climbing up from the worlds below. Why was it so important to have some explanation? But if he had to choose, James might go with the Navajo story of coming up right here into the world.

He let the Mormons take over as tour guides, since they seemed to be so enthusiastic and so lively despite their lack of caffeine. "There is a proven linguistic link between Aztec and Hebrew." The Japanese couple was fascinated, bursting with questions, and the Mormons had plenty of answers. "American Indians came from Asia? How long ago?" He knew he should straighten these guys out but he didn't have the heart to get all worked up on the subject of the Hebrew language. He was thinking of Angie again, wondering what his next move might be, or if the game were already over.

CHAPTER ELEVEN

⧗ **HE ADJUSTED THE** shower nozzle at Nolan's, making a sharp, narrow stream to get out the hay and to hurt a little, to perk himself up enough to visit Angie. By the time he had rinsed the soap off, he was feeling a little more confident. His breath still burned in his chest, and little hay scratches stung all over his neck. He rubbed hard with the towel and took a few hits from his inhaler.

He didn't want to get into some mess he couldn't get out of. He rarely allowed himself to walk away from short-term conflicts—like a shouting match, or with alcohol, a shoving match—but the slower, sicker, chronic kind of conflict like you found in families seemed to threaten life itself. Terri's family had been like that, always squabbling, always drama, and that was how her own personality had been poisoned. That's why, when he had been released from jail and walked the four miles across town to his parents' house, he did not tell them where he had been, and explained his arrival on foot by saying his truck was "in the shop." (When his father asked what was wrong with it, he had been tempted to say, "It got caught bootlegging.") James just didn't like that kind of fussing. So why was he now chasing another woman who would probably land him back in endless conflict until he hated her?

He rapped on Angie's screen door. The solid door was open and he saw the baby retreat from him. "Hello, hello?" he called comically over the country music.

Angie peeked out from the kitchen and turned the music down. It was George Strait singing the sentimental "Best Day of My Life." "Come on in!" she called.

He waited for her in the living room by the stereo and picked up a tape box featuring Strait's clean face under the Stetson. "You know why he wears a hat, don't you?" he said when she appeared beside him.

"It's my sister's."

"'Cause he's going seriously bald."

"You're thinking about Garth Brooks."

"All those guys are going bald, so they have to wear hats."

"Should I turn it off?"

"I can stand it. I'm tough, too."

She laughed and turned it way down. She was back in normal clothes, jeans and a T-shirt, and he could again see her brown, completely hairless arms. "It just kind of makes it easier to do housework. I always remember my mom cleaning harder when the radio was on. It was Hank Williams then."

"Yeah," James said, suddenly and strangely nostalgic for music that he had always heard and somehow always hated. "Did you get the job?"

She smiled. "Yes."

He put his hand on her shoulder for just a moment, then took it off, self-conscious. "Congratulations."

"Thanks."

"Listen, Angie. This weekend, some of us are going to a concert in Phoenix. You should come with us."

"Who's the band?"

"Cryptopsy."

"Who?"

"I got one of their CDs here."

It was *Blasphemy Made Flesh*, one of their earlier recordings, before Flo Mounier had fully developed his trademark stacked cymbals. Still, that big crashing sound dug in from the start.

She took the case and squinted at the cover, putting the CD in the player. They listened a little, then she said, "I can't understand anything he's singing."

"It isn't really singing, is it?" Roaring or howling was more like it. James took out the booklet of lyrics and read over her shoulder.

"Eew. I don't think I like this. Isn't it about some little baby falling out of a window? And they're sort of witching her into it?"

"Well, yeah, but it doesn't mean the *band* actually thinks it's a good thing. That's the point. It's basically in the point of view of Satan, or the forces of the dark side, whatever, death and destruction."

"I don't know. I was always taught to avoid all that talk about evil doings and, you know, 'adigąsh.'"

"I guess it's too much for some people to handle." He lifted out the CD and slid it back in the case. "So I don't suppose you want to go with us."

"I don't really see how I can, with the baby and all." She laughed. "I sure wouldn't want to take her along to hear that band."

"We could bring Nolan's baby, too. They'd be a big hit in the mosh pit."

She swatted at him, trying not to laugh. "I can just hear my mother shouting at me, 'Doo 'ájínii da!'"

"So deep down, you think I'm evil."

"No . . ."

Without thinking too much about it, James put his arm around her. He was glad he didn't think about it, because that would have messed it up. He was taller than she was, and he was a little off center, so his leg was up against hers, his hand on the hollow at the base of her spine as he brought her in against him, firm but not crushing her. His mouth was at her ear, and he felt her breathing against his neck. He liked her smell: faint fresh sweat, mutton, soap. He held her there, feeling that he was sinking into her. Then she turned her head slightly and he kissed her on the mouth. A nice one, not teeth grinding, just a touch of tongues. Not very long, but plenty long enough that there was no mistake.

She seemed a little embarrassed but still pleased. "I don't know what *that* was for."

"Uhh . . . congratulations? For getting the job?" They both laughed.
So there will be plenty of time. Go slow.

Nolan was on the couch with no baby in sight, listening to Napalm Death and smoking a joint. He offered it to James.

"Forget it, man. One dirty urine and I'm back in jail. Thanks to you."

Nolan took a hit, held it, and blowing out the smoke, rasped, "Fuck that. I thought we went through all that."

When James had first gotten out of jail he had asked Nolan if he had been set up. He said it seemed strange that the cop knew where to find the weed. They had argued on and on, and in the end James had been convinced that it was just bad luck. But he couldn't let go of the last of his resentment.

"Well, it's not you who had to pay the price. You can sit here getting high all you want to, and no one is threatening to lock you up." It was at times like these that Nolan's gold tooth seemed flashy in a disturbing way.

"It could happen to me, it could happen to anyone."

"But it happened to me." James couldn't keep out of his mind the possibility that someone had tipped off the cop somehow. Maybe not Nolan—what did he have to gain?—but maybe Chris Soros or the Mexican guy at the music store.

"Come on, James, you could have said no. You knew you were taking a risk."

"You can take the risk yourself, next time." After he said this, James felt his anger shift toward himself. "I wish I had known how much of a risk I was taking. All I can say is I'm glad Chris's supplier was skimping on him. I'd be a felon."

"Yeah, you're lucky."

James picked up Nolan's unplugged guitar and played along with "Mentally Murdered." By the end of the song his mind had unclenched and he was remembering that Angie had let him kiss her.

"Hey, maybe your mom could take care of Angie's little girl this weekend, since she's already minding the Beast."

"I can ask. But I didn't think Angie much cared for metal."

"She just needs an education."

"You trying to educate her? Eh, you teaching her a thing or two? You dog!"

"What!" James said. "I haven't done anything. She's married. Get your mind out of the gutter."

"*My* mind."

James blushed because he himself could hardly believe some of the things he imagined doing with her. "I'm not a rock star like you."

"I keep telling you, we don't even have a band anymore. Muzz isn't coming back from Albuquerque."

James knew the story: Zella had taken off in a huff, said she was going to get a job and live with her sister in New Mexico, and Muzz chased after her. Apparently she was being a bitch, not letting him in the door, probably seeing some other guy. But Muzz just kept going after her. "Well, if he isn't coming back, let me play guitar and you can play bass."

"I don't know," Nolan said lazily, his eyes bloodshot and glazed over. "It's probably not worth the trouble. I mean, nobody could keep to a practice schedule; we could hardly ever practice or do a gig when somebody wasn't wasted."

"Come on, man. Leon still wants to play, doesn't he?"

"Yeah, I guess so, but I don't know if he'd go along with totally reconfiguring the band. You'd have to learn all our songs, and we'd have to see how the chemistry is."

"Fine! So let's try it out. If it doesn't feel right, so be it."

"Okay. Find a place for us to jam, and then we'll talk it over."

James had a hard time getting to sleep that night. Being happy and excited for the future was as bad for sleep as worrying uselessly.

The next morning, it took an extra couple cups of coffee to get him going, but by midmorning he felt quick with his words. The first tour group was eight Elderhostel people. From the looks of them James worried that somebody would break his hip or wander off, and figured their questions would verge on the personal and irrelevant. But it turned out that several of them had been teachers and professors, and one sharp old guy had read the new book on J. L. Hubbell and his sons. "I think the verdict is still out, don't you? Who got more out of Hubbell's Trading Company, Hubbell or the Navajos?"

At lunch there was a birthday party for Littlesunday. Everyone tried to pin him down on his age, but he kept saying, "Ninety, maybe. Ninety-four, maybe." He looked in his wallet for the slip of paper with his birth date and census number but couldn't find it. "One hundred, maybe."

The ladies had brought a typical spread: casseroles, pasta dishes, Jell-O marshmallow salad, cake, cookies. The superintendent brought in a tray of chicken enchiladas that everyone went for. "You ought to try them," one of the weavers told James. "He really knows how to cook."

They were good, and Gabaldon sat down across the table from James and gave him the recipe. "The most important thing is how you pull the meat," he said. "Some people just cut it up, or even grind it up, but you have to pull it off the bone in strips, little strips. They call it machaca, pounded."

"But are you sure you don't pound it?" James said.

"Some do. I should make you nopalitos one day." His eyes got bright when he talked about food. "You don't just use them straight from the jar, that's the trick. You have to rinse them really well, get that slime off them. Then cook them with a little chile, some cheese . . ."

"You do all the cooking?"

"There's no one else. My wife is taking care of our house in El Paso. But even when she is here, she doesn't know a thing about cooking. The best cooks are always men."

The afternoon tour was another geriatric group, this time from an assisted-living facility in Sun City. They were herded around by both the driver of the van and a nursing assistant, but with twelve of them, once in a while a grandma or a grandpa strayed from the group. They had their eyes open, the way sheep did, but none of them really seemed to know where they were. After a while he gave up on the lecture and led them around through the usual stations without stopping. Some of them were out of breath when they got back to the van. "Okay, load up!" the driver said. "Watch your step, sweetheart."

James suddenly remembered the guy in jail, the wife beater, who had been accused of sexual harassment for saying "sweetheart." And where was Greenstone, his chess teacher?

When he reentered the store, James saw a familiar figure in serious conversation with the superintendent. It was Reverend Austin, who had come to Ganado when James was in middle school. His father had called him "an irascible person," privately, secretly, the way adults do. It was the first time he had heard that word. James remembered Austin as an asshole, an irascible asshole. He had once yelled at James and some friends when he saw them trying to cheat the pop machine in the Presbyterian Youth Center. He was a big figure, silver hair and beard and a red face, tall and paunchy, always in a clerical collar and a huge silver cross. Now he was leaning on the counter across from

Gabaldon, who looked like he wanted to be somewhere else, holding forth on some important subject, his cross swinging to and fro like a grandfather clock.

"No offense," Gabaldon was saying.

"None taken," said Reverend Austin, but clearly some had been.

Gabaldon caught James's eye and it seemed that he was asking him for help. Reverend Austin turned to James, and after a moment's hesitation smiled in recognition. His teeth must have been dentures, they were so straight and white.

"Well, if it isn't the prodigal son!" James was afraid he was in for a Protestant hug, but Austin shook his hand heartily. "I heard you were back in the area after a resounding success in the city."

James had no idea what the minister was talking about, and suspected he was mocking him. He had never had an adult conversation with the man, and his strongest memory was the pop machine incident. "Yeah, I'm working here. How's the minister business?"

"Oh, I've had the usual pastoral duties, the usual frustrations with the Presbyterian hierarchy. I won't bore you with all that. And I'm also involved in the Gore campaign. I am absolutely convinced that for the sake of the environment we must elect Al Gore."

"Yeah, I don't like Bush." The image that lingered in James's mind, stronger since his jail experience, was Bush as governor, sneering over the executions.

"And how are your parents?"

"Fine. Still in Flagstaff."

"You just decided to move back?"

"I like it here. I live out at the ranch, which is nice and quiet, and I have this job, which is kind of interesting, and I'm getting ready to form a band."

"What kind of band? Not some sort of satanic bat-biting act, I hope."

"Nah, I don't think we'd go in for that. You could get rabies."

"You know, with all the criticism from the Christian right, I think there is a real place for music in our ministry."

"No doubt." James was smiling inwardly, wondering if Reverend Austin thought he was going to play in front of his congregation one day. He remembered the trick with Christian pop-rock lyrics: substitute

"Jesus" for "baby," as in, "I just want to be with you, Jesus," and "I can't live without you, Jesus." James said, "We just haven't found a place to practice yet."

"Well, maybe you should think about using our youth center. Our youth pastor recently left, so our programs are in abeyance. It might be temporary, but I believe I could offer you the use of that space for a while, at least. Come on over after work and let me show you around."

The space was perfect, really: a big room in the building that was used for a day-care center, with plenty of electrical outlets. He shook Reverend Austin's hand vigorously. "I'm sure glad I ran into you."

The day was still warm and above, the light blazed like cinnamon on the part of the mesa they called Round Top. The sky was complicated, like an old painting. On the spur of the moment he walked across the wash and up the valley between the fingers of the mesa. There had been only a light rain in the early afternoon, so his boots weren't collecting big globs of mud. The rain had sent the smell of cliffrose into the air, not the intensely sweet scent of the flowers, but the complex, pungent odor of the resinous leaves.

There were many routes up to the mesa top, all sheep and cattle trails. He chose one that traversed a slope of tumbled sandstone and lake-deposit limestone. On top, he walked from one side to the other of the narrow neck and down the escarpments into the little valleys. At his feet, among the sagebrush, there were fragments of ancient pottery, and at overlooks, the remnants of parties, with fire circles, cans, and bottles. Somewhere in the sand, no doubt, there were traces of blood.

For two hours he walked along the crescent rims slowly toward the school housing compound, where Angie tended her child. He would have to be careful with Angie. He did not want to make the same mistakes again. No wild drinking, no jealousy, no carelessness. He would have to treat her right. No temper. He would have to stop whenever he didn't know how far to go.

CHAPTER TWELVE

▧ **WHEN JAMES SHOWED** up at Nolan's on Saturday morning, he was alone at his kitchen table drinking beer. Three empty cans sat on the table around him.

"Whoa, is this breakfast, dude?"

"Why the hell not? It's nearly eleven. Thought you'd never get your ass over here. Is Angie ready?"

The concert in Tempe started at eight, so they had plenty of time to get there if they left by noon. They were going to go in Leon's father's van but on Friday night Leon called to say his father had a big exterminating job to do, and all he had was a truck that was smaller than James's and would only hold two, so Nolan had to talk his parents into lending their car.

"I haven't seen her yet. You know, you can't drive."

"What are you, my mother?"

"I'm going over to Angie's. Maybe she's got some coffee."

Angie had agreed to come only after a sustained lobbying effort by James. His persistence surprised even himself. On Tuesday, when he showed up at her place after work, she had given him a glass of iced tea, and they sat on the couch holding hands. He was happy with this, even while he was amused by the television triteness of the situation. She was a little silly, asking why he thought she should go.

"Because I want you to."

"That's definitely not a good enough reason. You couldn't convince one person in the world to do anything at all with a reason like that."

"Okay, then, because you need to get out a little."

"Says who?"

"Okay, because you'll have fun."

"I doubt that. A whole building full of headbangers going crazy?"

On Wednesday she had cooked him dinner. She seemed to have planned it out: the chicken-fried steaks defrosting on the counter, potatoes boiling, gravy bubbling. She had cut up a cabbage and fixed homemade cole slaw. She gave the baby a boiled egg and some mashed carrots as well as some of the potatoes and gravy and served James as if she had done it many times before.

"Wow," he said. "I didn't know you could cook."

"What? How do you think I feed myself and my family?"

"Maybe the same way I feed myself. I open a can, or go visiting at dinnertime, like now." James felt he was as close to the subject as he had ever been, and thought he should take a chance. "There's just the two of you, anyway."

She had just sat down but popped up again without a word and came back with the salt. After a moment she cleared her throat and said, "Well, it wasn't always like that. Up until this spring, before he went back to Korea, there was him and both kids to feed and this was on base, which is not great housing."

"Where was this?"

"Fort Riley, Kansas. Explosions all day and all night rattling the cupboards." The baby was getting ready to throw a piece of egg yolk, and Angie said, "No!"

The baby delivered a challenge with a gaze of mild neutrality, knowing that at any moment she could change her mind and start screaming and wailing.

"That's why when he told me he was going to re-up again I said no thanks."

"And you came back here."

"Well, actually this is my sister's house. It's complicated. It's her house, she signed the contract with the housing authority, which says something about continuously occupying it. But she got a good job in Shiprock, so I'm staying here with the baby while my other girl is in kindergarten in Shiprock, with her. It works out, at least for now."

"She could go to kindergarten here, couldn't she?"

Angie hesitated. "She likes it there. She's crazy about her cousin, Evangeline."

"That's strange," James said. "You mean you asked a five-year-old if she wanted to live with her mother, and when she said no, you went along with it?"

"I don't think you should be giving me a hard time about it, James. It's something my sister and I decided on because of my situation."

He saw her eyes well up and said, "Okay. What do I know?"

After dinner he tried to get the baby to sleep so that he could snuggle up with Angie as much as she would let him, but the baby wasn't having it. She wouldn't sit still for a picture book, and she wouldn't let him roughhouse with her. She kept climbing over her mother, who had sat on the floor below where he sprawled on the couch. He had thought that her sitting there was a good sign, but her daughter was too smart for them both: he got only a good-bye kiss, and he had no chance to ask her what she meant when she told her husband "no thanks."

Every time he had gone to see her he had wanted to ask her about her husband—he thought of it as "straightening out the business with the husband"—but each time he left he realized he hadn't. On Thursday she gave him an iced tea and also the good news that her sister would be down for the weekend and that Angie would be coming with James and the others on Saturday.

"Great," James said. He had again been on the brink of asking about Malcolm, but she had just agreed to come with them to the concert and he didn't want to push his luck. He had been trying out ways of phrasing it: "So did you mean no thanks to all of it?" That seemed too vague. "Did you talk about divorce?" That sounded like an interrogation.

He was a little angry at her about it, though he hated to let this show. After all, didn't she realize he would need to know about this? Why didn't she just volunteer something?

He stopped by Nolan's before he drove back to the ranch and found that his parents had left a message for him to call.

"We were planning on coming out this weekend," his mother told him. "Thought we could see what you're up to."

"I've got the weekend off and I'm going to Phoenix with some friends."

"Oh." She sounded disappointed. "What's in Phoenix?"

"Cryptopsy concert."

"Oh, well, I guess I won't see you then. How is everything?"

"Good, Mom. The job's okay. The weather's good, some nice rains. You guys okay?"

He wondered if they had found out that he had been in jail. It wasn't the kind of thing that stayed secret for long. He might tell them sometime, but he didn't see a reason to now.

On the phone his mother was telling him, "Stay out of trouble, dear."

That was an indication that she had not heard about his time in jail, for she spoke about trouble in the generic way that would always be a part of her thoughts of her children. What was it about trouble? It was his role to get into it, had been since he was a baby, headed for the campfire or the deep end of the motel swimming pool. And it was their role to warn him against trouble, against more trouble, against his defining characteristic.

On Friday, Leon called to say they would have to go in two cars. He and Zendrick, the guitarist from Fort Defiance, would go together and meet at the motel. Now on Saturday morning Nolan was already half drunk and no one was answering at Angie's. The baby tromped into view through the screen door.

"Hey, Winona," James said softly to her, kneeling. She dropped the plastic toy she was carrying, which looked like a small AK-47. "Where's Mama?"

"Mama!"

Angie appeared and said, "I'm still waiting for my sister. She called at seven from Shiprock, so she should be here by now."

By the time Angie's sister Irene and her daughter arrived it was afternoon, and James was feeling rushed to get on the road. "You have to let me see my baby," she told him, cuddling her five-year-old, Reeba, who looked at her feet. "You are my baby, aren't you, Reebie? Aren't you?" Angie's finger was tracing circles at the base of the girl's neck.

A smile began in the corners of Reeba's mouth and then took over her face. "Nona's the *baby*."

"But you're my baby, too." James was glad to hear her say it.

He shook hands with Irene and said hello to her daughter Evangeline, the ten-year-old who had made the drunk-driving poster and had said, "That's the *point*." Now she didn't say anything; she was playing her Game Boy. Angie gave Reeba a hug but when she tried to kiss Winona good-bye, she kept wriggling and trying to get Evangeline's attention. After a few awkward moments James and Angie broke away.

In the car, James grumbled that they were supposed to have left in the *morning*. Then Angie reminded him that it was an hour earlier in Phoenix. "Actually what really pissed me off was . . ." James used his thumb to indicate the back seat, where Nolan was stretched out and already snoring. Angie giggled.

"I mean, Jesus Christ, first thing in the morning." He used to think it was funny when his friends got drunk. "These days I got less patience for that kind of stuff. I'm seeing my young drunk friends turn into the old drunk people I used to laugh about in high school."

"In high school I used to laugh at everyone," said Angie. "Almost all adults. I don't really remember why I thought they were ridiculous, or why I thought I was going to grow up to be any different. Anyway here I am, no better at all."

"Yup," said James. As he passed the turnoff to the ranch he said, "I should take you out there sometime." Angie blushed and said nothing. James thought that from her point of view he must seem to be a sex-crazed and dangerous man. "There's some hills with a lot of potsherds I could show you."

"Yíiyá." In the old way of thinking, Anasazi were dead, and their remnants were to be avoided. Now she thought he was a ghoul, but at least that was better than a likely rapist.

"While we're on yíiyá, up on that hill was where Rodney Kinlicheenie's grandparents used to live, on his father's side." James knew she remembered. No one they had been in school with would ever forget.

"It looks abandoned," Angie said. There were big patches on the roof where the shingles had blown off, and a gate hung askew by its lower hinge.

James felt the familiar shiver travel from his shoulders to his balls. Just past the turnoff the pavement was full of potholes and he had to slalom between them. Up and over one more low escarpment, and they were descending slowly into the broad, shallow valley, the air a little hazy with heat and recent cloudbursts. Stretches of the highway, for half a mile or so, were wet and puddled, sparkling everywhere, the clay hills shining in juicy reds and greens as shadows of low clouds rushed through.

James waited until she faced away from him, watching the landscape on the right, to reach over and put his hand over hers. She gave him a squeeze and smiled, looking not as surprised as he thought she should be. "Poor Rodney. We're lucky," she said. James had always thought that if Rodney had lived, he would have been no better off than if he were dead. Or perhaps he would have already died some other way.

Not far down the interstate stood a flaking billboard advertising "Truck Wash and Knife City."

"Do you realize," he said, "that after Rodney, there were no more knife fights?"

"I never thought about it. To me, that was the first time I had ever heard of fighting with a knife in Ganado. Two-by-fours and pieces of pipe, maybe, just spur of the moment stuff, whatever's handy when you're drunk and mad, but never a knife, a gun, something *premeditated.*"

"That's true. But, what's really interesting is a lot of us carried knives then. I did. I just liked knives, liked to show them to my friends. I used to love stores like Knife City. Ben and I used to make my father stop there every time we went by, and Dad hated to. Throwing knives, survival knives . . . We carried them, but somehow when we fought we never pulled them out."

"I remember you back then. Long hair, scowling at everyone, you and Nolan. Your evil laugh . . ."

James laughed. "We just wanted to keep things peaceful, get people to back off before they had a chance to *think* about starting something." Always stressed, alert to the constant danger. "You know, it's no wonder so many guys from the rez join the service. It's like after high school you're already accustomed to a combat situation."

"They just brainwashed you boys, starting from way back. So when on Career Day in high school the only ones who showed up were the recruiters for the army and the marines, nobody thought anything about it. Seemed natural. That's how they got Malcolm. Signed him right up."

"This is after the speech the principal makes about following your dreams, right?"

"Right."

"I thought about joining the army for a little while, just to make my dad mad. Navajo patriotism drives him crazy. But my plan A in high school was to become a famous underground cartoonist, and a metal star with my own plane. Now just cutting a CD seems like a pretty big thing. More or less out of my reach, you know?"

At the top of the long rise was the entrance to the Petrified Forest National Park, and from there west the desert spread out like a sea. Once, years ago when he stood on a hill beside the Pacific, he had felt, looking at the sea, that he was looking at a desert like this one, wide open.

Soon the dinosaurs began. A few years ago, not long after the last of the kitschy billboards advertising such attractions as "Indian Squaw Weaving Rug" had come down (replaced briefly by "A Navajo Weaver Practices Her Art"), statues of dinosaurs began to pop up along the highway in the Painted Desert. First they had been rather impressive, realistic sculptures in green and brown, but more recently, gaudy and comical prehistoric constructions appeared, upholding the artistic tradition of Route 66. Nolan, who had been lying on his back with his head on a pillow, cycling through periods of snoring and silence, sat straight up, staring at the Kelly green concrete tyrannosaur crushing a school bus on top of the mesa. "Wow, they're getting better and better!" Nolan looked all around and caught sight of a long-necked diplodocus with a child in its mouth. "I love this stuff. I wish they had it when I was a kid."

"Good morning," said James.

"Anybody getting hungry?" said Nolan.

They played the game of "who sees the first saguaro" as they descended to the desert, and all three of them called out at the same time. It was not long before they were slowly engulfed in the city. By Carefree Road James had to pay attention, as urban drivers zipped from lane to lane with an insolence that kept him on edge. The air began to smell of exhaust. The heat blasted up and out from the acres and acres of pavement. This was where a hard-core concert belonged.

Eight lanes of traffic. "I'm really surprised they don't have more accidents," James said. It suddenly struck him as improbable that so many humans had mastered high-speed driving on narrow painted lanes and curves. "As Mr. Utmost used to say, remember?"

"'It boggles the mind.'"

Nolan guided James through the streets to their motel in Scottsdale. "I reserved three rooms," James said.

"That was nice of you," Angie said.

Two hours after James checked into the motel, Leon and Zendrick arrived with a twelve pack and some chips and dips, and they all gathered in the room Nolan and James had claimed for themselves. Angie came from next door. They turned up the air-conditioning full blast, sat on the beds and the floor, and cracked one beer after another, joking and kidding each other, watching professional wrestling on mute until it was time to go out to eat and then head over to the concert.

CHAPTER THIRTEEN

⬚ **THE DOORS OPENED** about an hour before the band was supposed to come on, but there was already a big line, which moved slowly because everyone had to pass through a metal detector and the bouncers were patting everyone down. The mole on Angie's forehead was hidden by her frown and her movements were quick and jumpy. "Too many people," she said.

James thought all this was designed to make the scene appear edgy and dangerous, and therefore more appealing, but he said, "I guess they're worried somebody might take death metal literally." Angie did not seem reassured.

A bar was jammed up against the wall in the back, and they all got beers. The others disappeared into the crowd but Angie wanted to sit in back, away from the crush of fans standing around the stage.

"I've never seen so much dirty hair," she said.

He laughed at her, shivering in the over-refrigerated air. "Would you rather be in the middle of a crowd of skinheads?"

"I don't know what would be worse."

"Relax. Another couple of Coronas and you'll be able to enjoy yourself."

"No, I'm in the burp stage now. Once I start burping I can't get any more beer down."

"Not me," said James, burping loudly and patting his stomach. "When I burp, it makes room."

"Gross," she said. "Reminds me of Malcolm. So proud of all the disgusting noises he could make."

"I'd hate to compete."

He put his arm around her and she snuggled up. "It's freezing in here." She was wearing a light, almost gauzy blouse that gave a good view of the top of her breasts. She had goose bumps on her arms.

Finally, after several tech men walked on and off the stage, running equipment checks, the strobe lights started flashing, the stage was bathed in blue and magenta, and the band came on, swinging their hair around. In the middle of the platform sat the drummer, balding and with a small ponytail, surrounded by his drums and stacks of cymbals, tearing through the rhythm like a fast train. The vocalist in front of him growled in a long black leather coat. The two guitarists and the bass hammered away on the ends of the stage. The audience, standing in layers as close as they could come to the band, howled and cried out, flinging hair and giving the horn salute, adoration that could be mistaken for hostility. Between the standing crowd and James and Angie, a dozen young men were slam dancing.

Angie was giggling nervously.

"What's wrong?" he said, smiling.

"Nothing."

"Those kids up there? They're morons. Don't pay any attention to them, just listen to the music."

Angie sat quietly for a while, then was overcome again by giggles. Two of the slam dancers had banged heads, literally, and were staggering around. "Did they do that on purpose?"

"I don't think so," James said.

They had to lean over to talk in each other's ears. The simultaneous beat of the drums and the guitars caused a vibration in James's chest. "I like his bracelet," she said, cupping her hands. "*Bracelet.*"

One of the guitarists wore a spiky iron bracelet on his left wrist, and at the end of a song he combed his hair out with the fingers of this hand. The applause of the crowd was enthusiastic but compared to the amplified band seemed soft and anemic.

The strobe lights were particularly bright and unsettling. James had heard that they could cause seizures and wondered how you would know if you were susceptible. The lights had shifted to red and violet, and the effect was of a bizarre, staccato inferno of gyrating heads and bodies. For a long moment the drummer took over, sounding the cymbals in his trademark magnified clash. This was the mystery and power he was hoping to feel: the shiver began in his stomach and traveled both ways, up to his brain and down. The shimmering sound filled his head and he couldn't control the tears he felt. "Go, Flo!" he hollered. "Right on!"

Before long, James was glad to see that Angie had overcome her giggles and looked to be enjoying herself, smiling at the crowd and once in a while demurely bobbing her head for a few beats. She was giving in to it in her own hesitant way. The crowd beside the stage had grown, and a dense mass of bodies only a few feet away blocked their view. They left their seats and stood farther back.

The theater was at capacity, and the heat of the mob began to overwhelm the air-conditioning. "I don't guess it's any cooler outside," said James. They stayed through the break and the second set and watched while the musicians blessed their fans by grabbing their scalps lovingly and gently, and slapping hands. Then, before the crowd moved toward the doors, Angie and James walked outside.

"I don't see our guys," Angie said on the sidewalk.

The heat from the street still radiated up like an oven. At home it was almost never hot at night, and it made it hard to breathe here. "They'll get back, even if they have to walk. It's not far. I think they're all together anyway."

Back at the motel, they settled on the floor at the foot of James's bed. She said, "Sorry to be a wet blanket."

"No, I'm glad you came." They were holding hands and James gave her a light kiss. "Didn't you enjoy it at all?"

"No, yeah . . ."

"You just aren't into all the hangers-on."

"Just not my taste in music, I guess. But thank you for inviting me. I like being with you." They kissed again, and James lay down with his head in her lap. She played with his hair, which he had cut to get the job at Hubbell's but had started to grow back. "You've got Indian hair," she remarked.

"It's dominant," he said proudly. "Plus my dad ain't bald."

"Doesn't it seem amazing that so many people at that concert were Indians?"

"Why? I grew up with that kind of music."

"Not me. It always seemed foreign. In my family it was country-western. The farthest-out thing for my parents was like Waylon Jennings or Willie Nelson. Outlaws."

"Goes to show you we're a varied tribe. A lot of folks spend all their time going to song-and-dances."

"I like them sometimes. Especially the kids, all dressed up and solemn."

"Yeah, it's all good. Not my thing for sure, but I wouldn't begrudge anybody their own music. Tonight, that was pretty much my style. I don't know how to explain how it makes me feel. Angie, do you know how serious I am about music?"

"I've never really heard you play."

James sat up and stared into her eyes. She blinked in surprise. "It's the only thing I want to do with my life," he said. "I mean, I know I have to have a job, but it's always just going to be a job. And I guess I want a family." She smiled and he kissed her cheek. "But everyone wants a family. I want to eat, too, but I mean beyond the necessities, music is the one thing that means something to me."

She frowned in concentration, and her mole retreated behind the wrinkles in her forehead. "You're lucky. I don't really have anything like that. And it's not true that everyone wants a family. Malcolm doesn't, not really. I mostly think about my kids, what kinds of things are important for them to be happy, even for them just to survive. Let's get up off the floor."

Finally it was cool enough outside on the balcony to sit on the white plastic chairs and listen to the little misters spraying in the grass below. "We never had those kind of sprinklers in Ganado," James said. "Just the big oscillating kind."

"Those old ones are much more fun for kids to jump through. The water kind of knocks into you." Angie laughed. "That was the big summertime thing if you lived in the school compound. Kids who lived out on the rez would come in just to run through our sprinklers and get soaking wet."

"Anything for fun. Do you remember the guy, I think he worked in the maintenance department, lined the back of his truck with garbage bags and filled it up with water? In the summer he'd drive his kids all around, splashing and yelling."

"My dad said he ruined his springs that way."

"Cheap thrills on the rez. Driving your kids around in a mobile pool. Bingo, beauty pageants, cakewalks."

"You like being on the rez again?"

"Yeah, especially if I can get this band thing going."

"I'm kind of sick of it, all the gossip and smallness. If I could leave, I might."

"Where else would you be?"

"Well, when Malcolm re-upped I told him I wasn't living on the base anymore, and he refused to pay for an apartment in Junction City. I would have been happy there, I think."

"I think the rez is better for me right now. I just get pissed off in the city. I don't know anybody in Phoenix, but I'd end up hating everybody who lives here. Flagstaff isn't as bad, but I feel that way there, too: mean waitresses, fucking cops."

He pulled on her hand to guide her into his lap, and they nuzzled. He tried to put his hand inside her bra, but she said, "I don't think we should let things get too far."

"I'm not going to get you pregnant, Angie."

She laughed but looked sad. "That's the last thing I'm worried about."

"What is it, then?"

"I'm married, James. And until I can figure out how to get unmarried, it feels wrong to be starting up something with you."

They sat in separate chairs and stared ahead unhappily. James knew now was the time that he could really screw up, because he was angry and could easily say something to hurt her and ruin things for the future. But maybe what she was saying was that there was no future in it. "How do you figure?" he said. "About getting unmarried."

"I don't know. Please don't push me, James. I want to see you, but I just have to figure some things out first."

The way he was feeling—angry and wronged, jealous of this man he didn't know but who he was sure had mistreated Angie—confused him and made him want to come out with some sarcastic and final comment. But he held his tongue, waited the long moments before he simmered down. Finally he said, "Have you decided that you don't want to be married to him?"

"Oh, I've decided. I decided when I left Kansas."

"What's getting in your way?"

She sighed and leaned her head against his shoulder. "It's a long story."

James knew that he should not say too much. His anger was subsiding, but he still felt he was on unstable ground, like the quicksand out in the Painted Desert.

She went on: "It's all about the kids. And about the trouble he's going to cause when I tell him I want a divorce. Especially the trouble he'll cause about custody and child support—I know he won't abide by child support."

James had heard about restraining orders and courts taking money out of paychecks for child support; he'd heard plenty of ugly stories about divorce over the years, but he hadn't paid attention to how it actually was done. Not being married, it hadn't seemed important to him. "Well, what choice do you have? If you don't go through with it, you'll never get away from him." *And I won't have a chance with you.*

"True. The other thing is, I don't really know what to do with my life. Or I feel there isn't anything I can do with my life, except raise these kids somehow."

"I'm too young to have kids," James said. "I'm not responsible enough. I like kids, other people's kids, but I don't know if I should have any of my own."

"Well, you're more mature than your friends."

"That isn't saying much. Who knows what kind of trouble they're getting into even as we speak? My temper could get me back in trouble, too."

"Really? You don't seem to have much of a temper."

"Oh, jeez. I guess it's good you think that. Most the time it's under control."

"Well, it can't be as bad as Malcolm's. One time he hit me so hard it almost knocked me out, and I swear he woulda killed me if I didn't run out and hide at my girlfriend's."

Christ. I'd kill him. "Booze?"

"What do you think? Booze and just plain meanness. I don't know, it probably doesn't sound like much ambition, but my goal is pretty much to save up some money from this job and get my kids back under one roof, and keep Malcolm away."

"Is money the reason you don't take care of Reeba?"

"Well, that's part of it. I haven't been working, and Irene suggested it. It seemed like a good idea then, but I feel bad being away from her."

"Why don't you just tell your sister you want to take care of both your kids?"

She shrugged. "I should, I guess. Irene won't like it."

"You're the mother."

It was well past midnight and the traffic outside the motel had thinned out. The sprinklers had stopped hissing and a hint of freshness rose in the still-warm air. James didn't want to say anything. If he talked about Malcolm, that was keeping the man in their thoughts, and, like Angie, his goal was to keep Malcolm away. And yet in his silence he was seething. Being married to her didn't give him the right to mistreat her. He didn't own her. James hated him.

He squeezed her shoulder, still lacking words. A car parked in the lot below them. It was not their friends. "I wonder what happened to them," she said.

"I don't know. It's a big bad city."

They lay down on top of the bed when they could no longer stay awake. They did not remove the covers, they kept on their clothes, and James took care not to press too hard into Angie as he gave her a last kiss. His anger had faded into exhaustion and also into hope. It seemed like she was telling him everything, almost.

It was midmorning when Zendrick and Leon stumbled into the room. Angie groaned and rolled onto her stomach and put the pillow over her head. James sat up on the edge of the bed and rubbed his eyes. "Are you guys able to make any more noise?"

"Come on, man, we need to look for Nolan," Zendrick said.

James noticed an abrasion in the middle of Zendrick's nose that hadn't been there the day before. "What happened to *you*?" he asked, indicating his own nose.

"How the hell should I know?" said Zendrick.

Leon looked a little steadier on his feet than Zendrick did. Not really wanting to know the answer, James asked him, "What happened to Nolan?"

"Got any beer?" Zendrick said.

"Forget it!" James surprised himself at how furious he felt, and Angie sat up looking at him.

"All right, all right, don't get your dick in a tangle."

"I mean, Jesus, one of you's got to drive back today."

"I'm okay," said Leon. "I will be soon, anyway."

"So where's Nolan?" James asked again.

"That's what we don't know. I keep telling you," said Zendrick. He walked to the balcony doors and threw them open. The day was bright and the air from outside was like a blast from a blow-dryer.

Leon said, "The last time I saw him the bouncers had both of these guys facedown on the sidewalk. Nolan was pretty wasted, and of course he had to start mouthing off to them. For some reason they let this clown go . . ."

"Hey!" said Zendrick.

"But they were calling the cops for Nolan when we finally took off."

"Okay, what's the big problem?" James said. "Now we know where Nolan is. He's wearing an orange jumpsuit."

"We can't leave town without him, man," said Zendrick.

"Why not? I've got the car keys; you guys have your own ride. I can't stay down here. I've got an appointment with my PO."

"Your what?" said Angie.

"Probation officer. Don't pretend, Angie, I know you heard the whole story."

"And tomorrow's my first day of work," she told the others. "I can't just not show up."

James said, "Nolan's a big boy, and jail might teach him a thing or two."

CHAPTER FOURTEEN

▨ **"OKAY, LET'S SET** up, then we got to have a little meeting." The room in the church's day-care building seemed huge, and there was a cavelike echo in the empty space that made James feel his heart beat in his throat. They hauled their equipment from their vehicles and set up the drums, amps, microphones. James wasn't sure when he had taken on the role of band boss, but it felt natural. Probably it was because he had found this space, and it was to him Reverend Austin had just handed over the key.

The minister had met them at the door and took the opportunity to give a little speech, a kind of sermon. "One of the duties of the church in society is to give a boost to our young people." He went on about how music was a spiritual gateway, even though some fundamental sects feared and forbade music, and blah blah blah.

"Thanks, Reverend Austin."

It was Saturday afternoon. It was tourist season at the trading post, and James had been tapped for tour duty that morning. He would have been tired if he hadn't been about to finally jam.

"Who's got the extra octopus cords?" Zendrick said. "I need them here."

They arranged four metal chairs in a circle and all sat backward in them. "First," James said, "we have to agree to a few things, some ground rules, and hopefully it'll work out. The first rules have got to be Reverend Austin's rules. No practice Sunday morning. Quiet after ten. Occasional guests are okay, but no partying."

"Oh shit," said Zendrick. "What's the point then?" Everybody laughed, but Zendrick looked around and said, "What? I'm serious." They laughed again.

"Then there are rules we need to make as a band. When we have to vote to make any decision, majority rules. We need to agree on practice times and stick with it. And no drinking or smoking dope during practice."

There was a lively discussion about this point.

"If it's no fun, what's the point?" said Zendrick, clearly not joking. "Besides, some of my best music happens when I'm stoned."

"How about when you're drunk?" Leon asked. There was a tone of challenge in his voice; Leon had known Zendrick since high school.

"Not really."

The rule they adopted was to not practice drunk. It was okay to come to practice stoned, but no lighting up in the building because it would get them thrown out. James summarized: "What you do on your own time is your own business, but while we're trying to make music together, no being wasted."

"Should we be writing this down?" Leon asked.

"Are you going to forget?" Nolan said. "Jeez, none of us hardly reads music, and we all know lots of songs, so why start writing things down?"

"Well," said James, "I guess sometimes it does matter what you do on your own time. Like you, Nolan, after you'd been thrown in in Phoenix and if your folks hadn't bailed you out, we wouldn't be able to practice today."

Nolan turned red, or another shade, as his skin was so dark, the color of a bruise. "*Nishą*'? I seem to recall you had a run-in with the law not long ago."

James laughed it off, since everyone except his parents knew about that anyway and he was beginning not to feel embarrassed about it. "That's about all, right now, if we want to get started. We'll have to have other discussions when we start to get gigs, start to get paid and all that, but that's later. Let's jam."

James pounded away at an E-F-G-F progression, then turned his reverb up. Zendrick joined him while Nolan was trying to tune his bass.

"Hold it hold it hold it," James said to Zendrick. "You're like way out of tune."

"You're full of shit, man," Zendrick said. "If anybody's out of tune, you are."

Leon was warming himself up with his sticks and not paying attention. Nolan was laughing. "Okay, here's E," he said. It was the same as James's E's, first string and sixth. Everything in between was perfect.

"Okay, you now, Zendrick," Nolan said. "Here's your E."

He was a quarter-note flat. He had to be that much off, and Nolan laughed while James scowled.

"What?" said Zendrick. "It's perfect."

"You're flat!" they both said, and again Nolan laughed and James scowled. James wondered what was so funny about it; the guy didn't even hear it.

Zendrick tuned up some. "More," Nolan told him. Zendrick tuned up, this time sharp. "Whoa," said Nolan.

"Okay," Zendrick said and played a chord.

"Gimme that!" James finally said, grabbing Zendrick's guitar and tuning it himself. "See?" He handed it back.

"Jesus Christ."

Leon was about up to speed, getting into thrash mode, already starting to sweat. He ended with cymbals. "Okay! What'll we play?"

Nolan said, "Let's start with something we all know. How about 'Fade to Black'?"

James said, "Oh, one other rule. No covers. All original music."

"Like what?" said Zendrick. "We don't have any original music."

Nolan said, "What about one of the old Putrefaction songs? James, you've heard us. Zendrick, just fake it."

It was a disaster, of course. Nolan's playing wasn't inspired, but who listened to the bass? He should be glad they weren't playing country, where it's all oom-pa doom-pa. Nolan was pretty gloomy in general, like he had a headache. What was he expecting, anyway? It was the first time jamming together; they weren't going to be ready for the studio just like that. James was glad Leon showed more enthusiasm: he wasn't always perfectly accurate, but he could keep up with the guitars and sometimes double-time them, quick as a tweaker, though when he put his drumsticks down he was as laid-back as Mr. Rogers. Everything was okay with him. James had once asked him about this, before James had been arrested and could still smoke pot, when they were sitting around outside Chris Soros's hogan. "So how do you get like that, so that nothing riles you?"

"Well, you know I worked with my dad around all those chemicals. They're just now discovering that some of these insecticides are the best tranquilizers. It just doesn't seem worthwhile to get bothered about stuff."

"On the other hand, maybe it's because you can take out all your aggression on the drums so that you don't got any left for life."

"Could be. A couple of years ago I broke my hand and couldn't play. I did get pretty grouchy."

That's why it was so surprising that toward the end of that first jam session, Leon really lost it. Inspired by Cryptopsy, he had built his tower of cymbals much taller, and after a furious conclusion to another old Putrefaction tune, it collapsed onto the floor with a tremendous crash. "Fuck! Fuck fuck fuck!" He was still moaning, checking out every cymbal for dents as they packed up their instruments.

"It'll be better next time," James said. "Better and better. See you all on Wednesday."

James had seen Angie at work every day, but in the evenings since the concert, she always had something else to do: something with the baby, doctors' appointments, shopping. He was more and more certain that he had done something to offend her and was determined to clear it up. After the practice session James gave Nolan a lift back to his house, and he decided to drop in on her. There were all kinds of ways to mess this thing up, and one of them was to stop paying attention to her.

He called, "Hello, hello?" and walked in, which was what he had taken to doing instead of knocking. She was sitting at the kitchen table and looked up at him with an expression that confused him. It was not surprise, but a kind of frozen look, as if of fear or caution.

"What's up?" he said. "We just had our first jam session."

She didn't answer him but looked over his shoulder. Behind him he heard the bathroom door open, and a tall man his own age walked into the kitchen.

"This is my husband, Malcolm."

They shook hands without saying anything, eyeing each other carefully. A hard, bilagáana shake. Malcolm's hair was military short, and he had that flinty look the recruiters were after.

"James has been helping me out with . . . this and that. Malcolm just got back from Korea and he's on his way back to Kansas."

"How long are you going to be around?" James said. It didn't sound right. It sounded like *When is the coast going to be clear for me again?* Which was probably why Malcolm wasn't smiling.

"I'm not on R and R. If I'm not at Riley by oh-eight hundred on Thursday I'm AWOL."

James had planned to ask Angie to attend their next practice session on Wednesday, but it didn't seem like the right time to say this. Malcolm would be somewhere in Oklahoma by then, far from his wife and kids.

"Have a good visit. Winona must look bigger to you."

"Just three months since I seen her and she looks like a Mack truck."

There was the smell of mutton roasting, and Angie was mashing potatoes. He felt more than awkward. There was a kind of wariness in the air: not fear, but something like deference. *Wolves*, James thought. Wolves in a pack, testing each other out.

James left feeling betrayed. She must have known her husband was coming, and all week she hadn't said a thing. Now Malcolm was there in her house, waiting for her to serve him dinner. It wasn't long ago that she told James she intended to divorce Malcolm, someone he hadn't met yet, someone who was only an abstraction. Now he knew he was a tall, severe, and good-looking man, and wondered, with some sympathy toward him, if she had already told him, or was the bad news coming later? From Malcolm's confident manner, he supposed that she had put off discussing it. He wondered if he would be likely to get rough with her and if she would need help.

Or maybe she wasn't going to tell him, had never planned to divorce him, the father of her two children. One moment he was hopeful, the next dejected and anxious.

The sunlight was angry pink on the west side of the mesas and suddenly James felt that if he did not go off by himself, his irritation would lead him to trouble. He had Monday off, so he decided to spend the next three nights alone at the ranch.

In the morning the first thing he heard was sparrows around the house and in the junipers. He knew he would not be able to go back to sleep, as it was getting light, but he put his face in his pillow and lay still. Somehow while he was sleeping he had managed to nurse anger toward Angie, as now he thought of the things he wanted to say to her. He wanted to accuse her of not intending to say anything about Malcolm, of not intending to say anything to Malcolm about wanting a divorce, of playing James all this time, just someone to fool around with while her husband wasn't there. She and Malcolm had no doubt spent the night in the same bed, maybe even conceived another child. He remembered sitting with her on the balcony in Phoenix, talking quietly, and he knew his sour mood wasn't fair. But he didn't want to be fair. He wanted to imagine the worst.

His eyes still shut, he knew the sun was up because the meadowlarks were gurgling. It didn't make him happy, exactly, but it did make him want to get up. Drinking coffee on the doorstep, he saw Max down at the windmill filling the trough where two horses drank, the ones they had ridden several weeks ago. When James walked down to meet him he was standing on the ladder checking the water level in the tank.

"Horses came in, I see," James said.

"No, they didn't come in. Had to go get them. There was kind of a big deal yesterday. Beebee and his gang are at it again."

James hadn't thought of Beebee since the time they had seen him hopping over the sagebrush at his ranch, drunk and crazy. He had heard that they weren't able to pin the cattle rustling on him because he was mentally incapable of coming up with the scheme himself. Either that, or he had gotten off because his uncle was a judge. People said both things. But now there was more to the story. A sequel, always a sequel. James wondered if there is anything in the world that really ends.

"This time it was horses. Actually, the chapter has been talking about getting rid of the wild horses for years, and finally the tribe has money for it. Only they were supposed to check for brands, notify owners, all that.

"I'd been missing Spunk for a couple of weeks, since somebody opened the gate. I figured he would come around in a few days when he wanted grain or water, but a week, two weeks went by and I went out looking for him. Nowhere. I hadn't seen any tire tracks at the corral gate, so I didn't think someone had carried him off in a trailer. I lost the horse's tracks just right close to the corral.

"So I let it go. I figured sooner or later he would show up. He was probably out with a herd somewhere, the way it is around here." Max was chewing Skoal and he spit a little flood of brown drool into the dirt. "Well, Beebee and a pair of wetbacks had rounded up the horses, taking the chapter's money, and were fixing to sell them for dog food and keep the change. Only all our horses were in there, all the branded loose horses from every family in the area.

"Beebee claimed they were only doing what the chapter officials had told them to do, but the chapter vice president was there, as well as the head of the grazing committee. When I got out there—Chester had driven by to let me know what was going on—they were having a big argument, Beebee insisting that he would see to it that they lost their jobs. I thought somebody was going to get hurt. People ended up claiming their horses and there were only a few of the unbranded ones left in the corral."

"You think anything's going to happen to him?" James asked.

"I don't know. I figure sooner or later he's going to slip up somehow and they'll bust the whole ring of them."

"He doesn't seem like the criminal genius type."

"Ha! He's just doing what he's told."

"Who's telling him?"

"That's what I don't know. But somebody's contracting these wetbacks. Somebody's getting them to a meat packer who doesn't look at brands. Where were you yesterday, anyway? Could have used you."

"Working. Telling tourists about how Hubbell wasn't in it for the money or the women, just the noble cause of the Navajo people and the Republican Party. Then I jammed with our band."

"Since when have you got a band?"

"I don't know if I can really say we've got one. It was our first practice. Pretty rough around the edges at this point."

"Headbanger stuff?"

"Of course."

"It's like a chick magnet, right, being in a band?"

James was hoping to avoid the subject, even just the thought of it. Angie clearing the table and washing her husband's dishes. Helping him off with his pants.

"I don't have time for chicks."

Max laughed. "Anyway, I got the idea of looking into this rustling ring, but I don't know how. I was thinking of trying to get it out of Beebee. Get him drunk and ask the right questions."

"Might work," James said. "He's pretty stupid."

"That's assuming he knows something. He might just be a pawn in someone else's game that he doesn't even understand."

James had been looking forward to being lazy all day, making cups of coffee and tea, reading one of the books in the house, the Library of America volumes with the black covers. Not long ago he had picked up a copy of Thoreau, and had enjoyed reading about a canoe trip in the forest with an Indian man who talked stupid but wasn't. There was a passage where Thoreau described mistaking the sound of the wind from over the woods for a train, and James understood that.

But Max, as usual, had other plans for him. They pumped water from the tank by the windmill to the tank on the hill, which meant James had to go up and down the hill several times to check the height of the water and turn the valves. Then they both whacked the weeds around Max's mother's house that had grown tall since the rains. Some of these were the rank-smelling kind that attracted many doves. They would fly out of the weeds when you walked through, their wings making the urgent, odd sound, like rusty hinges. James remembered killing doves in the doveweed with his slingshot when his grandmother was alive. "Those *hasbídí* were the only things I had to keep me company. Now I suppose you killed the last one." He had heard the anger in her voice, at least the little bit of anger she was able to muster. But here were all these doves, long after she was gone.

That night he read some Thoreau and half of a Walter Mosley book, and then lay in the dark with his eyes wide open. Coyotes were yipping from time to time in the hills to the west. He thought of his great-grandmother's old hogan nearby, collapsed and slowly melting into the ground, as it had been from the first time he had seen it. He felt sure that Max was struggling uselessly to keep the old ranch from just blowing away, as it was bound to.

He didn't think he was being pessimistic. He didn't feel sad about it. It was night, and he was alone, but his mind was alert and like clear water; he could see things undistorted and the way they were. He had to make his own way in the world, even if everything he knew disappeared. He would play music no matter what, even if those fools couldn't get it together to play it with him. And he would find a woman, even if it wasn't Angie. And he would live where he lived and work at what he worked at, and not any of that would mean a thing in a short matter of time.

CHAPTER FIFTEEN

▨ **JAMES HURRIED INTO** Hubbell's five minutes late and almost bumped into Gabaldon, who was in the doorway, on his way to a Lions Club meeting. He frowned at James and said, "I'll talk to you when I get back."

It had to mean some kind of trouble. James went to work helping Littlesunday throw the bags of trash into the dumpster. He tightened a loom for Mabel, then helped stock groceries, and for a few minutes before the morning tour he hung around with two other employees, blabbing. He didn't really have his heart in either the blabbing—he didn't care about the rug auction on the coming weekend—or the tour, but he guided the herd through the dark rooms. "The china was shipped from Philadelphia."

As if anybody cared. What he wanted to do was welcome them to Ganado, this crummy little place that liked to imagine itself a real town, with a Lions Club of mostly white men—not conscious racists, of course. Gabaldon was there, Mexican after all, and hell, the Lions would be willing to include the right kind of Navajo if they could find one.

If he were able to give his own version of history, he would tell the tourists that this was the way it had been here for a long time: the would-be town of Ganado started as an outgrowth of Hubbell's enterprise, first a church, then a school, then a hospital, and all the housing those required. And as the Christians in the East and Midwest gradually gave less and less money to evangelize the Indians, Navajos moved into the Anglos' houses the way the weeds invaded their lawns, and the shingles blew off the roofs and weren't replaced, and stucco peeled from the gabled houses. This had all started before he was born. The old Navajos who had known the mission in its heyday complained about how run down it was. To James it had always been run down, but it was getting worse.

"See those signs?" James would point out to the tourists. "'No Hauling Water from Ganado Compound.' That's because of the drought. It's like that Guns N' Roses song: 'Ganado's my city, where the grass is brown and the girls are *ch'ízhii*.'" Of course none of the tourists would know that ch'ízhii meant rough and scabby.

Somehow he would bridge the old days to the new days and learn how to explain that after the heroics of the traders and missionaries, a twelve-year-old boy bled to death on the playground.

The tour he actually gave them didn't deviate much from the script. They weren't a very attentive group, anyway. A teenage girl walked behind her parents, picking her nose the whole time. He led them back to the store and spotted Angie behind the counter in her long dress and tsiiyééł. Her long smooth cheek was far from ch'ízhii. "How did it go?" he asked.

"Not so good. I'll talk to you later. I'm taking lunch at noon."

They met by the corral with the three burros. Gabaldon had exiled the burros to the farthest corner of the property from the weaving room and the trading post because they made so much noise. Across the graded road ran a line of black walnut trees, and beyond it, a dry old irrigation ditch. Angie was careful to keep the hem of her skirt out of the dirt.

"So did he leave?"

"He left. He's gone."

"Gone for good?"

"He better be."

"I mean, you told him you wanted a divorce?"

"Yes, yes, I told him everything."

"Even about me?"

"Pretty much."

"How did he take it?"

"How do you think?"

James thought Malcolm should like being rid of Angie, since he treated her so badly. He could have all his other women and not be bothered. "He didn't hurt you, did he?"

"No, not really. He pushed me around a little, is all. Threw some things."

James felt his face go hot. He wanted to find him and hurt him. "He already left?"

"He went to Gallup this morning to get the bus."

That was a relief. This kept James safe from violating probation. It wouldn't have looked good when he met with Wesson this week if he showed up with scrapes and bruises. "Just be sure you get a lawyer and file as soon as you can."

"He threatened to kidnap the kids. He said they were his kids and he wasn't going to let another man play like their dad. 'You're still my wife,' he said, and I thought, 'Not for long.'"

"You need to get a restraining order, for you and the kids, and you better call your sister about it, too."

"I'm safe as long as he stays at Fort Riley until they ship him out."

"Angie, I'm telling you, you *need* a restraining order."

"All right, all right. I just hate having to deal with it."

James started picking up the small rocks at his feet and chucking them over the walnut trees. It was something he had done since he was a little kid: at some point, if he was just standing around, he would start throwing stones. "Well, if it was up to me, I'd just whip his ass," he said, laughing.

"Frontier justice," Angie said, laughing despite her worried look.

They walked back to the trading post, Angie picking up her skirt. She said, "See you," going into the store. He watched her with a new feeling: that she was free for him to have.

Gabaldon called James into his office before the afternoon tour. The big man sat squeaking back and forth in his desk chair above a single small pile of papers stacked neatly, square with the corners of the desk. A calendar and a picture of his family stood in the corners near where James sat. It seemed odd that the faces of his wife and children faced the office's visitors rather than Gabaldon.

"How are the Lions?" James said cheerfully. He thought of Gabaldon and Austin and the guy who he had heard went around honking horns and collecting fines from members, most likely with a cruel little smile on his face. Gabaldon didn't answer James but started in a tone that reminded him of his old school counselor or a judge.

"When I hired you, I knew about your arrest and your probation, but because of your father I took a chance with you. I hope I didn't make a mistake."

"Did I do something wrong?"

"I know your probation officer and we keep in pretty close touch with each other. Nothing keeps me from telling him what I see."

"What is it you're seeing?"

"Seeing and hearing."

"What are you seeing and hearing?"

"Your band. Reverend Austin tells me he is helping you out, but he doesn't know if he was right to do this."

"Well, maybe I should see him about it."

"I would suggest that."

"Is that what you wanted to talk to me about, then? The band?"

"I'm just trying to look out for you. I'm sure if you don't get mixed up with the wrong crowd, you'll be fine."

"But you don't have other concerns? Like I'm doing the job okay, right?"

"I have no complaints with that. Maybe a haircut. It's starting to look a little shaggy."

It surprised James that he was able to smile and even shake the hand Gabaldon offered, thinking all the while, *Mind your own damn business.*

He needed to play—loud. James went early to the practice room that sunny afternoon, figuring he'd have the place to himself, but Leon was already there tuning his drums.

"How did you get in?" James asked.

Leon pointed to the open window.

"Man, we are all going to have to talk. Austin is already on my case, and spying for my PO. You're breaking and entering and in a little while the other two band members are going to show up reeking of beer and pot." James plugged in the guitar and tested the amp.

"What're you gonna do? You aren't their mother." Leon restacked the cymbals, then tied a cinder block to each of the stand's three legs. "There's no way this motherfucker's going to crash again."

James turned away from Leon and faced the wall and began to play big open chords, fast.

When James felt good, his music was good, but when he felt outraged, his music was the best. He pictured Malcolm touching her shoulder or her waist, and the chords rang out in perfect dissonant fury. By the time Nolan and Zendrick showed up he had gotten it all out of his system and felt all right again, like he didn't hate them all anymore. It was a pretty good session, working on an old Putrefaction song and one James had written called "Headless Surgery."

The main thing he kept telling himself that month was *Take your time. Until you know, don't do anything. Remember Terri, how after you gave in to her too soon she threw it back in your face.*

He was turning it over and over in his mind until it was almost driving him crazy. He was trying to think about Angie rationally, and this had never been the way he had thought about sex. In the past, if he had the opportunity for sex, and the girl wasn't with somebody else or too skanky and he wasn't too drunk, then that was what he had and he didn't agonize over it. Why was it different now? Burned and shy, no doubt, damaged by Terri.

He was at the ranch by himself, and rather than let himself go crazy analyzing the situation and himself, he picked up his guitar, and, imagining the amplification, crashed an E-F-G-F chord progression over and over, faster and faster. He growled spontaneous lyrics.

"Fuck your husband fuck your asshole husband."

She said it was over with Malcolm. If James slept with her and she later took Malcolm back, he would have wasted his feelings and would be wounded. But if he held back and Malcolm returned, he would have lost his only chance.

"Fuck your husband fuck your fucking husband." It was a song that didn't seem to have a second line.

In his more rational moments James also considered the fact that her older kid was being raised by her sister far away. Though Angie had explained that her daughter adored her cousin Evangeline, and that it was financially easier for her to live with Irene, he had never understood or even believed these explanations. What kind of mother wants her kids raised by somebody else? And what was wrong with her judgment in the first place, that she picked a lousy husband and had two kids? If she divorced Malcolm, would the military deduct child support? Or was she going to rely on James for that?

These things ate at his mind whenever his body was busy: when he was at work, when he was playing music, when he was out on the ranch cutting weeds and catching horses. His thoughts would ruin those fine days: the rains had pretty much stopped and it had grown cool at night. Some days, flocks of little clouds sped across the sky. Rabbitbrush turned whole valleys gold and the purple asters bloomed in masses. He couldn't sleep. He would play his guitar and after each quatrain growl the reasons for and against.

"Fuck your fucking husband."

There were the kids again. A bad mother? And she seemed to have no ambition. Not that James was driven toward some brilliant career. His brother had enough of that for both of them at fucking Stanford. But every now and then something would come up that reminded James that he had grown up with some privilege. They hadn't grown up like those deep-rez kids with their duct-taped boots and permanent third-grade reading level. His parents both worked. He had read more than a book or two. He knew how to ski—his father had taken him and his brother to Colorado several weekends every winter. They skied down the slope playing road warriors, blending in with the crowd. They did notice the occasional Indian, looking clumsy and self-conscious on the beginners' slope. Most of the time James felt that he was the same as Nolan, Angie, and Max, but there were these little differences. It was the same thing now that he was bothered that Angie couldn't think of what to do with her life besides her dead-end job (like his) and her family.

On the other hand, he could do a lot worse. She wasn't a bitch. He liked the way she laughed when he was talking bullshit. He reasoned that if it didn't work out with Angie, then he'd lost nothing. It wasn't something that you couldn't go back on, unless there was a promise or a child. It wasn't harming anyone—if Malcolm didn't like it, James didn't care, because Malcolm had his chance and had blown it. Then he would remember how much more complicated it could get.

When he started with Terri, he thought he had surprisingly good luck that the girl actually smiled at him in a nice way at something he said. She put her hand on his shoulder first. Every chance he took she gave encouragement. So dumb. Since then he adopted the Groucho principle, suspicious of any girl who would have him as her boyfriend.

He went from G to B-flat and slowed the tempo.

"Fuck your fucking husband."

He slowly realized that he would either sleep with her or keep agonizing about it.

"Fuck me fuck your fucking husband."

One thing for sure, he would use a rubber. Maybe even two. No use complicating things with a pregnancy.

The big cottonwoods in Ganado Wash were deep gold when he finally made up his mind, and the decision seemed exactly right. This was the day he asked her to come out to the ranch with him after work.

"What about Winona?"

"Bring her, too, of course."

He sat in a cheap aluminum lawn chair on the doorstep of his mother's house before the sun set, watching the changing shapes and relief of the hills, so familiar, always different. Angie was inside making tea.

He had sat here countless times at this time of day, and even in early childhood the view and the thoughts were the same. He remembered his grandmother talking about her own mother watching this same low sunlight on the hills to the east. How did he remember this? His grandmother never spoke English, but in his memory she was telling him clearly in the only language he fully understood. Memory is such a liar.

What had his great-grandmother seen? The dirt road was probably narrower and more crooked, but otherwise the land must have been almost the same. Maybe not the exact placement of all the junipers and pinyons, but maybe; they were old trees. Did she, this person he had never known, feel the same kind of yearning that he did? Life was harder then, so maybe people thought more about how to survive with less time for these sentimental ramblings. But he had been told that several of her babies had died, little bodies that she must have remembered were not with her in the world. She would have wondered what was beyond.

Angie came out with two cups of tea. Winona had gone to sleep, rolled into the crease of the futon couch, and her little snores were steady. Angie left the door open. "It's so quiet out here." He watched her as she gave him his cup and glided her ass into her chair in such a graceful, sinuous way that he could hardly believe it was possible.

"Yup. I love it."

"The sun's just about down," Angie said. "I always start to miss it around this time of day, start to say good-bye to it." The very top edges of the hills were still rimmed with gold, but soon that was gone and even the summits were gray, and the few clouds above began to turn pink.

The long rose arch of twilight appeared above the dark blue band of sky, leading the night westward. "*Nahoodeetł'iizh,*" said James, somehow remembering the word.

"Nahoodeetł'iizh," she repeated. She knew much more Navajo than he did. "What is that?"

"I think that's what they call what we're looking at, that arch."

"Huh. I never knew that word. And I don't usually see the thing, what is it, nahoodeetł'iizh? I guess in Ganado it's not flat enough toward the east, or I don't look for it, or something. But I remember seeing it as a kid sometimes, thinking that the dark part looked like a giant cave in the sky."

The stars came out: one, three more, then an uncountable number. "They were there the whole time," James said. He had moved his chair next to hers and they held hands, their arms touching from shoulder to wrist. He wondered why at certain moments skin felt so good. Skin that at other times might feel just ordinarily good, somehow wakening under his touch.

Then it was her face that came to life under his face—her lips, her lashes, her neck. Her breasts. Then inside, on the bed, he feasted on her breasts again. She said okay. "Okay for everything," she said. "Don't ask anymore." Hungrily he was licking her belly, her navel, and then, for a moment, holding himself back. "It's okay," she repeated. "Everything."

CHAPTER SIXTEEN

▧ **THE PINYON HARVEST** was on, and everywhere the nuts fell, greedy people were picking them. In the last couple weeks word had gotten around where exactly the green cones had developed and matured, and as they drove toward the summit, above the sloping grassland and below the ponderosa forest, with Winona nodding between them in the car seat, James and Angie saw the throngs of people crouched on the woodland floor. Some young families were so eager they happily ignored the old people's admonitions and jerked the branches and trunks to shake loose the nuts still clinging inside the cones. Buses from nursing homes and preschools spilled out their passengers, halting and hyperactive. It was lunchtime, and secretaries and division directors from the tribal agencies in Window Rock had sped out in their *chidí tsésọ'*, their Novas and Corollas, to spend a few minutes kneeling on the sunlit ground stashing pinyons in the pockets of their office clothes.

They hadn't been a couple for long, and when James spent the night at her place in Ganado he would still park his Nissan in front of Nolan's. Neighbors no doubt still gossiped, since she was married, after all, but he figured they would appreciate his attempts at discretion. Or perhaps laugh at his sneaking around. Tonight they drove with the baby out to the ranch. It was time his family knew about Angie. He stopped by at his aunt Thelma's house to see if she was interested in going pinyon picking.

Thelma and James's cousin Max were at the table with bowls of stew. "I been waiting for you to ask. Let's go tomorrow!" she said.

"Who's in the car?" Max asked.

"You'll meet her tomorrow."

James couldn't get enough of Angie, couldn't wait until she'd put the baby down and he could feel her soft skin against his lips. He wanted to feast on her. Winona could be an impediment. Sometimes when he tried to caress Angie she would laugh or scream at him, inserting herself between their bodies. What a brat. He did understand that Angie and her child were a package deal, and he cared about Winona in the general way that adults look out for kids, not letting cars run over them and that sort of thing. She was cute enough, most of the time. Tonight the baby was already asleep and didn't wake up as he carried her from the truck to her mattress. Soft little snores: one of her cute moments.

It was cool enough to light a fire, and they arranged two comfortable chairs with foot rests toward the stove. Angie put a pot of washed beans on the stovetop. Her looks had grown more interesting since high school, her body bulkier but her face thinner with bronzy triangles of wrinkles quietly bursting out from the corners of her eyes, a face that kept still as he kissed her, looking ahead with the smallest smile.

This woman should have had better luck. He remembered her back in grade school: cheerful, self-confident, playing rough and loudly on the playground, and in high school when she had become gentler, more sympathetic, one of the few kids who didn't make a big thing about his being half-Anglo. Now here she was, wife of an army brute who hardly saw his family when he was on leave, unappreciated and abused, no longer confident of herself, mother of two children, stifling some accumulated sorrow he did not fully understand. He wanted to treat her better than she had been treated, not so much to take care of her as to deliver her back to herself.

He put her bare feet in his lap and stroked her legs. "Don't you think it's about time I got to know Reeba?" He had seen her just that one time before the Cryptopsy concert when Angie's sister brought her down, and then only briefly.

"Any time you want to."

"Why wouldn't I want to?"

"I don't want to get into an argument."

He knew better than to go on talking, but what annoyed him and made her defensive was that she had given up her first child. Maybe it was just too hard with the baby, or a matter of money, or maybe some part of it was the girl's own choice, the way some Navajo mothers let their little kids fill up the grocery carts with whatever junk they want. Maybe Reeba liked being with Evangeline's family because she felt some basic deficiency in her own mother.

The fire crackled and he massaged her feet. She sighed, leaned back, and closed her eyes.

Early in the morning Thelma banged on the door while James and Angie were snuggling and Winona was barely struggling herself awake.

"It's gonna be a good day for pinyons," she said. "But we have to hurry up and find a good spot."

Within minutes everyone was getting ready. Thelma lifted up her skirt and ran from their house to hers and into the shed collecting things. "Don't forget the coffee cans." She gathered flour sacks and made sandwiches. They heard her shouting instructions to her son Max, who she thought was moving too slowly. "*Shá bíighah.*" He kept a few steps ahead of her up the hill from Thelma's house like a sheep that was being herded back into the flock. "We'll get a whole lot of them. While we're there," she told James, "you and Max ought to haul a bunch of wood." Once she started thinking about piling stuff up, she was off on her greedy streak and there was no stopping her. Loads of pinyons made her think of loads of firewood.

Max had pulled on his Tony Lamas and his grungy Carhartt, and obeyed his mother's every order. James thought that was part of his cowboy ethic, the same way he'd tipped his hat to Angie before he'd shaken hands with her, and the way he walked into the house like he'd just gotten off a horse.

Then Angie went after Winona who loved to run and squeal when somebody chased her. James deposited the chain saws in the back of his little truck, a box of Pampers, and lunch. Angie ran back in the house to get the pacifier. Max followed with his mother in her big Ford truck. "I'm not going in the rice cooker," he said.

The morning was already warming as the trucks crawled up the plateau on a series of dirt roads that became more and more primitive at each fork. They shifted and bounced according to the bumps in the road. Around the bend they saw sheep, and around the next bend the sheepherder, squatting under a tree and filling his pockets with pinyons.

"Everybody's getting in on it," said Angie.

They stopped near a clearing in the woods and Angie and Thelma and Winona, with coffee cans and flour sacks and diapers, knelt down close by the truck and started picking. James liked the line between Angie's kneeling thighs and calves, like a smile, and the arch of her shoulder as she reached in front of her.

James picked a few and ate them. First, a glance from the molars, then in the hand again, prying the crack open and extracting the white meat whole. When he was impatient he chewed them shells and all. He got a warning from Angie, who was changing Winona's diaper on the car seat. "Eat too many raw like that and you'll get a sore throat."

"I got some big nuts over here," Max called.

James whooped. "It's always good to have big nuts."

Angie lifted Winona and trudged back to join Thelma, who was steadily picking. Time to get busy. Soon the cold rains would come to ruin the pinyons and rodents would come to carry the nuts away.

"I thought you guys were going to get firewood," Thelma said.

"All right, all right," they muttered, and laughed, moving off into the forest.

Max carried his axe. James had the chainsaw in the case with the extra chain and folder of tools in one hand. He grabbed the chain oil and the motor oil with the other, then reached for the gas can. The chain oil dropped. Max picked up the can. "Man," he said, gesturing with the axe, "you're going to have to learn to use one of these."

"I could give you lessons in axe," James said. "But I represent the future. Technology. I'm going to invent a pinyon-picking machine next."

"It's the bilagáana in you, always trying to find a better way," Max said, tightening the chain. They had stopped by a standing dead pinyon tree. "But they already got one. I saw one in California, an almond harvester, but I'm sure it'd work for pinyons."

"You probably need ten Mexicans to run it," James told his cousin. "Or twenty Indians."

"No, just one guy drives the thing from tree to tree: he puts this set of padded clamps around the trunk and turns it on. In three minutes there's not an almond on the tree."

"No shit."

"I mean, if you were serious about a pinyon industry, Mr. Future Technology, you'd get rid of all these shitty little sheep camps and plant the trees in rows. While you're at it, why don't you invent some way of keeping track of cattle?"

"What's wrong with brands?"

"Ha," said Max. "We got brands, but in case you hadn't noticed, we don't find all our cattle. They just tamper with the brands. Can't tell for sure until the skin's off the animal. Cold-branding, that's a little harder to tamper with. I'd like to go over to that."

"Or we could bar-code under the tongue. Or plant computer chips under their skin like rich people use on their pets."

"I hear some guys keep track of their wives that way," Max said.

James looked at his cousin for his meaning. He didn't think he knew Angie's story, and fuck him if he did. Max had had more than one wife himself.

The plateau sloped gently to the south without many dips or rises. The vegetation was both ponderosa pines and pinyons, and there were junipers and cliff roses: *ndishchíí', chá'oł, gad, 'awééts'áál.*

Max had moved on, looking for the ideal tree, he said, pinyon or juniper, with a long thick untwisted trunk, free of rot, in a place where they could back the truck right up to it. From the state of the vegetation James could see this area did not get grazed much: up from the ground like little flags stood clumps of grama and wheatgrass with dried seed heads, and around the junipers in untrampled soil the black mossy cryptogams built up miniature castles. With sheep and cows free to roam everywhere, much of the reservation looked haggard and used up. This was a rare and unspoiled spot and they were about to spoil it. James saw it all before it happened: they would bag their ideal tree, removing it from the landscape, rutting the soil with their tire tracks, and littering the ground with wood chips and sawdust.

They stopped by a dead pinyon in a flat near where young Rocky Mountain junipers were growing. Globs of dried sap stood out on its black trunk. This was one James didn't mind cutting. While Max hacked away at the trunk, James put the chainsaw down, opened the case, checked the tension on the chain, filled it with gas, and cranked it up. By the time James turned back to the tree, Max had a hand on the trunk. He grinned. "Timber." When the tree crashed to the ground he said, "Man beats machine."

"Bullshit," James said.

In another few minutes they had trimmed the branches, then went after the next tree. By late morning they had taken off their jackets and were still sweating. James's arms were aching. Max showed no sign of tiring.

"Let's look for a *good* one now," Max said. They passed several standing dead trees not much smaller than the ones they had cut, but Max kept walking. At the head of a little box canyon they found a good one, and James's heart sank. It was an old Utah juniper, taller than most and with a magnificent thick trunk he could not have stretched his arms around. It had grown in the canyon bottom where water flowed from the rock walls, and the wood at its top, which reached above the lip of the canyon, had been blasted by decades of bright sunlight to a silvery gray. The trunk, heavy and solid, tapered in perfect proportion, and the major limbs angled off with grace and power. Its symmetry, James felt immediately, was meant to be a model for himself: strength and balance. Yet instead he carried a chain saw.

"This one's for American technology," Max said. "Fire her up."

"Nah, the tree's still alive," James protested, eyeing the smallest green tuft that the tree held high on one side. Max looked at it and laughed, and James shrugged. He sank the chainsaw into the first limb. Its nasal whine deepened, it wouldn't be a bad start to a death metal song: first a roar, then a shriek.

By midafternoon the truck was well loaded. James held a thin piece of wood and prodded at the pile, trying to find a gap between logs big enough to slide it in. They had left a lot of wood in piles to pick up later. "Let's get back and eat some pinyons," Max said. "Hey, did you hear about that hippie guy who brought in a big sack of pinyons to the trading post at Kinlichee? I guess he was out all day, or maybe two days, under the pinyons where he was herding sheep. Real weird guy, never took a bath, herded sheep for this family up on the mesa for food and shelter. He was from New York or some place. *Tsiiyogii.*"

"Yeah?"

"He took this big old sack into the trader and said, 'How much you pay for pinyons?' 'cause the guy didn't have any money and who knows, maybe he wanted to buy some soap. And the trader said, 'Let's see how much you got there; let's put her on the scale. Hm, it's mighty light,' he said. Took a look in the bag and started to laugh. 'What you got here mister is mostly dried-up sheep turds.'"

Just over the top of the plateau they turned into the clearing on the edge of which, under a huge ponderosa, the family sat on rocks and logs, Angie proudly smiling at her two big Blue Bird flour sacks of pinyons and her little girl. He parked the truck and walked down the almost imperceptible slope. James thought, with a little surprise, that he was looking at the woman—the married woman—he was sleeping with.

Winona squirmed in Angie's arms until she let go, then ran toward the men, yelling "Amos!" the latest version of her name for James. She hugged him around the knees and he offered his hand. "Dada," she said. "*Zhé'é.*"

"No, I'm not your daddy," he said.

"Amos," she said.

"James."

"Amos." They walked back down to where Thelma had already gone back to picking pinyons.

"*Haah,*" said the little girl, baby talk for "give it."

"This?" Angie said, handing her the green plastic coffee cup she had been using to hold the nuts.

Slowly Thelma rose from the prickly brown thatch of the forest floor and the pile of her skirt around her. Angie waited as she came with the pair of Maxwell House cans and emptied them into the flour sack. With her poor vision and moving so slowly, how did she collect pinyons so fast?

"There's still lots here!" Thelma said, starting again to fill the coffee cans, first with plinks as the pinyons hit the bare metal bottom, then with plunks as they piled up. Winona played with the teacup.

James lay on the pine needles, looking up at the clear sky. "I'm tired," he said. "But it looks like you guys can't quit." Clear squiggles floated in his vision against the sky, and he found he could keep them from moving by staring exactly above.

"It's hard to stop when they're all over the place like this," Angie said, passing over the dull gray shells of the empty nuts that had fallen undeveloped when the summer rains failed to reach them. "And I'm getting better at it. The only thing I hate is these needles that jab me under the fingernails."

James allowed himself to pick a few, eating half of them raw. He didn't have the enthusiasm that she did. The idea was to develop an economy of movement and a concentrated focus—or just dumb persistence.

Angie brushed away a locust shell from a little pile of nuts. "We used to have a sheepherder who ate locusts hot off the grill. 'Go get me some *wóneeshch'iindii*,' he used to tell us kids, and out we would go to go catch them because we liked to watch him. He'd take the insects by the wings and dash them on the hot stovetop, then pop them into his mouth. 'Crispy,' he'd say, and you could hear them crunch. 'Bring me some more.'" Angie imitated his slow slurred voice.

Thelma laughed. "*Shoo ya'*. A lot of people used to eat them."

James looked around for Winona who was sitting behind Angie playing with a stick. A warm yellow light fell onto the forest mat in patches and scented the air with pine. Thelma's gnarled fingers gripped their pinyon nuts with quick precision and her wrist disappeared into the old and spotty sleeve.

James glanced down the slope where Winona was walking toward a patch of cactus. "Uh-oh!" He ran and grabbed her and carried her back to her mother.

"*Ma'ii yázhí*. You little coyote," she told her daughter, whose smile made her laugh in spite of herself. James felt something like gratitude wash over him, a family feeling he was not sure he deserved. There were a few animate sounds and they were all the same sad tender song: a rustle in the yellow grass, a chipmunk's chatter, a lizard's footsteps, a raven drifting over the tall and breezy ponderosas. Reminders of something.

Angie poured another can luxuriously into the new sack. "Wow. I bet this is the biggest year for pinyons ever."

"No," Thelma said. "There's a lot now, but I remember one year when I was a little girl our whole family picked pinyons for over a week. We'd start before the sun came up, have a little coffee, and pick until it got dark and you couldn't see them anymore. Then we'd cook and sleep right outside in the woods and get up the next day and do it again. We had twenty-two sacks."

"Twenty-two. What did you do with them all?"

"We kept some and took most of them to the trader to pay off our bill. We took four sacks to some Hopi friends who gave us a bunch of big blue squash."

They went on picking until Thelma suddenly looked up and said, "Where's the baby?"

"That kid!" Angie looked around angrily, then in fear.

Thelma said, "I think she was playing over that way," pointing to where a two-track trail curved and disappeared downhill.

James ran in that direction, ahead of Angie. He had to find her baby for her. Angie fell farther and farther behind, breathing hard. He stopped to listen. The ragged needles of the few tall ponderosas were whipped into circles by a sudden wind. The sound approached a roar then died away. He panicked, imagining all the worst things for the little girl: snatched up by a tornado, devoured by a mountain lion. He could imagine Angie's fear, her anticipation of a terrible grief, which he now felt himself. A wisp of ochre dust flew up from the trail. "Winona!" Angie caught up with him and yelled, "Winona!"

A few more footsteps and the girl was in view, waddling down the track, merry but intent. James grabbed her from behind and the baby laughed. "Bad girl!" He clutched her sides and lifted her over his shoulder. James hauled her back up the hill toward her mother. Winona struggled hard against him, but at last settled down, overcome. "Dada," she said. "Zhé'é." This time he let it go.

CHAPTER SEVENTEEN

◈ **WINONA WAS ASLEEP,** thank God, although she wouldn't be asleep long. Just enough time to start some project, a pretty little dress for Winona, and then she'd be snuffling herself awake and that'd be that. Angie never really knew how long she had. She might go on snoring for a long time and she could finish what she started, or the brat could wake and it'd be over in a moment. Sorry, baby, you're not really a brat. Her face was clean after the bath that morning. So much stuff got all over her—food, snot—and now her face had that look of clear carved wax, her ear so perfectly formed. This one has been more trouble than Reeba ever was, and seemed to need Angie all the time. It was because when Winona was inside her she had seen that accident on the roadside, the body with the leg bent over its back. She tried not to look, but there it was, and the baby had kicked. Baby didn't like that.

With all the taboos that there were, you were bound to break at least one of them over nine months. No baby is born without some danger and disadvantage.

Was she allowed to use scissors? It must be all right because the cutting was for making something, not destroying something. She'd get it all pinned out before Winona woke up, maybe cut it out. More likely she'd get the pattern pinned and then Winona would wake up and grab the whole thing. Winona loved the rustle of the pattern paper. Made for trouble. Just like her mother.

She'd missed two periods and she didn't even want to think about it. Her periods always came exactly five days before the full moon, ever since her periods started, and then, weirdly, when her periods started again after each baby. There was no point in doing a pregnancy test: her fingers were puffy and she couldn't stand the smell of meat.

She felt the blood leave her head and her heart start to pound. There wasn't enough air. Stop it.

She knew she could stop it just by thinking about it. Didn't need a paper bag anymore. Just counted the breaths and made them slow and deep before her lips started to tingle.

Even with a condom. Malcolm hadn't wanted to wear one. "You're my wife," he said, as if that made any sense, as if he was *supposed* to get his wife pregnant, as if his purpose in life was to come home and deposit his sperm and then disappear again. Like the last two times. "Skin to skin. You're my wife."

James used a condom and didn't protest, though by then she might already have been pregnant and it wouldn't have made any difference. Was there any way to really know?

Was this Malcolm's revenge for her making him put on a condom, to impregnate her anyway, the little army wiggling its way through the microscopic holes in the rubber? He'd brag about how easy it was to have a baby, the little smirk on his face.

It was true. Those kind of men are too fertile. Every cliché of masculinity—the military uniform, the football jersey, the brawls, the cursing and spitting—makes them too fertile. Every sperm is an aggressive little baby fighting for its chance. Nice guys finish last, or don't even get a chance to finish.

Malcolm never considered her feelings, except in one sense: he wanted her to come. It was another way to command her. And when she came, she knew, despite what her friend the nurse practitioner told her, when she melted in submission, she opened herself to conceiving.

Or was it James, rushing in at the last minute, willing himself into fatherhood? This one *should* be his.

Winona's body shifted, her arm stretching over her head, and she sighed, her face still unrippled and quiet in unbroken sleep. Granted a little more time for herself, Angie pinned the right sleeve.

It wasn't fair. Hadn't been fair for a long time.

She hadn't thought about fair when she was little, hadn't questioned the family that was there around her. Her parents, both quiet and humble, *baa hojoobá'í,* already old, Irene like another mother, two almost unknown older brothers in Albuquerque and Barstow. When her father came home from cleaning the school, she would lie in his lap and play with his mustache.

When he died of sugar, they said, she was in third grade and wouldn't touch candy. They had to move out of school housing to a shack on the eroded clay banks of the wash. That may have been the first time she thought, *Not fair.*

But she was just a stupid kid like all the other stupid kids, shouting and receiving the schoolyard taunts and chants. "You got bit by the ch'ízhii worm." She hadn't been friends with everyone, but she'd had plenty of friends. And if she had enemies they were a combination of friend and enemy, someone she'd liked who'd become a teacher's pet or talked trash about her behind her back. Like Sylvia, who got a Manuelito scholarship years later when nothing was fair anymore. Sylvia, always talking about her illustrious family, how she was a descendent of Chief Manuelito himself, which was probably how she got the scholarship.

And Angie, in high school with ideas of college and no money, got talked into babysitting for Irene, which was how she wasted two years in Shiprock and met Malcolm and got pregnant with Reeba and started getting pushed around. It wasn't fair that Malcolm treated her like that even before they got married, or that her sister talked her out of leaving. "You only just got started together, things get better, men mellow with age," she said, although Irene's husband never got mellow; he just got fat and silent in an angry sort of way.

Not fair that she went from high school to baby care, and not even a start to what you might call a career. Even now she had no idea of what her career might be, though she did believe in theory that she could be anything. She hadn't been a great student but she could buckle down if she wanted to. She could see herself in a long white lab coat talking with other doctors in the halls of a hospital. Or arguing at a desk with another well-dressed lawyer. This was all TV. But if the actors could pull it off, when all they really were was actors, knowing nothing about being doctors and lawyers, then so could she.

She even read an article in the paper about some guy who pretended to be a specialist, a proctologist, who stole someone's diploma and set up shop. He'd close the curtains and knock his patients out, and when they woke up he'd tell them he'd stuck the tube up their butts and that everything was all right. He was rich and everyone was happy. He did it for years until they found him out. So if he got away with it . . . But that has to be harder than going to medical school: faking it, wondering when someone is going to bust you.

She was good at sewing. She'd made beautiful clothes without patterns. Her friend made expensive jackets with Indian designs and sold them to singers and soap opera stars in L.A. Angie had done a little work for her. She could go out on her own.

It was unfair, there was no doubt about that, but you could blame other people for only so long and then you had to do something about it if you were ever going to get out of your mess. She could go on arguing with Malcolm about child support and birth control but there was no future in it, she knew that. It was up to her now. It was fine if James wanted to help, but that was his decision.

It was up to her in spite of everything.

There was a buckle in the cloth she must have caused when she wasn't paying attention, thinking about her problems. She knew she couldn't do this without concentration. So she would think as she smoothed the wrinkle and repinned the pattern, and she would plan a career one step at a time.

The trouble was, no one around here had any ambition. You didn't even hear the word. Even Sylvia, who won the Manuelito scholarship, was raising babies. Two years into a full-ride, four-year scholarship she was back on the reservation sitting at home, probably making her baby some clothes. Everyone said that was what she got for having big ideas.

As they said about Angie, even though she had a job now: you're really suited to bringing up babies.

So how come Reeba was somewhere else? It was unfair that she was with Irene, who said that was the way it should be. When Winona was born and Angie said she was moving back down to Ganado and wasn't going to just waste away minding other people's children, her sister said, "How are you going to find a job when you're taking care of two kids? And Reeba loves Evangeline, doesn't want her out of her sight. We have a big house." On and on she went, wouldn't let up, the same way she always did and ended up having her way.

What Irene didn't say exactly was that Angie didn't have what it took to be a mother. Didn't have a husband who was reliable, had no money to speak of, and didn't have the whatever it is, the *seriousness*, that makes a mother. And Angie was afraid she was right.

But so what if she was going to be here alone with two babies anyway? She was not going to give up her job, not going to give up unrealistic hopes even though she knew that's what they were, not going to give any of her kids away again. No matter what, she should bring Reeba back down. She was almost old enough to actually help rather than just make things worse. Maybe she should do this even if her period came tomorrow with a lot of bleeding and cramping as there would be since this wouldn't be a period but a miscarriage. Then she could stop having to tell people she had another daughter she wasn't raising, stop trying to explain to James that of course she was her mother even if for a while Reeba was living with her auntie.

Not fair.

James, who seemed like a dropout, was maybe the only one with big ideas, talking about his music.

How was she going to kick Malcolm out? She had told James she would. But if she did, would James rescue her? It was risky. How was she going to tell Malcolm she wanted a divorce if he didn't even write to tell her where he was?

Here she was planning her moves with James and she hadn't even broken it off with Malcolm. She just hadn't been able to say anything before he went off to Fort Riley. But really she wasn't planning her moves with anyone. If something happened it wasn't because she planned it. Nothing ever went according to plan, not her plan, anyway.

How was that buckle in the cloth still there, or there again? She needed to keep her mind on one thing, which was impossible. Out came all the pins again, then back in once more.

She had known James as long as she could remember. His family was always there. His mother was Navajo and he grew up here so he understood things, so he wasn't an actual *alien*, but his father was white, and she probably had always known he was privileged and maybe even rich.

He mentioned branding cattle, so his mother had cattle, which Angie's family did not. He once mentioned skiing. Unfair, but she didn't know enough then to feel much resentment.

She'd puzzled then about his half-white face, familiar but a little unusual, interesting, his nose a little flat, his coloring a little pale, three or four freckles on his nose that somehow made him look like a mouse or a cat.

But he had never sat in the front, never sucked up to a teacher, was sent to the principal's office plenty of times, even though his father was a principal too. Maybe nothing happened to him in the other principal's office because of some Code of Principals that determined their sons were safe from each other. He was partly a bad boy (and this was partly good) and any advantage he had of being half white and being a principal's son wasn't really there anymore. He had not excelled in school the way his younger brother had (no one from Ganado had seen anything like Stanford Law School) but that might mean he just couldn't accept bullshit the way Ben could. The intelligence genes might still be there.

She hadn't seen the fight when Rodney got stabbed. She can't remember where she was then. She remembered hearing about it. Kids whispering. James's face, grim, not talking.

She watched his face grow thinner and stronger and more interesting over the years. Indians were better looking, usually, but their looks were kind of boring. Dark eyes, sharp features, prominent cheekbones, downturned mouth—the image of Malcolm's face, or so many others with tiny variations. All the way across the reservation there was another guy who looked almost the same, like cutting out a thousand little dresses from the same pattern. White people, on the other hand, weren't one type but had every possibility of ugliness (and occasionally, almost by mistake, of beauty). Noses like red rubber balls, little mouths like bass, explosions of freckles and scabs, tufts of curly orange hair. Then put an Indian parent with a white parent and you never knew what you were going to get. Generally not *really* ugly, and always a little different.

Now she liked his face and remembered the secrets of his body.

He had that crazy side: his music, his friends, though he didn't party the way some of them did. He did know what to do in bed. Was James one of those exceptions, a nice guy who knew how to fuck? None of her girlfriends had described a guy like that. Maybe he was faking the nice guy stuff.

She knew James wasn't really such a nice guy anyway, from over the years. She'd seen him fight when he was a boy. He was into metal, after all, though not the lipstick and leather pants but the horn sign and head-banging, sweat and shouting. Couldn't be *that* nice.

Malcolm would have called her a scheming bitch, but there was nothing wrong with trying to think it through a little ahead of time, like she should have done with Malcolm.

James already liked her, and that wasn't due to any scheming. According to him, he'd noticed her a long time ago, way back in grade school, then later when he thought she was cheering on that kid who picked a fight with him, and she didn't really remember who she had been cheering for, whoever won, probably. Now he was grown up, had a square jaw, hard muscles, and a deep voice, and he went to bed with her. Married or not. Pregnant or not—but even she hadn't known for sure then. Malcolm had been gone then, but James knew he was out there somewhere and he had slept with her. So he couldn't blame her; he had only himself to blame.

And if they all went pinyon picking and he fell for little Winona, whose fault was that? Might as well blame Winona for making him smile.

The baby moved and groaned a little in that cute delicious way that on the other hand might mean she was going to start waking up and raising hell.

Where had Malcolm been while his baby daughter was lying on the couch making cute noises? Back to his base and then off to some other place like Korea. He'd had just a few days to see his kids and where the heck had he been?

She was not going to let herself hyperventilate, also not going to get so down she couldn't get up. She had to take care of Winona, and she had a job. She had already put it behind her, already told Malcolm that she was tired of being treated like a piece of crap. When he wrote she would write back to tell him it was over. He would show up and threaten her. She wouldn't be afraid. She would tell him to get out. There was nothing he could do to her. She would be holding the baby, and he never hurt the baby. He would say, "You mean a divorce?" and she'd say yes. That way she wouldn't have to use the word. And he would call her a scheming bitch, but this time it wouldn't be a scheme; this time she'd do it.

The nurse practitioner—the one who didn't believe what Angie knew to be true about orgasm—explained to her the most likely time of the month to get pregnant. She also said that abortions were easiest before twelve weeks. What was it about these white women that allowed them to say such things so easily? Did they have sex without thinking about it? They probably weren't any different from anyone else in that respect, but they could talk about doing in a baby like it was nothing, talk about *aborting* a baby in the same tone of voice you would say you were changing a baby's diaper. Well, this was the kind of thing nurse practitioners practiced talking about, though it did seem a white girl sort of thing. Angie knew some Navajo girls who had abortions and for sure there were plenty of others who did and just covered it up. But they all were *hok'eed* forever, their insides haunted like homes where people had died.

Winona was stretching and her eyes were half opened and there was no going back on it now. Awake and fussy, soon to be running around the room grabbing things. She never just woke and smiled like Reeba used to do. Winona thought if she was awake it was reason enough to complain.

But it was miraculous: the dress was cut out, and perfectly. She would sew it when she had a chance, another time.

CHAPTER EIGHTEEN

▧ **JAMES'S PROBATION OFFICER,** Mr. Wesson—like Smith and Wesson—lived and worked in Flagstaff, making regular rounds to the reservation from there. His short federal hair stood up straight from his craggy head, and he had one of these handshakes that was a kind of competition for who could break the other's hand. Not long after the pinyon expedition, James had a scheduled visit with him at the chapter house. First came the handshake. Then Wesson ordered the piss test.

"I don't think I can go," James said.

"Oh, just squeeze out a few drops. We don't need much."

What made it nearly impossible was that Wesson insisted on following him to the urinal and watching him. "That's the procedure."

"I don't care if that's the procedure, I can't piss when you're staring at my dick."

He did turn his back and James managed to fill the cup partway. He handed it to him with a glare. "Jesus Christ."

They went back to the office and Wesson said, "It better come out clean."

"It will."

"From what I hear you're hanging with a pretty druggy crowd."

"Austin's been feeding you a bunch of bullshit."

"It seems like you would be grateful to Reverend Austin."

"I appreciate the practice space, but that doesn't give him the right to mess with our music or to spy on me."

"James, my job is to make sure you don't violate your probation."

"Okay, okay, do your job. Bust your ass. You won't find anything."

James had no trouble staying straight and sober, but he worried anyway that the urinalysis would turn out positive. What if that little bit of passive inhalation of Nolan's fumes showed up in his piss? He didn't know how those tests worked, and could only hope he came out clean. He was spending a lot of time with Nolan, and Nolan was spending a lot of time stoned.

Putrefaction had a gig coming up, a Halloween concert in Gallup, and they felt pressure to practice a lot. They could play only half their dozen songs even decently, and there didn't seem to be enough time to work on them. Almost every scheduled practice session was ruined because one or another of the band had some reason he couldn't show up or adhere to the rules. Zendrick's trouble was having a large family that was always pulling him into someone else's mess. Nolan was dealing pot as much as ever, and he never practiced when he wasn't stoned. All of them fuck-ups, no discipline.

James called Wesson the next week just to make sure.

"Yeah, you came out clean," said Wesson. "Why are you worried about it?"

"I just wanted to hear you say it."

For the rest of the month, at least for a couple of hours, the band managed to get together almost every evening, and gradually took rough control of their songs. All original. No fucking covers. Besides Angie, the band was the best thing in his life, and he tried hard to keep the other members from messing it up. No matter how much he wanted to straighten up and stay out of trouble, he wasn't about to give up metal.

It was Angie's idea for them to wear makeup at the concert. At first he thought of KISS or some other glam band.

"But it's Halloween," she said. "Don't you think anyone else is going to have a costume?"

Not sure if there would be a place for it at the theater, Angie helped them do their faces with black and white stage makeup before the drive to Gallup. James was amazed at how much he enjoyed the look of his face painted like a murderous zombie, and he made Angie deepen the black below his eyes to accentuate it. Angie carried a wig and put on long black fingernails, but she was the only one in the van with no makeup.

They were in Leon's father's van. Leon was dressed like Dracula: white face, a cape with a high collar. The uh-oh lights and siren went off just as they crossed the New Mexico line near the Nazarene elementary school. Some kids playing on the playground stopped and stared.

"Aren't you a little old for trick-or-treating?" the cop said. He was a New Mexico highway patrolman, an Indian.

"We got a concert in Gallup," Leon told him, trying to sound ordinary. James was glad he didn't do a Transylvanian accent, which he had been rehearsing.

"Who's playing?" the cop asked. "License and registration."

"Us. *We're* playing. Putrefaction."

"Your right brake light is out."

"Oh, give me a break."

"I'll give you a citation. You've got two weeks to get it fixed. What is Putrefaction, one of those gangster rap bands?"

"No, it's death metal. The real thing."

"Maybe I should run all your IDs."

"No call for that, officer. Not for a brake light."

"I'll be the judge of that." And they sat there for close to an hour while he ran them all through the computer. Angie wasn't carrying ID, but the cop let it go: a woman, and no costume. There were no outstanding warrants, thanks to the fact that Zendrick carried his brother's ID.

The street was cold and nearly dark when they entered the remodeled downtown movie theater. The stage was a little shallow and the lights guy didn't know what he was doing, but the sound was loud and clear and there was plenty of room for the audience, since there wasn't much of an audience.

It was an all-ages show and there was no liquor, and most of the people he saw milling around between sets were kids wearing shirts from eighties bands. Black Sabbath. AC/DC. Iron Maiden. Destruction. Twenty-first-century kids, the younger generation, and they were still stuck on those old groups. Some of them were even smiling.

"Where is everyone? I mean, where is everyone our age?"

"'Amá Da'alzhishídi daats'í," said Angie, laughing at herself. That was one of the bars in Gallup that had a name in both languages. The Roundup, in English. 'Amá Da'alzhish, Dancing Mothers, named for the women who stomped their boots and wiggled their tight-jeaned asses while their kids stayed at home.

Two songs into their set they began to relax. Just as they were about to hit the opening chords in "See You in Hell" some guy in the crowd started shouting something. The way the lights were glaring, no one on the stage could see him very well, and at first it wasn't clear what he was saying. Then James heard him call out Zendrick's name. "You pussy! You cocksucker!" James looked at Zendrick. "You know him?" James asked. Zendrick started taking off his guitar. "Let it go," James said, "he's just an asshole."

"Right," said Zendrick. "There's a lot of bad blood between him and my cousin. I don't care what stupid shit he says about me, but someone's got to teach him to shut his fucking mouth in front of all these people." Just then James saw with relief that two bouncers had the heckler by the arms.

That night they sounded *good*. Even Zendrick, whose adrenaline put more power and precision into his playing. Everyone in the band felt it, you could tell, and they were feeding off each other's energy. But no one in the audience noticed or gave a damn. One kid asked them to play a Metallica song. James told him, "We don't do covers, man."

By early November the tourist season was all but dead, though they didn't lay people off at Hubbell's until the middle of December. James would give a tour whenever there was a big enough group. Most days there was hardly any heat in the sunshine outdoors, even at noon. After work one day he lay on Angie's couch in the long rectangles of the late sun. The sun through windows was still warm. He'd drunk a beer and it had made him sleepy. He wasn't sure if he was thinking or dreaming.

Winona walked over to him and put her sticky hand over his face and laughed. When he opened his eyes and blinked at her she laughed again, turned, and took two steps away from him, then turned to face him, grinning. He blinked at her again and she laughed. She started to paw his face again but he sat up on the couch. "Angie, come get your pesky kid. I gotta take a dump."

The bathroom, more than any other room, was hers: little pink shells of soap in little dishes enameled with floral designs, towels with lace at the borders, a pastel blue plastic trash basket with yellow daisies. He sat on the toilet looking for something to read. This was when he missed literacy in Navajo homes the most. A small cardboard box lay on top of the used tissues in the trash, and he picked it up, thinking at first it was for tampons. *Great, no sex for a few days.* But the box said: "Answer. Quick and Simple. Home Pregnancy Test."

"What the hell!" he yelled. He rummaged around for the test strip itself but didn't find it. He washed his hands and brought the box out, and put it under Angie's face. "What's this?"

She was trying to get Winona to sit at the table in her high chair. "Just what it looks like."

"How'd it come out?"

"Positive."

"That's a relief."

"Is it?" she smiled.

"That means you're not pregnant, right?"

"No, positive means I *am* pregnant."

"What's positive about that? You already got two kids, and I've been wearing a condom every time."

She shrugged and smiled.

He sat at the table with his head in his hands. Winona called for his attention. "Amos? Amos!" He looked at her and she laughed.

"What's so funny?" he said, and she laughed again. "You're in a weird mood," he told Winona.

"You're in a weird mood, too," Angie said, putting out the macaroni and cheese.

"What do you expect?"

He ate in silence, ignoring Winona's attempts to flirt with him. He took his plate to the sink and told Angie he was going to the ranch.

He kept thinking, *How could this possibly happen?* He hadn't been careless, and they'd never had a condom break or slip off. Driving down the highway in the twilight, his mood shifted from moment to moment. It was a complete disaster, his life was ruined. Then he'd imagine himself a father, a good father, interested in his kid. Then he would remember that Angie had two others who would also look at him, at least somewhat, as a father. That was too much.

But if this was a fact, then he couldn't just run and hide. How could he abandon Angie? Abortion would make this whole complicated mess much simpler, but he couldn't imagine bringing up the subject with a Navajo woman. Her smug little smile when she told him she was pregnant.

Here he was with a married woman with two children, now pregnant again with his kid. What had he been thinking? He had been hard up and lacking imagination, unable to think of any better woman out in this small place. *Kiyaa'áanii* and *Áshįįhí* women were out—at least he didn't have to worry about clans on his father's side. And no taters. No bitches or whores. And of course it had to be someone who liked him. That left Angie.

He lit a fire in the stove and sat in the big chair with his feet on another, thinking and dozing from time to time in the dark. What would it be like with a house full of kids all the time? Why was he thinking about taking on Malcolm's mess?

Maybe it was *all* Malcolm's mess. It wasn't all that long ago that he was here. And how come he had to discover the pregnancy by finding the box in the bathroom?

There was too much to think about. He kept waking every couple of hours troubled by a new question: What kind of mother was she, would she be? What would his own mother say? Once he woke up dreaming his father was telling him, "What kind of fool are you?" It was not the kind of thing his father would say, but it was exactly the pitch and tone of his voice. James hoped, as he drifted back to sleep, that it all would be somehow clearer in the morning.

In fact it was no clearer to him in the morning. They met at midday out by the burro corrals. The last yellow leaves clung to the branches and the ground was stained with walnut hulls. He thought he should remember to collect some for his mother to dye wool.

"I'm all mixed up, Angie," he said, propping himself on the fence, his forehead on his arms. "Maybe I should feel happy about this, but something isn't right."

"No, it isn't right," she said. "I'm just getting to know you again. You didn't ask for this. I'm still technically married to Malcolm."

"Technically."

"Well, the truth is I don't want to be married to him and he hasn't been a good husband for a long time."

"And now you're going to have a baby."

"Yes, we are."

"Are you sure it's *we*? It's not Malcolm's?"

She turned quickly away from him but didn't speak at first. She made a low choking sound, then finally said plainly as if talking to someone who wasn't there, "I *knew* this would be the way it was."

"Knew what?"

She faced him, furious. "I *knew* you'd say something like that. Try to get out of it somehow, pretend you'd never come home with me, act like I'm trying to trap you."

James was miserable. "Well, that's just it. I guess I'm stuck with you." He took her hand and stood there with her against the fence, saying nothing, feeling no better.

As the days went by and the autumn nights turned cooler, James thought less about the shock of his new situation and more about the implications of it. How was he going to provide for a family? He wondered if his parents would be able to help them for a while, and then realized that he hadn't even faced the idea of telling them. And there was still the unsolved riddle of Angie's own family, of her missing daughter, Reeba. If he was going to take care of Angie, she was going to have to take care of her own kids, and he was going to have to get to know her. "I have to at least spend some time with her. You can't put it off any longer, Angie."

He suggested they go up to Shiprock to see her, but Angie said it would be better if she came to Ganado. "I don't really get along with my brother-in-law."

"What's he doing raising your kid, then?"

"Him? He's not raising her. He works twelve hours a day and hardly says anything when he gets home."

"You know, I don't see why she can't live here with you. She goes to school, right?"

"Reeba's in kindergarten. But then what do I do with her when she gets out at two thirty?"

"Couldn't you get someone to sit with her for two or three hours?"

"Not for free."

"I could help pay for it."

"You better wait before you make an offer like that," Angie said.

Angie called her sister and she agreed to bring Reeba down for the weekend. They could eat on Friday night, and then they could all go to the flea markets in Window Rock and Gallup on Saturday, then head back. "Reeba's in some program at church on Sunday," Angie told James.

"Are you going to tell your sister you're pregnant?"

"No, not yet. Not until I can feel the baby move."

James felt relieved. He didn't want anybody thinking about him yet as a father or provider. He hadn't gotten used to the idea himself.

By late morning James heard Irene arrive at Angie's. He was sitting on the couch with Winona and a bowl of cut-up apples. He had tried to feed them to her, but she had more fun when he let her put them in his mouth, and she gave him a hard time when he wouldn't let her take them out again. Reeba was the first one in the door, and she ran over to her little sister and tried to make her laugh. Winona held out a mushed-up apple piece.

"Reeba, get over here," Irene called out, briefly shaking James's hand. "Get the plates from the car. And tell Evangeline to put down her Game Boy and bring in the chicken."

"She doesn't listen to me, Auntie."

James could see the resemblance of the little sisters in their fine noses and light complexions. Reeba was a little darker than the baby, pretty in the way that almost all little girls were pretty. She stood quietly beside Irene's daughter Evangeline, who let herself be coaxed out of the car to sit silently in a chair, still absorbed in her Game Boy.

James brought in the buckets of chicken and put them on the table where Irene indicated. Here she was in Angie's house for two minutes and she had already taken control.

"Reeba didn't want to come," said Irene. "And she wouldn't come without Evangeline. But she's had her nose in that thing since we left the house."

"Nobody asked me if I wanted to come," Evangeline said, not looking up.

"How did you do in that poster contest?" James asked Evangeline. It had been almost six months since James had first met her, and she looked at him blankly.

"You drew a drunk driver and someone flying out of a pickup."

"Oh," she said without smiling. "I got third place. They cheated."

Evangeline pushed away Reeba, who wanted to play with the Game Boy. Reeba started to cry.

James reached over to pat Reeba's shoulder but she stiffened and stared at him. "What?" he said, laughing.

"You're not my daddy."

Irene and Angie made the náneeskaadí bread while the fried chicken and mashed potatoes that Irene had brought warmed in the oven. Angie had fixed green beans and sweet potatoes with marshmallows. She had put out some pinyons, which Winona went straight for. "Don't let her get them," said Evangeline to Reeba. "She'll put them up her nose."

Angie bragged to her sister about all the pinyons they had picked. "You ought to see James's aunt. She uses both hands."

Irene turned the bread on the skillet. "I wanted to go, but I couldn't get nobody to go with me. I didn't want to go alone." She lowered her voice. "You wouldn't believe. So many people ran into those bi'éé' daalzhinígíí."

"Bi'éé' daalzhinígíí?" Angie said. It meant "black-clothed people" and sounded to James like Catholic priests.

"Gangs."

"Why would they be there?" Angie asked. James laughed.

"Really!" Irene frowned. "They steal people's bags of pinyons and sell them. They're giving three fifty a pound now."

Everyone ate hungrily, and for a while the conversation was reduced to pass this and pass that. James asked Reeba, "Did you go trick-or-treating?"

"At Halloween," she said.

"What did you go as?"

She stopped chewing her chicken and shook her head, not understanding, and when Irene said, "She was a pumpkin," Reeba squeezed her eyes shut and shook her head violently. Winona looked at her sister from her high chair and laughed.

Reeba glared at James and said, "I *wanted* to be an *angel*. And my daddy's a *soldier*."

Irene nodded and said, "We're all proud of your daddy."

Reeba hadn't taken her eyes off James. "You're not a soldier."

James thought of a few things he might say to her, but none of it would make sense to a five-year-old. Finally he said, "I can play the guitar."

"So what?" said the little girl, turning away from him. "My dad does, too."

"Okay," said James.

Evangeline carried the dishes to the sink and Irene and Angie washed them and wiped the counters, talking to each other in low voices. James knew they were talking about Malcolm. Irene was saying, "Oh, she was so upset when she found out he was on leave and he didn't come to see her." James wondered if the whispering tones would cause Angie to spill her pregnancy secret.

"He said he was going to go see her," Angie was saying. "I kept telling him, 'You know she's going to find out you were here and then she'll be mad.' He said he would and then he'd disappear and wouldn't say where he'd been, and pretty soon it was time for him to go back."

James sat in the living room with the girls, who didn't seem to be listening to the women's conversation in the kitchen. Winona was crawling over Reeba, who was sitting on the floor and trying to push her away. James was hoping Angie would stop talking about Malcolm, and when the topic drifted to clothes at Wal-Mart versus Target, he relaxed.

"Want to read a book?" James asked Reeba. She shook her head violently.

"Come on, it's a good one." Reeba stayed away but Winona spent a few minutes cuddling up to James and trying to turn the pages with her smudgy hands. Reeba laughed at her, and James felt that was a very small step in the right direction.

He put a videotape in the machine, some cartoon with a feisty princess that caught the eyes of both Reeba and Evangeline, and James went into the kitchen to drink coffee and listen to Irene and Angie talk in the mix of English and Navajo that seemed to be their common language.

"Do you think she hates me?" James asked. It had just occurred to him that maybe that was not the problem; maybe there was something actually wrong with Reeba. Was it because of the way she was being raised, or did Angie unload her on Irene because there was something with her not quite right?

"No, she just doesn't know you," Irene said.

"She isn't usually so rude," Angie said. "It's because she's mad at her dad."

"Oh, well. Maybe she'll get used to me."

"She will if she sees more of you," Irene said. "Once she gets to know you."

Angie kept giving him looks that seemed to say that she was sorry, and it did help to keep him from feeling totally miserable and out of place, but before long he finished his coffee and stood up. "I guess I better be going. Getting dark. Nice to see you, Irene."

"Nice to see you."

"Bye, girls." No answer. "See you, Angie."

"Bye."

"I'll see you tomorrow." He wanted to kiss her, or at least put his hand on her shoulder, but he wasn't sure what at this point was to be known, and what he was supposed to keep secret from whom.

"Right."

As he left, Evangeline was complaining that she would have to sleep on the floor next to Reeba. "She slobbers."

This was going to be his life?

CHAPTER NINETEEN

⬛ **HE TURNED THE** ragged pages of the magazines in the waiting room in Fort Defiance, which was full of pregnant women and small children. It was Angie's first prenatal appointment, and they had already taken her to the back. The only other man in the waiting room, who was watching over two toddlers, gave James a sympathetic nod. He nodded back. What comfort was that solidarity? They were both fucked.

The assistant called his name and he followed her. "Your wife wants you there when they do the ultrasound." Where had she got that idea, *wife*? The doctor was a short, brown-haired woman with bags under her eyes, yet she smiled a lot and Angie seemed to like her. The doctor herself did the ultrasound, smearing a clear blue jelly under Angie's navel with a sort of narrow box connected to the monitor by a cord, waving it back and forth as staticky lines formed and unformed shapes on the screen. All at once the lines came together and James saw the unmistakable curled back of a baby, and the legs wiggling slightly. *His* baby. What he was going to live for, from now on.

The doctor made some measurements on the screen. "Looks like just about thirteen weeks," she said.

Angie tried counting the months forward, then asked when she was due. James watched her doctor write a prescription for vitamins and an order for blood tests, and he did his own math, counting the weeks back. The doctor shook hands with both of them.

James drove them toward the summit, the broad top of the plateau, halfway between Fort Defiance and Ganado, first silent in a hot way. Then the words broke free. "You're a liar," he said.

"I am not."

He pulled off at the picnic area, and she sat at the concrete table covered with graffiti and pine needles. She wouldn't look at him. He grabbed her by the shoulders.

"So what were you thinking? That you could pass this baby off as mine?"

"I never said it was. When did I say it was?"

James started to answer but he was afraid that he could not remember her actually claiming that it was his baby.

Then she said, "What difference does it make?" She was turned away from him, making sniffling noises.

"Difference? You're joking."

"Well, it could be yours."

"How could it be mine? The doctor said thirteen weeks."

"She doesn't know that for sure. And if I'd met you sooner . . ."

"Angie, that's bullshit. Cut it out."

She stood up quickly from the table, lurched a few steps toward a stand of big pines, then slumped to the ground, sobbing on the cold pine needles. "I counted the weeks. I tried to decide if it was possible. Why don't you try to understand? What was I supposed to do? Malcolm coming home drunk and pissed off. So many nights . . . Food for the baby and this new one, how am I supposed to do that without somebody's help?"

"Give them to your sister to raise."

She took a noisy breath in, then said, "You're awful."

"Have an abortion." He turned away as she sobbed, her forehead on the forest floor. He sat in the car and watched her, feeling cruel, not minding being cruel, until after a few minutes she opened the door and sat down.

He drove in silence back to Ganado and stopped at her house, the engine still running.

Her face was red and wet with tears. "James, don't be like everyone else. No one wants to take care of anyone. Why can't you stay with me? What kind of future do I have with Malcolm?"

He had no answers.

In recent years Thanksgiving had become disagreeable to James: all the

Indian-pilgrim shit, the same crap they'd fed him back in kindergarten when they had made construction-paper turkeys and horns of plenty. Plus it meant sitting at a crowded table and eating too much, then jockeying with cousins for space in armchairs or on couches, holding in big farts. This Thanksgiving, though, he really didn't know what to do. He had avoided Angie for two weeks, and in fact avoided everyone as much as he could. Thelma and his mom had already started making plans for a big dinner at his parents' in Flagstaff, and he didn't even want to be there. He had a week to think of excuses to be away, but knew that they wouldn't be accepted.

He didn't want to talk about it. What was he going to say? That he dumped her? This was a case where you really couldn't say who dumped who. To explain, he would have to go into the whole business with Malcolm and how she had briefly snookered James, stupid, stupid James. He knew he hadn't ever been completely fooled; he had pressed the point, asked her the questions, but that even made it worse because it made it clear that he believed because he wanted to believe. His stupidest moment was when he first watched the moving shapes of the ultrasound and he had believed it was his kid, wanted it to be his kid, loved the idea. Stupid!

Maybe he would be able to talk about it soon, but not until he had made up his own mind. There were nights when he was ready to go back to her. He imagined pleading with his eyes, saying, "Look, I don't care if the baby's not mine." What a lie that would be. Not much different than the barstool lies before one-night stands, but worse. More consequence.

Then he thought of giving her an ultimatum: if she wanted to be with him, she had to give up custody of all Malcolm's kids. The cruelty shocked him, to even consider this. He thought of Winona's smeared face laughing at him, calling him Amos.

It wouldn't work, anyway. She wouldn't do it. What she wanted was for someone to help her take care of her children, not to give them all up.

Back and forth he went, angry at himself for not making up his mind, angry at Angie for not letting him know, for trying to trap him. At least he was pretty sure she was trying to trap him. But he missed her comfort, her skin.

"I don't know *what* the fuck to do, I don't know *what* the fuck I want, I don't know *what* the fuck I want to do." He could actually say it out loud, here on the mesa top where there wasn't anybody around. Foxtail grassheads waving, chickadees chipping, vetch pods rattling. The seed head stalks of mullein stood tall, almost dry, some leaves brown and papery, some yellow, limp like washrags, some still green.

Before he could talk to anyone he had to have the conversation with himself. Striding along the rim, among the pinyon trees, here without cones or nuts, he advised himself. "So what are you saying, fool? That you should take Angie back despite the fact that she *lied* to you? Despite the fact that she's pregnant with her husband's baby? I mean, my god, man, you don't *have* to stick with her."

He answered himself in a much less confident tone, "It feels like I do."

As his advocate, he said, "Does it feel like you do because you're so crazy about her or just because you're so crazy?"

"I don't know."

"Or just because you're feeling sorry for her, feeling guilty? Jesus, that's too much loyalty. I mean, do you really want to take this on? Do you really think you have a duty to her just because the two of you had sex? Do you even want to fuck her again, knock up against her pregnant uterus? Water another man's baby with your semen?"

He argued loudly with himself, and as he followed the sheep trail around a curve in the rim and over some rocks, he came upon old man Littlesunday walking with a homemade cane, his few goats browsing on the cliffrose nearby. He looked at James and smiled, started to laugh a little. James said "Yá'át'ééh," and passed by, embarrassed. "Yá'át'ééh," the old man said, finishing his laugh.

He couldn't stand it any longer, and at work he told Angie he wanted to come over to talk that evening. He tried for no facial expression and saw that she was doing the same.

"Okay," she said.

He stopped first at Nolan's, where the Beast and Winona were sitting on the floor in front of the TV, watching a cartoon. "You running a day care now?"

"Yeah," Nolan said. "For free. You got any kids that need watching?"

James looked at him with narrowed eyes. Did Nolan know anything? "I'll be back in a while."

James walked in Angie's door without knocking. He thought he should knock, but he wasn't going to. She was putting clothes in laundry bags, her expression grim. She didn't stop what she was doing.

"Did you even tell Malcolm that you were divorcing him? Are you actually going to divorce him?"

"I told you, James . . ." She tied up the bag and set it next to a big box of Tide.

"It's not like before, Angie. I don't know when I can believe you anymore."

"James, listen to me. I never said it was your baby. I never did. That was your idea." She was looking at him now.

"Well, you never said it wasn't."

"I didn't *know*. I still can't really accept it. When the doctor said I was thirteen weeks, I was thinking, how could that be?"

"You never missed your period?"

"I do sometimes. I just thought I *couldn't* be."

"Angie, I'd like to believe you. I can't say this about anybody else, but I love you, and I really want to believe you. But I don't."

"Then act like you love me," she said. She wiped her cheek with the front of her wrist.

"I'm acting *just exactly* like I love you, Angie, you should be able to see that. And it hurts. I can't stand it."

"I don't know," she said, controlling her tears. She sounded stern now, with some authority. "I should have told you more about what I was thinking. You know I was thinking about other people, too, not just my own self."

"Do you mean that I'm just thinking about myself? I am thinking about everybody else involved: you, your girls, your *husband*."

"Who I'm *divorcing* . . ."

"Are you?"

"Yes."

Her tone was hard. They were arguing now. Good.

"If you even cared," she said.

"I did care. But now . . ."

"Now what? Now that I told Malcolm I'm divorcing him, and now that I'm going to have a baby, you think this is a perfect time for you to split with me? Great timing. Good for *you*. But what about me? My family already thinks I don't know how to be a mother. They don't like Malcolm but they like me being with him more than me being a single mom. And now that I find somebody who is actually a nice guy and might have some kind of a future . . ."

Nice guy? At first he thought, *Wonderful, I'm a nice guy. Maybe she meant idiot. Future?* A future with him sounded bright to her because he'd be slaving for three children who belonged to someone else? He was going to be angry again, and then there would be no way back. "Angie, I can't talk about it anymore." He turned to the door, looked back at her once, and almost tripped as he left her house.

At Nolan's the kids were still on the floor watching the cartoon. "It's so fucked up," James said.

"I kind of thought you two had split up."

"We did, I guess. But I'm not really sure."

"Well, none of my business," said Nolan. "Though I could've told you a long time ago that you don't want to mess with women that's got kids."

"It's not that, really. She's pregnant."

"No shit."

"It's her husband's baby. She got pregnant before we started fucking."

"Oh, that's nice," Nolan said, and laughed from somewhere deep. James had a full view of his gold tooth.

"I knew I shouldn't have said anything to you. What's so fucking funny? I never said anything about your wino girlfriend."

"Until now, anyway." Nolan laughed again, his wide chest shaking. "All I mean, man, is that chicks never cease to amaze me, the things they do. And as for us, we're all chumps. I don't know if the next time around I'll be able to benefit from my own wisdom from experience, you know. Love is blind."

"Well, I feel blindsided."

"Well, if you think about it," Nolan said, "maybe it's a good thing. I mean, she was really setting you up. She's got these kids, and along comes a guy with a little drive, and also some family support and maybe some money from his parents, and he's a nice guy. Knows how to fuck her, too, eh."

"Fuck you, Nolan." But that was two people in a row who said something nice about him.

Thanksgiving was all arranged without him, as usual. His mother called him at Hubbell's on Monday and told him to be at their house in Flagstaff by noon on Thursday.

It was still morning when he arrived and all the warm, drowsy smells were familiar from every other Thanksgiving: turkey, pumpkin, cinnamon. His mother and Thelma were taking things in and out of the oven and the refrigerator. He came over to her and gave her a hug. "Hello, dear," she said.

Max sat on the couch watching the TV where giant balloons bobbed above a New York street.

Out from the bedroom that had briefly been James's came his brother Ben, whom he hadn't seen since he'd gone to California two years ago. His body seemed even stringier, and he was wearing a pair of expensive-looking city shoes. They gave each other a strong hug with slaps on the back. Behind Ben, standing with an awkward smile, was a pretty white girl, tall and thin, her shoulder-length blonde hair waving a little near her ears. "This is Francine." They shook hands. It was an Anglo woman's handshake, a squeeze and a tug. So far from the nearly passive touch of the soft palm he remembered from his grandmother. Handshakes were a tricky thing, and once in a while he would misjudge, as when what started out as a Navajo handshake ended up gripping and pumping. A kind of handshake a Navajo member of the Lions Club would give.

Soon the ladies called out "Da'ohsóó," and they all gathered at the table. This was Thelma's time: the Long Prayer. As James semibowed his head and heard Thelma's low-pitched murmur thanking the holy ones for the family and friends and the food and on and on, he thought of the painting by a Navajo artist he had seen in a downtown gallery on this very subject. A family in front of a table of food, most heads bowed, a grandma admonishing a giggling child.

Thelma made special mention in her prayer of Ben and his girlfriend, but she did not pronounce their names—those who came from far away—and the whole prayer was in Navajo, so it was lost to Francine, and maybe to Ben. James wondered how much Navajo his brother still knew.

His father was very friendly with Francine. They had arrived from California Wednesday afternoon and he had apparently already grilled her and knew some things about her. Now he asked, "Are your parents having dinner in Berkeley?"

"Yes. My sister and brother are taking their families to their house."

"So you are their baby?"

"I guess I am their baby."

It was strange, James thought, passing the food, that there were no actual children here. He found himself missing Angie's kids, her niece, and especially Winona. "You're in law school, too?" James asked her.

"We're in the same class. We actually met at Legal Services in San Mateo." She turned slightly toward Ben and smiled shyly.

"Why, you both got into some kind of trouble?" James asked. Everyone at the table laughed, and he laughed too, though he hadn't meant it as a joke.

Ben said, "It's like cheap lawyers for poor people. We're just doing paralegal-type work there."

"Paying your dues before you hit it rich?" James grinned at his brother, who smiled uncomfortably. James felt that perhaps he had seemed envious of Ben, which was the very thing he wished not to convey.

"Actually, it's the kind of law we both want to do. At least partly."

"James has a new job, too," his mother said. He knew it made her happy he was working, but he wished she wouldn't talk about him in front of everyone. When she had called him earlier in the week she told James he could bring someone with him to dinner. He had told her there wasn't anyone, and she said that Max had told her differently.

"That's all over," he had told her. Now he said to his brother, "I've got a job at Hubbell's. Tour guide. But it's a seasonal job that's about to end soon. Hopefully I'll get rehired in April."

"That sounds just about right," Ben said. "Leaves time for other things. Are you doing any music? You still have, what was it, Ataxia?"

"Nah. That exploded. The bass player exploded. Meth. But I'm in a new band." Even now it hurt James to say it, but Ataxia was better than the band he was in now would ever be. "Putrefaction."

"Great."

"What do you play?" Francine said.

"Guitar," James said. *Know what that is?*

"What kind of music?" she asked sweetly.

"Death metal," he said, loving to say it, loving to see her face fall.

"Oh."

Ben asked James if he had listened to any good new bands.

"Most the new stuff I don't like. Have you heard the new Nile? And Dying Fetus, of course."

"How about Cannibal Corpse?"

"Nah, they haven't come out with anything in the last year or two. Plus they kind of bring back bad memories, since Terri and I got together at one of their concerts."

Francine blushed and Ben said, "Bittersweet, huh?" with an exploratory smile.

"Just fucking bitter," James said. "Only that's like ancient history."

"Is there somebody new?"

James knew that Ben felt he was on shaky ground, and he was. Since James wasn't sure himself where things stood with Angie, what could he tell his brother? And when he didn't even want to think about Angie, why talk about her?

"Fuck, no."

Then Max, the asshole, asked why James hadn't brought his girlfriend to dinner.

"We split up," he had to say. "I think."

"Oh," said Max.

They were on the pies and a little sluggish when Max brought up what he was finding out about the rustlers.

"Not another accident?" James asked.

"Rustlers! You're kidding," said Francine. "I thought that was only in Westerns."

"Then we're in a Western," Max told her. "No more accidents, no more dead cows on the interstate. They shut down the cattle company near Holbrook. The brand inspector finally got around to inspecting."

"Well, that's good," said James's mother. "I never did like those people; they seemed like shady rednecks."

"Well, that won't slow them down much," said Max. "And James, guess who's just been accepted into the Ganado Lions Club? Beebee. Yes! And you know who nominated him? Your friend, Gabaldon."

"He's not my friend, he's my boss. And how come I never heard about this?"

"It just happened this week. I was talking with my buddy Ray Montoya, who's in the Lions and tells me shit."

Francine asked, "Is there really someone named Beebee?"

"Nickname," James's father said. "There's a lot of nicknames around here. What *is* his name, anyway?"

Ben's brow was furrowed in concentration. To no one in particular he said, "I wonder what you could do about rustling. If you weren't able to catch them red-handed, maybe you could sue the grazing committee for derogation of duty."

"I'd prefer to catch them red-handed," said Max.

After the meal Francine ended up on the couch between Ben and Max, and James could see that Max was trying to impress her with cowboy stories. That old one about the lightning bolt and Max falling with the horse over the mesa wall. She was playing along, smiling at him and saying, "Oh really?" Ben was trying to look pleasant, but had heard all this bullshit before; James knew this because they had talked about it years ago. That's just the way their cousin was. And Francine, perhaps, was just the kind of white girl who would fall for it.

James grinned at Ben, whose pained smile turned to a laugh of recognition. James suddenly felt a surge of affection for his brother, who knew him better than anyone. "You should come out to the rez while you're here. Sit in on our practice session, see the ranch."

"Man, I'd love to. But we're heading back to Phoenix in the morning to fly back."

"Oh. Busy people, you two." Ben just looked at James, understanding too well that James was disappointed. "It's okay, some other time."

Why could Ben not have stayed longer, or showed some interest in the ranch? The answer was that they had things to do in California. James understood this, and this understanding, this refusal to feel envy, proved he loved his brother—he checked now and then to make sure he did. He really wanted his brother to succeed and to have a good life. But did his success have to be so completely standard—law school and blonde girlfriend and helping the unfortunate?

James's father sat in the chair next to James. "So when does the job end?"

"December fifteenth."

"What's your plan for after that?"

"Well, I guess I'll look for a job, but it's only three and a half months."

"You thinking about staying out there for a while?"

"I might. I like it. It's peaceful out at the ranch, and someone ought to be there. Max isn't there half the time."

"Well, don't just stay out there contemplating your navel because *someone* has to be there."

"I got plenty to do besides contemplating my navel, if I ever did think about contemplating my navel. There's lots to fix up. And I want to do some reading. I've got a band and we're getting better."

"Well, that's good, son. All I mean is don't do what you do because of what someone *else* wants."

"I don't plan to," James said.

Before long Ben had stretched out his legs and rested his head on the back of the couch while Max went on entertaining Francine, and James had slumped sleepily in his chair. His father suggested they all take a "constitutional" around the neighborhood. At first James was glad to get out into the cool air, but three doors down, who should be raking leaves and crushed acorns on his lawn and driveway but Mr. Wesson? At first it hadn't made sense, seeing his probation officer out of context. Did he work part time as a landscaper? He had tried to stay back behind his brother and Francine, but his father and mother walked over to Joe, as they called him, and chatted with him. "These are my sons, Ben and James." Mr. Wesson was smiling when he shook Ben's hand, but by the time he had looked James in the eye, he took on a poker face. "Hi," James said. Then, without another word, they were walking down the street.

It was a close call. James thought it might have been easier if he had just told his parents about the arrest and his probation, so he wouldn't have to sweat out moments like that, the same way years ago he had wanted to tell them all about the day Rodney was killed, but couldn't. Now once again he kept silent, already knowing what they would say. He could deal with whatever angry words his father had for him—in fact, he would respond with his own anger, and this was a way he could lift himself out of even worse feelings. But his mother would just cry, and he didn't know how to deal with that. It just made him sad, and there was no way out.

The group had spread out by the time they were back at the house, and James and Ben decided to hike awhile in the woods while the others made coffee. James felt a little desperate to talk with Ben now that he knew he would be gone again soon. He didn't want anyone's pity. Ben was usually careful enough not to boast or seem to pity him, but James felt like he was back in middle school, missing the boat over and over again. He enjoyed talking about the amusing, even ridiculous events of their childhood. But just behind those stories James knew, and Ben probably knew, were the others, the lowest points in James's memory, like where the fog slid down in the lowest valleys.

Climbing toward the boulders at the base of the mountain, they reminisced about their school days, all the teasing and arguing and fighting, the scowling teachers and all their ridiculous quirks: the rodeo clown, the coach. Mr. Herring. Elbert Herring, the one they called Elbert Utmost because he was always telling kids to do their utmost. Kids he had known when they'd been preschoolers together, now in a gone world. And the cowboy country types he had never encountered until first grade, and who rarely spoke.

And James was there again, in that low place, remembering the terrible feeling of waking up in the morning facing another day at school. Back then his mother called him grumpy and said he'd gotten up on the wrong side of the bed. But life was hell. Ditching was the only pleasure on a school day. Then when they were called in to talk to the counselor the first time, when he'd finally called the teacher he'd been resenting for weeks a bitch, that was the scene: his father angry, his mother crying. James pulling balls of linty wool from his sweater and letting them drop to the floor.

"It wasn't easy for you," Ben said.

Ben often made James understand what he didn't want to understand. "It wasn't any easier for you," James said.

He and Ben had not talked about when Rodney died. For years that had seemed unnecessary. Ben had been there too, farther back in the crowd of onlookers while Rodney and Lennerd pushed each other. Soon after the stabbing Ben had said to James, "You told him to teach him a lesson." He was letting James know that he knew he was stricken with guilt. James could picture his brother now as a judge, with the same stern assurance as any other.

In those days his father was often upset with him, telling him that he didn't know where his behavior was leading him. "There is so much at stake. You can't just flunk out of school. Just try, James." But now that he was on his own, his father had seemed more settled, less panicked than he had been when James was in high school. James was not sure he liked this any better, since it seemed to mean that there was less at stake, that his fate was already decided, that his father felt disappointed but was resigned to it. He no longer had any expectations of him, as if he saw no triumph in his future.

James and Ben sat on a flat boulder warmed a little by a spot of sunlight. A single wasp appeared, buzzing and dipping from rock to rock. "Probably wondering where all the other wasps are," said James.

"Look how close to the ground he's staying," said Ben. "And how slowly he's buzzing around."

"Late in the season," said James. It scared him a little when he felt like this, as if he were at the bottom of a dark hole. He wasn't going to kill himself because that required an effort and a desire, and now he didn't have either. It was just that he felt his life was already over. "Don't stay away too long," James said.

CHAPTER TWENTY

▨ **"COME ON, ARE** you still sleeping?" It was Max who was knocking loudly at the door.

"Jesus Christ, what's the matter with you?" There was the faintest rim brightening the east below a jet sky still full of stars. James was in his boxers and T-shirt and turned back to his bed after he opened the door for Max. His eyes felt gritty and he knew his hair was probably comical, sticking up like half-dead weeds.

"Look," said Max. "I'll make some coffee, and you get ready."

"Ready for what?" James said into his pillow.

"To look for some cows."

James groaned. "Why don't *you* go look for cows?"

"Ever think I might need some help? We been missing several cows and their calves for quite a while. Most of them are branded, but there's one cow with twins that are still slick. Those are the ones I'm worried about."

"Oh, man, I don't feel like riding all the way out into the Painted Desert looking for fucking cows. It's too cold. I didn't sleep too good last night."

"Quit whining, you wuss. Get dressed. I already got your horse saddled up."

He could see the horses' breath and their own. The stars at the eastern horizon were starting to fade. They rode slowly, the horses dipping their heads with each pace. All but the brightest stars were gone. Traces of pink appeared in the thin clouds that partly overcast the eastern half of the sky. As they rode up the gradual slope James could distinguish shrubs and rocks at the horses' feet. Then, at the top of a rise, the bright gold light of the sun hit them. Now the horses picked up their pace and James was just beginning to think.

"It's getting worse," Max said, his hand on the back of the saddle, turning toward James. "I got some friends who work at the cattle company this side of Holbrook, and they say every day they take in stolen cattle."

"I thought you told us they closed it down."

"Ha! For a week. Some punishment, huh? I believe some cash changed hands."

"You know, it doesn't really seem like keeping cattle is worth it," said James.

"You're just now figuring that out? No one's getting rich off those dumb animals except the rustlers, but what else are we going to do with our spare time? Sit around all day like you with your gloomy thoughts?"

"Right, looking for stolen cattle on a freezing morning is going to snap me out of my gloom."

"Okay, what you probably need is to get some young pretty hooker . . ."

"No, that is not what I need. It's probably what *you* need, you sick fucker."

They could see Beebee's place in the valley as they rode across the hill, avoiding the path of the coyote who trotted north, looking back over his shoulder. The sun emerged from the clouds from time to time, but there was no warmth and the wind had picked up. They took cover below a little cliff that blocked the cold breeze, and rested for a while. The soft sandstone crumbled easily, riddled with little arches and cavities, ancient lake deposits that had always reminded James of bones and skulls. Max offered James some Skoal, which he declined, not trying to conceal his disgust. The last time he had tasted that brown wintergreen mess was in the seventh grade.

"What'd you think of Ben's girl?" Max asked.

"Nice enough. You seemed to like her just fine."

"Yeah. Cute, but not really my type. It's hard to imagine his life out there."

"He was meant for that life," James said, surprising himself. "He was always going to be some place like that. He doesn't really belong here."

"Yeah, well, *she* sure doesn't. She held her own, though. Must have been scared to be around all of us."

There was a rough noise across the hill by a juniper, not far from where they were resting: two ravens were trying to drive off a third, all squawking, and from time to time they rose a little ways into the air, then landed again in the same spot, where they picked at something in the ground.

"Your folks seem to like her okay."

"Shit, anything Ben does they like okay."

Max strode across to where the ravens had landed and James followed. He stopped, knelt down, and showed the big boot tracks to his cousin. "Something's going on," Max said and walked toward the ravens, who hopped and flew off, croaking. He reached down into the poked-at dirt and lifted out something orange. "Damn." He dug a little more. "Son of a bitch."

James saw that what Max held was two ears from a cow, with Max's notches and his brand on the orange plastic ear tag. He dug a little farther and shook the dirt from a square foot of hide with Max's brand on it. The blood was still a dark red, clotted with sand.

"The mother of the twins," Max said. "I wonder where the rest of her is."

James followed him down the other side of the hill to where they crossed over a little arroyo, where mushlike green offal out of a cow's stomach spread over the sand.

"We're on the right track now," Max said and followed the little drainage to where it dropped off about twenty feet. They looked down and saw in the gorge among the white rocks the rest of the hide and the legs of his cow.

"So what now?" James asked.

"What do you think? Somehow I don't think the grazing committee is going to help us with this."

"You could take in the evidence. It'd be pretty hard for them to ignore it."

"Hell, ignoring is what they're best at. I can hear them now. 'How do we know you didn't butcher your own cow?'"

They got back on their horses and James followed his cousin toward

Beebee's house, where a thin stream of smoke came from the stovepipe. James felt his heartbeat quicken. He wanted to turn his horse around and head back home, but Max was determined and there was no use trying to talk him out of it.

They hitched their horses to a smelly ailanthus tree and walked up the stair with the broken railing onto the narrow porch. Max knocked.

"*Wóshdę́ę́*," they heard. For such a big man, Beebee had a surprisingly high-pitched voice. He was putting more firewood into the big cookstove.

"Cold," Max said, taking off his gloves and shaking hands. James noticed Beebee's shake was like his old grandmother's.

"What you guys doing out here so early Saturday?"

"Just getting a little air," Max said.

"*Gohwééhísh ła'*?" he offered, putting three enamel cups on the table and pouring the coffee from the big pot on the stove.

"Nice and warm," James said, his hand surrounding the cup.

"You here by yourself?" Max asked.

"Course I am," Beebee said, since everybody knew that his wife left soon after they got married.

"Hey, I hear you're a Lion. Congratulations."

Beebee laughed. "A Lion. Yeah, I'm in the Lions Club so I guess I'm a Lion." His laugh was a hee-hee-hee that went with the long braids that he wore down his front, tied with buckskin like one of those AIM people, Lakota braids on a big stupid Navajo man, light on his feet, enjoying his visitors, as if he were trying to be his own mother. When people offered *gohwééh*, they usually meant food, too, so Beebee actually slapped some dough and laid it in the hot lard. With a fork he laid the pieces of fry bread on a paper towel on the table. It tasted good, like James's mother's.

Max asked in a loud and steady voice, in a tone James thought he clearly intended, "You got any fresh meat?"

"Sure," said Beebee, opening his propane refrigerator and pulling out a big joint wrapped in cotton. "I just butchered . . ." At that moment James saw something happen behind Beebee's eyes as he narrowed his lids at Max. "Are you eccusing me?" He reached behind him and gripped the cast-iron skillet.

"*Eccusing* you of what?" Max said. "All I asked for was fresh meat, which I see you got."

"What do you know about fresh meat?"

"I don't know anything," said Max. James shook his head.

"Oh yes you do."

"It could be anybody's animal," Max said.

"I seen you guys. What did you find up on the hill?" Beebee lifted the skillet. Out of the pocket of his Carhartt, Max brought out the ears and the square of branded hide and laid them on the table. Beebee put the skillet back on the stove and picked up the evidence. "One dead cow ain't worth a whole lot of trouble," he said. He lifted the lid of the burner with its handle and threw the hide and ears into the deep orange fire.

Max and James left Beebee's and faced the ride back in the windy cold. James didn't want to say much but couldn't resist: "You backed off because the big moron had his hand on a skillet."

"Well, yeah," said Max. In a less defensive tone he added, "We're just gonna have to do it some other way. Find out who's behind all this stuff. Beebee's not the great mastermind."

"Ha, that's a good plan. That's good thinking," James said.

CHAPTER TWENTY-ONE

▨ **IT WAS A** bright Saturday in the best season to be in northern California, what they call winter, and Francine was visiting her parents across the bay, so Ben decided to work on his article at the picnic table out in the yard. He thought he wouldn't be too distracted. It was quiet in the neighborhood, with only an occasional bark from a dog on the next street, and the birds, whatever they were, some little California birds with rosy heads, flittered from the bare plum tree to the ground and back up to the tree again and chirped in a way that he thought couldn't possibly distract him from stern consideration of the history of Native water rights. It was early in the evolution of this article, which he was writing for his own *Law Review*; he had already done most of the research and needed a little freedom of thought and fresh air to begin to form the argument that would be the core of his essay. Later he would need a closed room with no windows, but now he was inhabiting a distinct phase of his work that required a day without constraints and slippers instead of shoes. Francine had been ready to go early, and she let her blonde hair fall amiably into his face as she kissed him, leaving him most of a pot of coffee and wishing him a good day. No, she had said, "Have a *productive* day," and he'd heard the italics as a stipulation.

He poured some coffee into the big blue mug—it was Francine's fair-trade stuff, which was a little too bitter so he poured in some milk—and went out into the yard in shorts, a T-shirt, and slippers. He put the mug and pen and yellow legal pad on the slatted redwood table and sat on the detached bench. The coffee was good. Three rose-capped birds seemed to be playing tag. He told himself that the thrust of his work this morning was to develop a reasoned argument, something that would at least earn the first-glance respect of the mythical unseen judge Ben had learned to keep in mind as the audience for all his essays and legal arguments, words with enough loft and generality to rise above and obscure the origin of his case in his rage born and nurtured by the historical review he had just painfully completed. This was always the first step when it came down to the writing, to disguise the passion the subject provoked, to speak slowly and deliberately to the exact degree that history and precedent required crazy fury. The law as war.

He wrote at the top of the blank lined page: "Aboriginal Rights." Halfway down the page he wrote: "Abrogations." Then he thought of the windmill out at the ranch and the sound that it made going around and around in a moderate breeze, the water pulsing between trickle and gush, and the liquid song of the meadowlarks and the calls of the blue quails that depended on the tanks and troughs and what spilled out of them, the muddy rivulets that wound down into the stock pond, the metallic song of the slightly off-center sucker rod as it was pulled up and down and up and down by the galvanized blades above.

This is going to get harder if I let it, he thought. He was familiar with the lure and danger of nostalgia. There, too, was a potential source of creativity—he'd read a volume of Proust and got the idea that for him there had been no other source, which seemed like the kind of self-indulgent emotion a sickly homosexual who spent all day dressed in pajamas (Ben looked at his slippers) would rely on—but for Ben it was just as much a drain to his creativity, because what could you do about the past? He thought he had to start to treat his childhood the way he had seen busy lawyers treat their families: they kept their wives and children preserved in pictures on their desks and bookshelves while they worked most of a day's hours in offices and courtrooms as if to tell themselves this was why they did it; the babies and children were the reason they didn't see them. And it made no sense for him either: there were other reasons he didn't live back home. He would think of them in a moment.

He wrote: "Winters (1908). Tribes reserved everything not expressly relinquished or unequivocally abrogated by the federal government."

His neighbor appeared in her backyard with her garden hose in one hand and waving at him with the other, and sprayed the shrubs at the back of her house with a silver arc that landed on their waxy leaves with a tropical patter. He waved back, thinking that that was Indian water, if not unequivocally relinquished or abrogated. "Nice day," she said, and he agreed. Her name was Janine, and she was a widow in her sixties who spent a lot of time in her garden, even getting down on her aging knees and pulling weeds hour after hour. There was a low redwood fence separating her yard from Ben and Francine's, which they were renting cheaply from a law professor who was spending the year in England. Several times Janine had brought Francine cut flowers from the yard— peonies, daylilies, roses—and the two of them chattered happily with the bouquet between them. There was a bird feeder hanging from a large oak in Janine's yard, visible to Ben as he sat at the picnic table.

"You haven't seen Artemesia, have you?" Janine asked.

Ben remembered that this was her cat, a huge gray animal that frequently escaped from her house. He said he would keep an eye out, but lowered his gaze and wrote on his legal pad, "Adjudications," then added "Duress." He heard Janine turn off her hose and close her back door. Across the street he heard a car start, the dog bark, and two children calling to each other, the placid sounds of the benign neighborhood.

Perhaps spurred by the children's voices, he remembered a school trip to Narbona Pass, though then, in the eighties, it was still called Washington Pass. At the highest point along the highway over the Chuska Mountains, there was a picnic area by a pasture with scattered clumps of oaks bordered by thick blue spruce. It was spring, not long before school-out, the third- and fourth-grade classes stuffed into yellow buses that wound slowly up the grade like a procession of elephants, then exploded out into the pasture at the summit in yells and laughter, wild running and chasing in the air still sharp with the smell of snow patches melting on the cutbanks of the little stream. Soon they were splashing in the water, racing impromptu boats of bark and leaves, engineering dams and canals. This was more water than they usually saw on the ground; the wash at Ganado was a trickle by comparison, even in the three or four miles where it flowed permanently; this was a stream, not a wash, with pools of tiny silver fish that faced the current together and darted away from third-grade feet and strings of lumpy algae.

Ben remembered exploring along the stream in a group of boys that waxed and waned in solidarity: sometimes he was in a little group, sometimes by himself. Around a corner he came upon James, Rodney, and another boy crouching by a greenish pool. Rodney had a tiny frog in his hand and they were gently poking at it to jump. James told Ben they needed to find another so that they could have a frog race, but they couldn't find one: there were large groups of black tadpoles in the pools, some of them with rudimentary legs, but all still with their tails and bound to the water. Rodney had the only mature frog, and he let it jump back into the water where it swam, in its froglike way, to the underwater shadow of a rock.

It was a different world on Narbona Pass, and being in it with all the children he knew from school was strange and exciting. It was cooler than home, and the wind sounded different blowing through the tall spruces. Three horses he had never seen before grazed below the black cliffs and in the distance, in an unbelievable blue vastness far below, the New Mexico desert spread out all the way to the shining mountains. The magic of this high place was the water.

The water, Ben thought now, so shallow and so narrow, so rare, so little. Then it seemed a flood, infinite, eternal. More water was flowing than most of them had ever seen. Yet he would later see and hear the voluminous rivers, even in the Southwest, carrying huge flows of water he knew to quantify in cubic feet per second, having gathered the trickles and freshets of his Native childhood into great American rivers quenching thirsty farms and cities far away.

He wrote: "Practically Irrigable Acreage."

Now he remembered precisely the sound of Rodney laughing as the frog jumped from his hand, far away in time and distance, and felt the dreadful tug of unrecoverable events, which he knew put him at risk of paralysis. And he could not let himself be so distracted from his task. Somehow he had to harness this memory of the little stream in the pasture on Narbona Pass to the service of his legal exegesis, had to push through the temptations of nostalgia and forget the sound of the laughter of the dead.

He moved down the bench a few inches so his paper was in the shade. If he was going to have any influence on the congressional briefing this spring, he had to finish his article.

He wrote: "Time Immemorial." There were words in the law that were quaint, almost poetic. Despite its history of running roughshod over Native communities, it could admit in such a grand and uncompromising phrase that there existed "Ancient Priority Claims."

One of the problems he was struggling with was the idea of quantifying rights. It was a way of closing the door. Before you put a number to it, you had infinite rights under *Winters*. The rights were limited only when quantified.

This was when he needed to turn up the metal and hear *fuck you fuck you fuck you.*

He still listened to metal, became a different person when he did. He didn't follow the new bands but relied on James to tell him what was good. The people Ben worked with liked stuff like bluegrass or Celtic or Wilco. And his own temperament, in public, was similarly tame. But as for what he really wanted when the frustration built, it was to put his earphones on and turn it up. Francine was always telling him he'd ruin his hearing.

It was painful to still love your brother, your brother who was never going to change, who didn't even want anyone to make things easier for him or to make things easier for himself.

He could go to the law library and maybe keep his mind on track. But he knew he'd just look at the women, and it would be Stanford and a million miles from home and what he was writing about. A squirrel appeared on a low branch of the oak next door that held the bird feeder, and tentatively approached it. Janine had attached a complicated squirrel guard out of tin, a cone that was meant to protect the seeds from his grip, but the squirrel had figured this out and hung by his back legs from the branch, lifting the feeder by its chain until it could momentarily spill seeds on the ground to where he pranced down to feed.

Francine had been saying that they should not travel for a while. There was too much going on. They could spend Christmas with her parents and possibly her siblings, maybe go up to the cabin at Tahoe for a day or two, but not back to Arizona again. However, since their visit at Thanksgiving she wavered, and Ben worried—not seriously, but in amusement—that she was impressed with his cousin Max, all of course the fault of Max, for this was all he knew how to do: impress women and go to bed with them, even have kids with them, then leave, and though of course Francine was no idiot like the women who had really fallen for Max (he couldn't even remember a single name of any of Max's wives or girlfriends), Ben just thought it was ridiculous that she smiled at his stupid cowboy stories and said, "Really?"

Ben knew Francine thought she liked his family: she had told him this many times. It was not just Max's bullshit either. She said his mother was sweet. His father, she said, "doesn't seem to put a lot of pressure on you," and he'd answered that it was only because he put pressure on himself, and that she should ask James, since if there was anyone who had chafed under their father's high expectations it was his brother, who had developed what he needed to resist the pressure. "The pressure was there, for sure. Still is."

"But," Francine had protested, "it's not like in some totally white family where all they care about is the kids getting ahead."

He had left it at that. It was true that the family was not "totally white," but that brought up a topic that he didn't like to spend much time on, not with Francine.

He suspected that Francine in some sense had been disappointed in his family, expecting perhaps that they would still be living on the reservation. She knew better, of course, but his stories from his past had mostly been about Ganado and seldom about Flagstaff, and she was always asking him about the reservation, about Navajos, and seemed to care less about the other, less interesting half of his ancestry. Her parents—both academics—were always ready to discuss topics related to Native Americans. He didn't mind: he welcomed direct talk after four years of Stanford where his fellow students either apologized to him for no reason or made him uncomfortable with jokes about scalping or too many chiefs.

And she didn't know his family, no matter what she thought. She had said he was well adjusted; she also thought his brother was well adjusted and that he had rejected a life of accomplishment because he had read a little Thoreau and had high principles. She seemed to be in awe of Thelma, who had more of an accent and used Navajo more often, at least before Ben told her about Merwin.

He should have known better. They had met at Legal Aid in San

Mateo; he was working on behalf of tenants of a notorious slumlord while she was completely absorbed in a domestic violence project. Even her supervisor thought she was too enthusiastic and personally involved and had asked her if there were a similar dynamic in her own family of origin. She was aghast and explained that it was precisely because all the men in her family were gentle and supportive that she felt so deeply shocked and offended that the women and children among her clients had to endure the things they did. She was similarly taken aback when Ben had told her that Merwin used to stay out for days at a time and would come home smelling of alcohol and women to argue with Thelma and throw things at her. "You saw it?" she asked.

"A couple of times. Sometimes we would stay over with her when we were kids."

"Why didn't she leave him?"

"She did. For quite a few years. We were glad; we thought he was gone. We didn't like him; he called James Little White Man, that sort of thing. Then when he got sick he came back whining and she took him in. She always had to have somebody who needed her."

"Enabler."

"I've heard the word." And he felt it was part of the jargon that owed more to social work and pop psychology than the field of family law, a word too trite and dismissive to be applied to his own family, a family that was admittedly more complicated than she had thought. It was perhaps a good thing that she was beginning to realize some of the details and nuances of where he came from, that it wasn't some sort of exotic pastoral; maybe it wasn't so good, though, if she ended up sticking on other reductive labels and imagined him originating in a rural freak show.

He took a break and went into the kitchen for more coffee. The kitchen was neat and clean, and the appliances were new and pretty. The law professor whose house this was had nice things from the kitchen to the library to the bedroom. The light outside the window was strong but at this time of year not unmerciful. There was little fog on this side of the peninsula. In the refrigerator he found some treats that Francine had bought at Whole Foods: some spicy olives and marinated mushrooms and St. André cheese, which he spread on a sesame cracker. He thought of the Navajo word for mushrooms, *náá'ádįįh*, which means "makes you go blind," and he wondered what kind of Navajo he was to be eating them with such pleasure.

It made him sad that he would have to give up everything in his early life to make a go of it. Francine didn't know that; she thought everyone always had choices. It was of course absurd that he was spending so much effort at becoming an expert in this area of law so that he could get away from the reservation and live in Washington. Where else would an expert on this branch of federal law live? What kind of job could he get at home? (He was still calling it home, against all reason.) If he decided to go to Window Rock he wouldn't be any closer to making a better future for Navajo people but instead would be dealing with tribal politicians as criminals, perhaps as a liaison between the gaming commission and the mafia.

Francine and Ben had begun to talk about making a life together in a place like Palo Alto or Georgetown. Francine could work in family law at the federal level, though she didn't mind staying in California where her family was and there were plenty of grassroots kinds of things she could get behind. She liked that he was up and coming.

Ben was happy to be up and coming, if he was, and happy about his work, which he was doing well, and everyone thought he was exemplary. He liked to be recognized for being smart, and also for being ethical. He believed in the law . . . sometimes.

Back in the yard he wrote, "The Tribes' unique property and sovereignty rights are under attack in the courts and in political arenas." And he thought, *Which way should we lose it? If we quantified our water rights and sold them, white farmers and city people might howl because they'd become accustomed to using Indian water for free, but was that any better?*

He had always liked school, ever since his first class with beloved Mr. Soros, but it took him a long time to realize he was smarter than James. Sometimes he still wasn't sure, and he knew that his superiority was limited to the sort of verbal quibbling that defined a lawyer's intelligence. James's talent for music, for instance, certainly exceeded Ben's, and maybe it was a more comprehensive and well-rounded intelligence, as it wasn't just frontal lobe and Broca's area but also drew on emotion and intuition and muscle memory.

Ben knew that James thought he should have more interest in the ranch, in actual life on the reservation. In figuring out some way to keep the neighbors from stealing the cattle.

Now he was trying to keep others from stealing the water. But the settlements would cost money the tribes didn't have, and it would all go to lawyers. Navajos called lawyers *agha'diit'aahii*, which means "they win for you," like the racehorse you bet on. But they win for themselves.

It's just that there was no other way to fight injustice except through the justice system, even if the greatest injustice was done *through* this system. Look at Indian history. Look at any history. What were the counterexamples? Desegregation, the civil rights movement. But then, look at the failure of Reconstruction, the retrenchment of the right wing. Laissez-faire again. The chipping away at Indian land, the land dispute and relocation.

It made him mad to have such two-edged weapons, and that's why he liked death metal. Banging his head felt better than thinking circles around it. But he was smart and had to put on a suit and fight them in court. He could say "Your Honor," even if James couldn't.

It hadn't been easy for him to see his brother. There were always the complicated feelings, Ben wishing James could try harder, could succeed at something, and the slights he felt, realizing that he did not like Francine. (Ben hoped she didn't know, and he would never tell her.) But now he felt some bigger discomfort than what he was used to feeling, some real despair. James seemed much older now, and sadder. As if he were beginning to realize his opportunities were fewer. Even when he talked about his band and how they were sounding better, it seemed as if he were telling a joke or a lie.

It was tugging at him; James must have been able to tell. When they talked of the people when they were kids in school, the deep-rez kids, the teachers with their nicknames. James had yelled something before Lennerd had stabbed Rodney—was it that Rodney should teach Lennerd a lesson, or that he should back off?

He did remember that as the moment when he decided he was going to live off the reservation, to make as good a life for himself as he could. There had always been fights at school—Ben remembered a couple James was involved in—but no one had ever seen knives. There were rumors of knives, even guns, over the hill in Fort Defiance or up at Shiprock, bigger and rougher communities, but nothing more than fists there in the schoolyard, and even the drunk adults, if they had some stupid jealous argument, would reach for a two-by-four or an empty bottle rather than have the meanness and foresight to carry a weapon. Now life on the reservation seemed incredibly sad, and it was impossible to imagine bringing one's own children up in it. Before that he could see himself as some kind of tribal functionary, and there were by then Navajo doctors and lawyers, but they seemed corrupt as well, landing in the papers in scandals and crime.

Rodney's funeral was open to all his school friends; they were encouraged to go, and there were a lot of them there, all baffled and quiet. It hadn't felt real at the time. Rodney had actually died. Ben kept thinking, *I'm not going to stay in Ganado.* I can be a half-and-half anywhere in the world. I could learn Spanish and live in Mexico and everyone would think I was Mexican.

And here he was in California, his face blending in with the general mix, some of the Asians wondering if he was one of them, or more likely what they called Eurasian. Somehow that blended together better, like one continent running into the other somewhere around the Urals and the Caucasus, not like "American Indian half-breed" where they couldn't even figure out what words to use. So he was happy to be Eurasian until they knew better.

Either way it was a disguise. Here in the city everyone was disguised, all acting like they belonged here but all from somewhere else. Investment bankers from some little chicken-farming county in Georgia. It wasn't so much that they all wanted to wear their ties and their jackets and their expensive shoes, but that they wanted to look like they belonged in them, belonged here, far from where they started.

Ben decided that there was no way around it: tribes must negotiate water settlements, and the best ones possible. It wasn't fair, it wasn't enough, but without negotiating and without quantifying, all the water rights in the world were just on dry paper. He glanced over the fence at the bird feeder where two of those rose-capped birds were feeding and all of a sudden a claw appeared from below, obscured by the fence, and one of the birds flew up and away and the other was carried down out of sight by the gray claw and two feathers fluttered in its absence.

In a moment the neighbor was in her yard fiddling with the sprinkler. She smiled at him. "Schoolwork?"

"Janine, I think your cat is in your yard. I just saw it kill a bird."

She stood there smiling at him. Sometimes she seemed hard of hearing.

He repeated, "Your evil cat just jumped up and grabbed one of the birds in the feeder."

"Oh my," she said. It looked as if she didn't want to believe it, but she said, "Cats *are* hunters by nature."

"So is that why you keep the bird feeder full? Is it really a cat feeder?"

At first she smiled in her deaf way, but soon her expression became one of offense and disgust, and she turned and went back into her house. It didn't bother him. That was part of what he did, making people understand what they didn't want to understand.

CHAPTER TWENTY-TWO

AT THE EMPLOYEE Christmas party, James drank his plastic cup of pink ginger-ale punch and ate cookies in the shapes of wreaths and bells. He was brushing crumbs off the front of his shirt when he heard Gabaldon's voice behind him and felt his big hand cup his shoulder. James suppressed clenching.

Gabaldon was jolly, playing Santa Claus without the suit. "Are you going somewhere for the holidays?" he asked.

"I thought Saint Barts," James said, and watched Gabaldon's face register nothing. "How about you?"

"The wife and I are going to visit family in El Paso. And we'll visit my brother Mike in Amarillo. These cookies are good, aren't they?"

"Mr. Gabaldon," James started, tasting a little acid in the back of his throat, "I was just wondering about my chances of getting rehired in the spring."

He frowned and looked toward his shoes, which meant he gazed at the tip of his gut. "You like working here, don't you?"

"Yeah." Of course there was a lot of qualifying he could do, but this wasn't the time. He needed the job and had actually gotten to like some of the tour-guiding. He had been mentally working on his tour speeches and reading some of the Library of America books his parents had at the ranch. He had found a quote from Thomas Jefferson telling Governor Harrison that his plans for the Indians "must be kept within your own breast, and especially how improper to be understood by the Indians. For their interest and their tranquillity it is best they should see only the present age of their history." He'd carried it around on a scrap of paper until he knew it by heart.

Gabaldon was smiling now. "You certainly did a good job with the holiday decorations."

"Thanks." One of James's last tasks for the season was to "deck the halls," as Gabaldon insisted on calling it, in an old-fashioned, "tasteful" way, and he sent James out into the forest to cut ponderosa boughs, which he wired together and then twisted around the posts in the store. James had been glad to get out of the store, as he wouldn't run into Angie, who never said anything to him these days anyway, and beautiful woodpeckers called as they flew between the tall pines, and the ice crystals that frosted the forest's bed of needles crunched agreeably under his boots.

Gabaldon drank the last of his punch and rocked on his feet, preparing to move on and talk to his other employees. "Well, ordinarily we offer the seasonal jobs back."

"Good."

Instead of smiling, Gabaldon narrowed his eyes. "What's this I hear about you and Beebee?"

"Nothing."

Gabaldon kept his eyes narrowed for a few seconds, then suddenly his face relaxed. "Well, Merry Christmas," he said and turned to talk to one of the weavers.

It suddenly occurred to James that it must have been Gabaldon himself those years ago, who paid the "surprise" visit to school as Santa. Who else was big enough? They all tried, but none of his classmates managed to remove the beard, which only brought out more of the kids' sadism. All naughty, none nice, no merry gentlemen, they jabbed him in the ass and grabbed all the candy they could.

James drove to Gallup the next day, son of a bitch. In his chest he felt pressure to buy stuff for his parents, his brother, his friends. Maybe a gift for Angie, a peace offering. He wasn't sure. He had his last paycheck in his wallet and his inhaler in his shirt pocket, which he had to keep pulling out to take little puffs. The cold air and the hurry of shopping kept him wheezing. The highway was packed with other people who had been sucked into this holiday folly.

His first stop was at the bank in Window Rock. There was an ATM, the only one between Gallup and Tuba City, but taped onto the monitor was a handwritten cardboard sign saying, "Out of order. Please use another one." A big pothole yawned on the blacktop on the other side of the ATM, which took some sharp maneuvering. He was aware of the risks, had once seen a new Taurus high-centered on a pothole in the parking lot at the KFC nearby, wobbling like a teeter-totter.

Just then, four *yé'ii bicheii* swooped by, pale impersonations of the gods who were seen only in this season, skin ghostly white, tight buckskin masks, making their muffled owl hoots. James stopped the car immediately and they pressed their hands at the window until he opened it. Spooky blank faces, spruce collars. One of them had on a pair of red Converses.

James dug out his wallet and took out his last twenty. One of the yé'ii bicheii stepped up to him, holding out a fawn-skin bag, then backed up and came at him again. No hoots now, but an almost mechanical *tickitickitickiticki*. Finally on the fourth approach he opened the bag and let James deposit the bill. The yé'ii bicheii ran away with the others to knock on other cars, their fox skins bobbing behind them. They didn't thank you or bless you like the bell ringers at the Salvation Army kettles; this was more of an extortion, a heist that people tolerated, even welcomed. Now he had no money in his pocket, but he was strangely glad that it had been these representations from the holy world who had taken it; he was afraid not to give it to them, the same way yé'ii bicheii had always scared him on those cold dark nights when his parents led him and his brother through crowds of people and smoke and eerie sounds. Who knew what kind of punishment they would mete out if he refused? James also felt proud that these beings still walked the earth, following their own rules, making the muted sounds of their own non-human language, running in their kilts and *kélchí* past balloon versions of Rudolph and Santa outside the stores.

Between Window Rock and Gallup he passed the liquor store called Navajo Lounge, a rectangular building with peeling white stucco. The central door and the two windows on either side made it resemble a skull, with drunks swinging in and out of its maw. People had referred to the liquor store and the littered grounds around it as Navajo Beach, for in good weather men and women sprawled out in oblivious, sunbathing poses. Out beyond the butane tank, amid patches of snow, lay a corrugated culvert where a dirt track crossed a dry wash. It was where the drunks crawled to have sex, and it was called the Tunnel of Love.

Love. There was a song there. In back of the liquor store, *love*. Galvanized Tunnel of *Love*. E-G-B-flat-G . . . E-A-flat-D-G-C-G.

Angie talked about love when she meant child support. And he craved her bare legs around him and called it love.

What was he doing back out on the reservation, anyway? Here he was, about to spend the last of his money, money he had partly earned telling lies to tourists. A job he was kissing his boss's ass to keep. Just to stay in this depressing, poor, run-down home of rustlers and drunks, fuck-ups and burnouts, a place with no opportunities. That's the prospect his parents described to him when they moved to Flagstaff. "There will be more opportunities for you in town," they said. He thought they meant opportunities for jobs and for school, but maybe they too were thinking about the other opportunities he seemed to be lacking here: an honorable living, a community of good musicians, the right kind of woman.

He might give it a little more time to make sure he had explored all the possibilities. There was the girl who rented out videos at Montoya's, who was happy to flirt with him as he told stories of when he had her job years ago. There was that teacher's aide who seemed to like him, the short one with the breasts that he sometimes thought seemed to weigh her down.

That line of thinking hurt.

He found an ATM in Gallup that was a little dented on the outside but worked. Some things worked here, although there were potholes and sidewalks that disappeared twelve feet above an enlarging arroyo. Flagstaff was a little better. It all had to do with what percentage of the people were Indians. The more Indians, the crappier they kept it. Who was going to complain? The Mexicans and Arabs who owned everything in Gallup and sent their money somewhere else would give you a look meaning, *Who and where do you think you are, chief?*

In order to spend as little time as possible in Gallup, which was always unpleasant but at this time of year about the worst, he had narrowed down and firmed up his Christmas list. He would get his mother a Pendleton coat, and his father either a fancy fishing knife or a Leatherman. He had spent some thought on his brother's present. If he could find an English judge's wig at the costume store he would get him that and it would be funny, not completely mean, though it might be kinder to buy him a few CDs. James knew he could find him some music he'd like, because Ben, surprising to some people before they got to know him, loved metal. (Did Francine know that?) He just wasn't keeping up with it as passionately as James. He never had. Much better to get him the CDs than the wig. If Ben wanted to be a fucking lawyer, who was he to make fun of him?

He couldn't find a decent Leatherman so he went to the sporting-goods store that had a few fly rods. As he came out the door with his father's fishing knife, he passed two Navajo guys walking down the side-walk, a rural type more common when James was a kid, self-conscious and out of place in town. They were both about James's age, brothers or cousins or close friends, judging by the way they seemed both familiar and rough with each other. The taller one spoke in Navajo into the ear of the other as they walked awkwardly, knocking each other a little, sober but somehow stressed, tensed like wrestlers. They wore beat-up Wranglers, a little baggy in the seat. Shovel butts. Mud on old boots.

"Let's get out of here," was what the one guy said to the other in Navajo.

On Christmas day, after the presents and turkey, James and his parents went for a walk in the woods behind their house. The snow flurries had just started and were lightly coating the oak leaves and pine needles on the forest floor.

"Why don't you come back to town?" his father asked.

"I've thought about it, since I've got no job again. Pretty sure no woman again."

"Oh yeah?"

"Forget it, Dad." He wasn't going into it, and he thought of his bed on the reservation, cold and lonely, the woodstove not quite warm enough. They walked a few more steps, then stopped at the top of a rise, winded, and waited for his mother, who was walking slowly behind them with one hand on her hip and the other gripping her aluminum walking stick. "But I have thought about moving back to town."

The snow was falling fast enough now to collect in soft crescents on the tips of their boots. A woodpecker called and another answered with a flutter of wings, a red swoop into the upper branches of a ponderosa.

"What are you two talking about?" said his mother.

"About whether or not I should stay out on the rez."

"I'm glad you're taking care of things for us out there. But don't listen to Max. There's no use getting mixed up with their range warfare. And I don't want to hear anything else about married women." She walked on ahead of them slowly, clacking her walking stick. What was a Navajo woman doing with one of those? "I suppose you thought I was in the dark. I still know plenty of people in Ganado."

He followed her up the rocky slope and said only, "All that's changed." He might have told her that the married woman thing was over and done with, even though maybe it wasn't, or that she wasn't married anymore, or soon wouldn't be. He couldn't tell her both. He could tell her that he was also done snooping around with Max when he already knew damn well who was behind the rustling, but that was too long and complicated. "All of it."

"Maybe you should come home," she said.

"You mean Flagstaff? Is that what you mean? The only thing is the band."

"What?" his father called out behind him. "The band?"

"The band. Music."

They walked a few steps in silence until his mother said, "You ought to worry more about yourself and less about your friends."

He didn't know why he bothered explaining. "Mom, it's the same thing, me and my friends. I can't make music by myself."

In fact he had considered telling the guys they just didn't know how to make music and walking away from everything. But he stubbornly hoped for a breakthrough, something that would make them serious about the music, something that would lift them out of that weak, bland sound they had fallen into.

At about the same time James was walking with his parents in the snowstorm in Flagstaff, it was snowing in Ganado, too, and the cops had set up roadblocks in the usual places. "I was wasted," Nolan told him a couple weeks later, after he was out of jail. "I could hardly talk to the cops. I couldn't tell where I was supposed to drive. The center stripe split in two and I couldn't decide which one to stay to the right of."

"Jesus, it's a good thing they got you off the highway."

"At first I was pissed off about spending my white Christmas in jail but then I thought, *I could have killed some little kid.*"

"*Yáa.*"

"Or I could have had the Beast in the car with me. Would have been a felony, then. This time I'm not making no excuses, not going to say they got me for Driving While Indian. Who knows, it might be a good thing. Now we both got to take piss tests, keep to the straight and narrow. Our music might get better. What do you think?"

CHAPTER TWENTY-THREE

▨ **IT WAS COLD** and windy all the way to Dilkon where Joe Wesson hit a dust-colored reservation mutt hard and head-on in a splattering thump that left no doubt. It had wandered slowly across the highway, not once looking up with care or curiosity, cockleburs in its side hairs, dirt in its face, distemper in its brain, no value to anyone. Still, it was one of God's creatures, and Wesson hadn't *tried* to run the darn thing over.

He parked on the side of the chapter house and checked the front of the car for damage: just blood and a few clumps of curly brown hair on the bumper and left headlight, but he was glad it was a Department of Corrections vehicle and not his own. Bobbi Ann wouldn't have liked that.

The chapter house was empty except for a bulldog-faced chapter secretary named Truman, who sat at the long fold-up table in a veteran's cap and with a cup of coffee. "Hey, Wesson, how's life treating you? Where's Smith?" It was his invariable joke, and Wesson didn't reply, not because he was irritated but because it was unnecessary. He thought that having the name of an arms manufacturer suited his job as probation officer. People kept their proper distance.

"I'm okay except for my sciatica. How about you, Truman?"

"Can't complain." He wiggled his ass in the metal chair, which wasn't big enough to hold it. "Who's supposed to see you today?"

Wesson looked at his watch. "First one's already late. Headed for jail this time."

"Is that the Salabye boy? He's already in jail in Window Rock."

It annoyed Wesson that the jurisdictional overlaps kept him from knowing about his probationers' every misstep, and also that the local man knew more than he did just by word of mouth. The reservation was a redundancy and an anachronism.

"Here's your next one," said Truman, who was facing the door. "If he makes it."

Wesson turned just as a thin man in denim jeans and jacket—his Canadian tuxedo—stumbled just inside the door and rose awkwardly from his knees. Wesson knew he was in his early thirties, but his face contained marks of both a younger and an older age: red and greasy, cystic and scarring acne all over his face, and many streaks of gray through his loose long hair. He walked a bit unsteadily toward them until Wesson spoke up.

"I can see you, John, so just stay where you are. I don't want to smell you."

Truman sprang out of his chair with surprising agility and escorted John back out the door, his arm around him. When he returned to his coffee he told Wesson, "I'll try to talk some sense into him by next month."

His third and last appointment reached the table, one of those who made it worthwhile: barely thirty, newly Christian, eyes aglow and ready to tell him how many days and hours he had been sober. Getting a lot out of the domestic violence classes. No nonsense about the peyote church. He mumbled a little prayer for Wesson to have a safe trip down the road.

Wesson drank a half a cup of coffee with the chapter secretary, then gathered his folders. "Take it easy," Wesson said.

"Easy does it," said Truman.

Not so very long ago a gray cold day like this would have suggested the pleasures of a dark bar, chatting with a pretty alcoholic woman, perhaps a big glass of Southern Comfort. Something brown, a little sweet, a whole lot of warmth. Wesson imagined it sliding down his throat, the glow in his stomach. The momentary craving passed, as it always did. He just had to swat those demons down like flies. He was a lucky man. He could be dead, or still in a fog. He had his job, he was helping people, he had his faith (though it could be stronger), he had his A.A. group, even though he was feuding with one or two guys in it.

He was happily married. Forget the sweet warm brown liquor and barfly. Bobbi Ann had risen before him that morning, and when he shivered in his underwear and peered through the blinds at the snowplows whose scraping had awakened him, she was there at his side in her satin robe with a cup of coffee. She later gave him oatmeal with raisins, which he swallowed with customary difficulty as the sound and smell of bacon snapping in the pan gladdened him. "Oatmeal to counteract the effect of the bacon on your heart."

"Is that what it does?"

She was nothing if not sweet, and he was a better person mostly because of her. No longer drunk and foul mouthed. But how did her telling him to drive safely make him safe? It was typical of her magical thinking, and one of the reasons he wished she would stop teaching Sunday school. It was okay to tell little kids that God was always watching you, but these fairyland ideas that God had a plan for everyone—didn't that interfere with free will? How long would those kids believe it?

In Flagstaff that morning the roads were plowed and the cinders were spread by the time he was on his way. He had swept the light snow off his government car and waved at his neighbor Ray Claw, who had already steered his snowblower back and forth across his driveway and was working on his sidewalk. He would be seeing the man's son in a few hours, and he probably had no idea.

Now snow reappeared on the roadside just above Dilkon and deepened the farther east he traveled. This was a tribal road, so it was poorly maintained. The Indians were always complaining about self-determination, but every time they took on a responsibility they refused to meet it. For years now the tribe—the Navajo *Nation*—had been making noises about taking over the federal probationary services, but they'd never do it. Or if they did they'd be sorry.

He recited the serenity prayer to himself, for there wasn't a darn thing he could do about Navajo politics.

The voice on his new tapes was earnest and enthusiastic, upbeat. That was the main point, the "Way of Hope." The author in the picture on the box of cassettes stood smiling, his feet apart like Orion, a slim, graying man in his forties in slacks and a well-cut sport coat over an expensive collarless shirt. He looked like right after this taping session he was going to get laid. Wesson had accurately predicted his voice from his picture—a baritone inflected enough to sound sincere, not so coached as to sound like an actor or a politician. What he was saying was something he believed.

> When we are in the presence of a successful person—we can define this however we want, but I find there is general agreement on who is a genuinely successful person—we may feel deference, and respect, and admiration, but we don't feel envy. You may ask why not, for is it not human nature to envy people who have done better than we have? But once I noticed this phenomenon it came to my attention again and again: the truly successful person inspires loyalty, not envy.

This was the first tape he was listening to now, as he drove slowly among the icy potholes above the winding course of the Pueblo Colorado Wash, and the voice (confident, triumphant even) went on to tell you how success—making money, getting promotions, winning personal disputes—all depended on not even considering the possibility of failure.

> One of the key steps in getting what you want is to stop striving for it, to admit your own helplessness, and to surrender your fate, as it never was and never will be in your own power.

There was a familiar ring to these words, though so far the subject matter had been disappointing. There wasn't enough on addiction. As he got closer to Ganado, side one ran out and he didn't turn the tape over.

None of this positive thinking was likely to do him much good with the two probationers he was going to see here: James, his neighbor's son, who had been on his roster for six months for bootlegging and running marijuana, and his death metal bandmate Nolan, whom he hadn't yet met. James wasn't into the Way of Hope. Death metal was pretty much Satanism, as far as he could figure, though you didn't hear that word much lately. Those days when he went around warning communities about baby sacrifice were over—it occurred to him that James and Nolan might have been in middle school when he was giving his presentations to middle school classes—and kids had gone from spray-painting pentagrams on boulders to joining actual gangs and cooking actual meth. But the roots were the same, and ancient.

The culture these boys had come from was not one of redemption but of decay, and their unsavory, even disgusting music was part of it. They hid their repulsive lyrics with that heavy growling chant, but if you deciphered them, they encouraged base and illegal acts, mayhem and torture, and glorified putrefaction and death. Even the names of the bands were of necrotic diseases.

Over the years Wesson had come to believe in good and evil. It was surprising how many people refused to understand that the battle between these absolutes raged every day. As a child he had been impressed with the cartoon figures of demon and angel perched on left and right shoulders arguing their sides of the case. And he still imagined moral struggles in those terms. You had to swat the demons down like flies.

Wesson's supervisor in Pretrial Services kept reminding him that it wasn't against the law to like metal music or to play it, but wasn't that naive? They put all kinds of other restrictions on their probationers: who they could associate with, where they could go. And it was clear enough to Wesson that this was degenerate music and a bad influence.

The question had come up months ago when James had mentioned the Cryptopsy concert in Phoenix, and Wesson had decided against trying to forbid it. He believed he would have been justified in forbidding it on the basis that the concertgoers were "criminal associations," but he hadn't wanted to start off with James on the wrong foot, with no trust at all. And he was glad that he had restrained himself, for he had gotten to feel sorry for him, being half Indian and all.

Wesson wasn't a bigot. There were plenty of white guys married to Indians, and that was usually a benefit to the Indian spouse, kind of lifted her out of the mess of her origin. Maybe those mixed marriages were okay. (His father—who *was* a bigot, Wesson would be the first to admit—would have called them mongrel families.) Certainly those couples hadn't been thinking about the effect on their offspring, but that wasn't the kids' fault.

He pulled up to the chapter house, avoiding the area where the asphalt had fallen away, and stretched before walking up the two steps. Even short drives made his sciatica worse.

This chapter house never looked pretty, but it was always clean. Or rather, someone was always cleaning it. Beneath the smells of cleaning were the lingering odors of wood smoke, wool, and leather, and of infrequently washed rural Indian bodies—he didn't care what anyone said; they smelled different. Today the smell of Pine-Sol was strong. A skinny woman in matchstick jeans and an oversized Sun Devils jersey pulled a wheeled bucket across the floor as she ran a mop back and forth across the gray linoleum. He said hello to the short hefty woman in the kitchen and smelled the coffee coming from the big enamel pot on the stove. "Did it snow a lot in Flagstaff?" she asked.

"Not much more than here. And they plowed it all by the time I got started. Should I set my stuff up in the classroom?"

"Go 'head," she said. "I'll bring you some coffee."

The blackboard in the little room hadn't been erased from the last alcohol awareness class. In big letters in the middle was the word CRAVING and off to the side CHOP WOOD and PRAY. In the corner somebody had drawn a cartoon: the big-nosed Indian from the "In Cahoots" strip, slouched against a wall, drooling with a thought balloon empty except for a bottle of Mad Dog. Wesson erased the board, thinking that his clients would think he had drawn the cartoon and was a racist. Not that he was politically correct, but even he could see the "In Cahoots" Indian wasn't exactly a positive image. And to make it more absurd, he knew whoever had drawn on the board was an Indian, and so what did that say about racism? He was just putting the eraser in the gutter when a chubby young man walked in the room and said his name was Nolan.

"Joe Wesson. Mr. Wesson to you." He let him know by his handshake that he meant business. Nolan went back out the door and returned with a stroller containing a baby who was almost too big for it.

"This isn't a day-care center."

"Sorry." Nolan had a southern look, like a Pima or a Mexican Indian: fat, dark lips and that startling gold tooth. Like the ones in the Bogart movie who end up bringing fruit to the old American prospector.

"Where's the baby's mother?"

Nolan gave him a look and said, "Beats me."

Wesson didn't appreciate hard looks from his probationers, but he didn't push back this time. "Single father?"

"Yup."

"Well, in the future you need to make arrangements."

"Okay."

This was good, not the same kind of lip he usually got. James would have said "whatever" and Wesson would have had to say, "No, not whatever. Let me make it clear for you. I'm the only one standing between you and jail." But this guy was a little softer. Compliant.

They sat across the table from each other while Wesson sipped his coffee and took his time with his paperwork. He went through the schedule, the rules, and had Nolan sign the usual places. "Think you can make it through the year?" Wesson asked him.

"One way or another."

"Your buddy James will tell you the time passes quickly. It's already been six months for him."

"I know. I can't say how it's been for him, but I actually see this as a good thing. Driving around drunk—I'm a father, for Christ's sake."

Wesson winced, but he never nagged his probationers about taking the Lord's name in vain. There was too much else to cover. "You going to meetings?"

"Yeah." Nolan laughed. Not a good sign.

"What?"

"Some of those dudes, their stories."

"You have to remember all of them have the same alcoholic failings, even though some of them may seem to have succeeded."

"I don't know," said Nolan. "I don't hear any real success stories. And I don't envy any of them."

"Well, just keep going, keep listening. It's the only thing that works."

The baby was fussing, straining against the straps of the stroller, wanting to toddle across the room to the chapter house kitchen where a couple of women were mixing dough and brewing coffee. Nolan undid her straps, and, dressed bulkily for the weather, she waddled as best she could. Wesson had a good feeling about Nolan, who might even be a positive influence on James.

Speak of the devil. There was James with his oily hair and black and red Cannibal Corpse T-shirt. He and Nolan performed a three-part handshake. *Not so good, too subculture,* Wesson thought. James's laugh was a little too loud, a little too evil. "Welcome to the club," James said to Nolan, who retrieved his daughter from the ladies in the kitchen and wheeled her back out the door. "Later."

Wesson tried to figure out who was the ringleader. It was clear that James was the more defiant, but there was something disturbingly equal in their standing. James already sat at the table with his arms crossed, recalcitrant and frowning, so Wesson didn't bother with a handshake.

"How's it going?"

"Fine."

No smile. Wesson had never seen James smile. That was true of a lot of his guys. Tough guys. He didn't try to make them smile, but when they did he knew their visits would be easier. Except for the real con men, who started off smiling and offering you a sincere desire to change. Rather have no smiles than big smiles at first. James leaned back in his chair.

"Still working?" Wesson asked.

"Got laid off. It's a seasonal job." James shifted his weight a little, arms still crossed.

He knew James had been giving tours at the local historical trading post. "Looking for another?"

"I think I'll be able to hang on till April." James glanced at his right boot, which was crossed over his left knee.

James had an interesting, slightly confusing face, like a lot of these half-and-half kids. Not kids anymore, a lot of the mixed-bloods from the seventies were grown, full phenotypes now, no longer just the idealistic notion of their miscegenating parents. The combinations were interesting. Not to mention the occasional Tiger Woods, with his ambiguous face and skill and money.

"I'm not sure that's a great idea. One of the conditions of your probation is that you have gainful employment." Wesson found himself mirroring James, crossing his arms over his chest and leaning back in his chair. If he was going to be a tough guy, and show that he could physically hurt him, then Wesson could do that, too.

"It's just a furlough."

"Still."

"Come on, man, you know how it is out here. What kind of job you think I'll find here for three months?"

Always pleading for special treatment because it was the reservation. How the heck do they expect to get ahead with that hooey and that attitude? "What do your parents think about you hanging around unemployed with all your friends wasting time all day?" In the old days he would have said "jerking off" instead of "wasting time," and perhaps it would have been more effective.

Wesson had been intending to mention James's parents for some time, to say something about how he respected them (though he meant his father; he didn't know the little Indian woman) and that he was surprised to see him in his neighborhood in Flagstaff. But James didn't let him. He sat up in his chair and leaned toward Wesson. Heat rose in waves from his face, and there was something in his eyes more dangerous than anger. *Some kind of intelligence*, he thought.

"Just a minute. There's no fucking need to insult me or my parents."

Since Bobbi Ann had succeeded in convincing Wesson to deal with his profanity issues it was hard for him to know what to do when he heard it. The words were still there, but he never spoke them. Yet people like James had this idea that if you didn't curse or take the Lord's name in vain you were weak. And Wesson was still tough, still a caged panther.

"You don't think that idleness is going to make it easier for you to drink and do drugs and get into more trouble?"

James looked at him like he was somebody that had reappeared after dying a century ago, then gave a little snort of a laugh. "You mean like the devil's on one shoulder, saying, 'Go on, James'?"

How did he know? They weren't so different: Wesson had a lot to teach him. He had made all the same mistakes. Wesson was sure that many of James's problems could be solved by the Twelve Steps. But the longer his silence, the less Wesson thought he could break it by suggesting such a thing.

"Well, you should be working."

James put all four legs of his chair on the floor and his elbows on the table. "Don't worry about it. I'm staying busy. I'm reading up on my local history. And my cousin is always thinking up a never-ending set of chores for me."

"We're talking about Max? From what I hear he may not be the best example for you, either."

Wesson watched James's natural color return as his lips pursed and then relaxed. He was clamming up. They sat in silence for a while, then Wesson brought out a plastic cup with a blue screw-on lid from his briefcase. "So I guess we'll find out if you're staying away from your old habits. How is it going with your drinking and smoking weed?"

"Whatever."

"You don't think I'm serious?"

"Of course you're serious about your Twelve Steps. *My* name is James and I am *not* an alcoholic."

"It's called denial."

"Can't win, can I?"

Wesson pushed the plastic cup over to him, sprinkled the blue powder in the toilet, and waited for the specimen to be delivered. At least he didn't have to watch James urinate anymore. When they started the monitoring program Wesson had to stand there and watch as the guy pissed. Did James think he enjoyed it?

The trip back through the nearly empty landscape to Flagstaff seemed long, and it got dark early. Wesson wasn't in the mood to listen to the tapes. He wasn't in the mood to hear a successful person (a *fucking success*, he thought but didn't say). And as he got toward town, just past the reservation line, he saw the lights of the Two Bar Three ahead on the left. It had been there as long as he could remember, a liquor store and dingy bar serving local working types from around Doney Park and the reservation nicknamed the Two-by-Four. He slowed momentarily, nodded slightly toward his left shoulder. You can't listen to their arguments; you can't even let them talk. You got to just swat them down like flies and drive on past.

CHAPTER TWENTY-FOUR

▧ **CONSIDERED OBJECTIVELY, EVERYTHING** sucked. Here he was out in the sticks in the middle of winter, no job, no girlfriend. With heavy snows, travel on the dirt roads was hard enough, but on top of that, his tires were nearly bald and his truck was leaking oil. He should have been depressed.

Instead, he felt pretty good about things. He got up when it was getting light, well rested and feeling strong. He had a little money and he could always ask his parents for payment for work around the ranch. And he was a cheap bastard, didn't mind eating corned beef and potatoes three days in a row. Add in a can of jalapenos the third day. It was great not to have to get up in the dark and drive to work, fighting snowdrifts and mud. When the weather was bad he built up a fire and read his books, wrote songs, and played his guitar. He was comfortable.

He tried to keep his mind off Angie, and sometimes it worked. Then the old body rhythms asserted themselves: *horny* was the word that first came to mind, but that was just part of it. *Lonely* summed it up better, horny and lonely. He did not masturbate because he knew he'd hearken back to their times together, but then he would dream, and wake, furious. She needed to leave him alone, the sneaky liar, but he remembered her curves and her moles and her hands, too, and when he thought of her tears he didn't just think *sneaky liar* but also *poor Angie*. What was driving him crazy was that he felt two ways about her; he couldn't just make up his mind.

Then he'd do a little work around the place, splicing wire on the fences or washing windows, and that natural, healthy, good feeling would come back. And he could always rely on the music to help him that way. He was writing songs and playing his guitar for hours, getting ready for band practice.

And the changes Nolan was going through helped James as well. Since Nolan had been arrested and forced into what he had started calling *recovery*, he had become serious about everything, including the band. Their practice schedule was Tuesday and Thursday nights and most of Saturday, and Nolan was always there first. One snowy evening James was ten minutes late and Nolan was sitting outside the locked door looking angry.

"I almost skidded out," James said.

"I don't know why the fuck we said six o'clock since no one is ever here then."

James opened the door and turned on the lights and they stomped the snow off their boots. "Right on," said James. "I'll let you be the enforcer."

James was later sorry he had said this, because when Zendrick and Leon showed up Nolan let loose. "Fuck, man. Didn't we decide on some rules, like for instance you are not going to show up to practice drunk?"

"Who's drunk?"

"I smell it on you, don't deny it."

"Shit, man. One beer."

"Yeah right."

James was glad Zendrick didn't take it any further; he just tuned up and ignored Nolan. Not long ago Nolan wouldn't have been able to smell it on Zendrick and wouldn't have cared if he had. It was a good thing he wasn't drinking, but he was extending his strictness to everyone else. Nolan, of all people. He was the one who made them play a song over as many times as it took to get it right. Of course James backed him—he was the original hard-ass—but Nolan took it up a notch, becoming enough of a pain that Zendrick started to complain he wasn't having fun anymore.

"Fuck you, then," Nolan told him. "If it's not fun for you we'll find someone else."

Leon just laughed. "You guys need to chill."

"Right," said Nolan. "Chill us with a shot of DDT."

After that session James had to go up to Zendrick and tell him Nolan didn't really mean it. "You know, it's like they say, he's on a dry drunk."

"Well, he could use a liquid drunk, I'd say."

"He'd probably agree with you. But he knows that if he did, he'd end up locked up."

"He doesn't need to be a jail guard to stay out of the slammer."

Zendrick stayed and somehow became aware of when he was out of tune and learned to correct it. Leon's blast beating, too, was more precise, and he stopped missing the important attacks.

Nolan was also trying hard to book the band, saying that they needed any kind of exposure they could get. He set up a show in Gallup on Groundhog Day, the first Friday in February, where they were to play between two Albuquerque bands that were better known. "It's a real opportunity," he kept saying.

Zendrick thought they should dress up like groundhogs. It was fun last Halloween when they got all glammed up, even though the concert was a bust.

"What's a fucking groundhog, anyway?" Nolan said.

"It's like a gopher, a prairie dog, a *dlǫ́ǫ́*."

"Forget it." Nolan acted like he was deeply offended, like Zendrick had suggested he get up on stage in drag.

James just laughed, but at the moment he laughed something sad slapped him behind the eyes: he remembered their last Halloween and the gentle pressure on his cheek as Angie put on his makeup.

"You moron," Nolan told Zendrick. "We'd look like Alvin and the Chipmunks up there, singing about plagues and the end of the world."

Zendrick said, "Jeez, what's happened to you guys' sense of fun? Besides, isn't plague from prairie dogs?"

After practice one night James stayed over at Nolan's house. He decided that instead of struggling over the muddy roads again he would wait until early morning when they would be frozen solid. "Sure," said Nolan, "but we'll have the Beast." His parents had somewhere to go that night and when they arrived at his house from practice his mother said, "At last. I just fed her and she wants to go to sleep, but she's fighting it. Now's your time to be a daddy. Nishą', James. You need to practice being a daddy?"

When they left, Nolan bounced a big red ball at his daughter, who bent over clumsily and managed to throw it back in his direction about half the time. She had a goofy one-note laugh she let out each time she put her stubby arms around the ball. "She's growing up," James said.

"She's a megabrat."

"What did your mom mean asking if I needed practice being a father?"

"Probably nothing." The Beast kicked the ball into the kitchen and stumbled after it.

"Because Angie must be showing by now and your mom might be wondering . . . how I fit in."

"Yeah, she is showing. She was over here the other day. There's no hiding it."

Nolan was just leaving it there, and the pause was getting long, so James took a breath. Since he'd come this close, he might as well finish telling him. "It's not mine."

"Yeah, well, the timing didn't seem right."

"I suppose it *could* be mine, but according to the doctor it's off by like a month."

"Well, there you go then. I figured. I don't see you guys together."

"You mean we don't seem right together?" The Beast had thrown the ball, which had landed at James feet, and she was complaining about his inaction.

"Pick up!" He rolled it back into the kitchen.

"No, man," said Nolan. "I got no opinion about that shit. I mean I haven't seen you guys together since way before Christmas. Figured something was up."

"What'd she say?"

"She mostly came to talk to my mom, I think. About feeling the baby kick, not being able to sleep, and my mom saying she'd start knitting a blanket, all that kind of thing."

"She say anything about Malcolm?"

"I don't know. Like I said, she was mostly talking to my mom. You know how they do, dropping their voices about an octave and turning the volume way down, almost whispering, saying *oh my* and *oh really*."

"Well, I don't think I'm ready to be a father."

"It's a blessing," said Nolan, and James was shocked by his vocabulary. Appalled. Horrified. Must be from the A.A. meetings.

As February came closer the band added Wednesday to their practice schedule. Everyone was on time to their sessions, and sober, and enthusiastic that their music was getting better. Most of the songs they ended up doing were ones James had written, though Nolan and even Zendrick submitted a couple. Nolan usually did the vocals, though James often joined in.

One of James's songs was inspired by his brother's *Law Review* article, which had arrived in a padded envelope with the comment "Hope it's not too boring." James had to use the dictionary a couple of times—Ben was always showing off this way, but James supposed he had to—but it was not boring. On the contrary, James found himself infuriated by the situation Ben was describing. The coin toss for Indians: heads you win, tails we lose.

Thirst! Die of thirst, savages! The sun will bleach your bones!

The first few takes of the new song James waited for Zendrick to hit that last note before the transition, where they were supposed to pause three beats before hitting the new accelerated rhythm.

"Okay." James stopped everything, trying to be gentle. "Let's try it again."

But the second and third times Zendrick was late again. "Zee, get your head out of your ass!"

The fourth time Zendrick deliberately fucked up, everyone could tell, and Nolan said, "Look, asshole, I told you before, we can get somebody who's willing."

"Come on, chill," said Leon, hitting his tower of cymbals.

"Chill?" said Nolan. "How can you chill any more than you're chilled? You're permanently chilled. You ever wonder how many brain cells you've lost to your addictions to alcohol and who knows what?"

Leon stared at Nolan and James guffawed. "Addicted to pesticides? Okay, let's skip that song. How about 'Masters of Mutilation'?"

The next Saturday they tried "Dry Genocide" again and at the tricky transition, Zendrick was there just when he was supposed to be. And Nolan, too enthusiastic, was crying shrilly, "Die! Die! Die! The sun will bleach your booones!"

"Shit," said James, who couldn't keep from grinning. "Sounds like a slasher movie."

Well before the date of the concert James thought they were ready, and he began to feel there was such a thing as overpracticing. The element of spontaneity and surprise was gone, and they began to make mistakes they had already overcome. The songs were losing their power; he didn't feel it anymore. They agreed to take a break for a week, and James went into a little spell of hibernation at the ranch.

He was reading on Monday morning, turning the brittle pages of one of the old books that he had borrowed from Hubbell's, when he heard wheels spinning and an engine revving down the valley. The last couple of days had been warm and the roads had gone from snow-packed to alternating sections of slush and ice, and most people were avoiding them. Max was tackling one of the slushy sections with his usual determination, and James laughed as he watched the big four-wheel-drive slice slick ruts into the roadway. You couldn't accuse Max of being patient.

He parked his truck near the windmill and walked up the hill toward James, who stood on the doorstep in his socks, his book at his side, his place marked by one finger pressed between the pages.

"You just getting up?" Max said. He was wearing overalls and work boots and had smears and spackles of red mud up to his chest.

"Rough ride?"

Max snorted. "Could have used your help out by Repent or Perish. But no, Jamie boy was all warm under the covers."

James wasn't ready for the fist that landed on his shoulder, intended as play, but too hard. He rubbed his deltoid and winced. "What's with you? Why aren't you working?"

"Closed the plant down. Another fire. Manhole covers flying up in the air again right and left. Explosion in the alkylating tank."

"Anybody hurt?"

"Not this time. Fucking lucky, too. We been telling them for months."

"So you get a vacation."

Max snorted again. "They might lay us off for a few weeks, but it'll be twenty-four-hour shifts when we go back."

"So you get a little vacation till then. Come on in, have some coffee. You want a shower? I can turn on the water heater."

While his cousin cleaned up in the bathroom, James threw some more wood in the stove, poured himself some coffee, and continued to read about Hubbell's famous guests. There were photographs of Maynard Dixon and Dorothea Lange, and a quote from her that made him snicker: "We went into a country which was endless and timeless. The earth, the heavens, the changes of seasons, I'd never really experienced until that time. Then I became aware." At the end of the chapter was a story about how the model for one of Dixon's iconic Indian males once got into a drunken rage and tried to stab the artist.

Around noon James heated up some stew and he and Max ate it with some fresh Zuni rolls and a cherry pie that Max had brought. With food in his stomach Max was less critical, but he couldn't stop picking on James for not doing everything he himself would do if he were able.

"At least you could check it out down toward Beebee's and see where the cattle are."

"Maybe when it dries out a little."

Max was worried about his mother. "She puts up with all the old man's shit. You would think that now that he's helpless and depending on her for everything that he'd . . ."

"Show a little gratitude?" James had heard it before and wondered why Max was expecting the impossible. Maybe because kids always expect their parents might change.

"He's worse than ever. Doesn't like the food she gives him. Too much pepper, not enough salt. Doesn't like the way she drives. Says it's her fault they amputated his leg. Says she didn't cut his toenails right."

"She should dump his ass in the nursing home. I know he's your dad . . ."

"She should."

James told Max that things were going well with his band, and that they had a concert scheduled. "It's the first time we'll actually be ready to play. Hopefully they won't embarrass me."

"Maybe I should check it out, borrow one of your grisly T-shirts and blend into the crowd. Not my kind of music. No offense. Can't understand what they're singing, if that's what you call it."

"Nobody listens to the lyrics anyway."

"That's what I don't get," said Max. "I like my songs to tell me something. I want some kind of story. At least a picture of something in my mind. You guys pretty much just growl, right?"

"Yeah. No tear in my beer kind of bullshit. Admit it; it's just too heavy for you."

"What's wrong with a little simple humanity? You know—love, heartbreak . . ."

"Divorce, cheating, getting drunk . . ."

"Yeah, all that stuff."

"Metal's more about the mood. What you feel. It's not a story. It's an attitude."

By midafternoon Max got restless and started splitting the wood in James's pile. James started stacking the split logs and raking up chips. The work got into the kind of rhythm that grabs hold of you, and two hours must have gone by when they stopped. James made some more coffee and they ate some more pie. Max said that he had tried to arrange a visit with his girls, who now lived in Denver, but his ex-wife wouldn't let him. "She won't even let me talk to them."

"I don't guess I'll ever have kids," James said, pained as he flashed on Winona and the new baby forming in Angie.

"You're better off without them. I loved having them, then I didn't have them anymore. I read the other day where people without kids are like ten points happier than people with them. I believe that. There's a lot of pain involved with kids. But if you have kids and then you don't, that hurts the worst."

James was sorry to see his cousin go, slipping through the muddy roads under the pale sky, the noise of his fishtailing the only sound in the cold valley. The last light from the sun, gone so early, was the faintest pink and orange on the bottom of the thin overcast, and by the time the dome had bled out to blue and gray, Max's truck was over the hill and all James could hear was his own breathing.

The concert was at the same remodeled theater in downtown Gallup where they had played on Halloween, and James was sure they were all thinking about that fiasco, that paltry audience, the terrible sound system. And Leon, as he drove them in his father's van into town, reminded Zendrick that he wasn't supposed to pick fights with the audience. Leon had meant it as a joke, but Zendrick took it seriously.

"That guy was trying to start shit with me. If he's there again damn straight I'll toss him out."

"That's what they got bouncers for," Nolan said. "Besides, there's going to be no trouble. I feel golden."

The headliner band was Abortion, from Albuquerque, but in the middle of the first set their guitarist broke three strings and had some sort of argument with the management, and Putrefaction went on early. The crowd, which had been swarming in an unruly line outside the marquee when they arrived, was loud and lively, pointing horned hands at the stage. Their clothes were black or camo and there was a lot of long and untied Indian hair.

Leon asked James as he set up his drums why he thought the crowd really came out for Groundhog Day. "Guess they seen the movie."

The crowd was with them from the first song, and they couldn't do anything wrong. James smiled over at Nolan after the opener, "Planet Blood," and Nolan screamed "Fuck, yes!" They played "See You in Hell," which had bombed on Halloween, and now the kids were loving it. Before them was a moving mass of hair, a sea of bobbing bodies obeying the beat they were providing, like worshipers of the metal priests they must be. They screamed when they played "Dry Genocide," and the relentless "Masters of Mutilation," and the hyperactive dirge of "Necronomicon." James felt like a magician, making the mob feel what he felt. They all played like they'd never played before, not in their private, separate imaginations, not ever in their practice sessions where quibbles abounded and blame blew up around the notes. They were all playing their own fantasies and at the same time they were playing together, a convergence of rage and desire. James had traveled through the landscape of death to feel, for a few moments, pure contentment.

CHAPTER TWENTY-FIVE

N **THE WORD FOR** mud is *hashtł'ish*, which sounds like a boot coming out of the stuff, and it was the time of mud, when everyone on the reservation wished the season would pass or that they were somewhere else with more asphalt; where you could see through your windshield and walk with the lightness of feet clad only in shoes or boots; where each trip off the highway didn't require a provisional kit of chains and a shovel and two jacks; or where the highway led to a paved road, which led to a paved driveway, which led to your own spotless front door. Or to your parents' front door. James couldn't be blamed for taking a break and coming to town for a few days.

First stop was the car wash. Then a shower and a change of clothes. Hi, Mom, Dad.

In Flagstaff the streets were dry. He stomped over the pavement, leaving clumps of pink and beige reservation mud in little piles until he got to the path into the forest where the snow still lay unmelted. He walked toward the tumble of boulders where the mountain got steep, and happened upon a small herd of mule deer browsing on the mountain mahogany and *awééts'áál*.

Funny that he would find such a scene so near town. The five deer, which looked at him calmly before stepping away into the woods, would have been shot long ago on the reservation to feed somebody's family. Wilderness was something related to town; he couldn't think of a word in Navajo with that meaning.

Farther up the slope, where the trails proliferated and became smaller, more for wandering animals than purposeful people, James heard the incongruous sound of a radio sports announcer, the waves of excitement above the tide of monotonous chatter. He looked up to where the noise was coming from and saw a figure where the boulders leaned against each other to make a sort of cave. A man was sitting against a vertical rock face, his legs outstretched, and he rose awkwardly to stand, looking up and down the slope in James's direction.

"Greenstone!" Until that moment James had not considered that he was looking for his old cell mate, but now he wondered if this had been his goal all along: he knew this was "his" area of the woods and felt glad to have found him.

Greenstone looked bewildered or nearsighted, staring at him from his place on the boulder, and finally said, "Is that you, James?"

James followed the rain stains up to where Greenstone was standing and shook his hand. "So this is where you live."

"Welcome to my humble abode." James looked at the stuff strewn around: a sleeping bag, a tarp, socks draped on a rock, mounds of food-stuffs in boxes and cans, tea bags drying for reuse. Blankets heaped up, plates and pans stacked here and there, a smudgy fire pit. An old radio tuned to basketball.

"March madness," Greenstone said. He grabbed his leg below the knee with both hands as he sat, and James saw pink plastic between the sock and the pants leg. James had somehow forgotten that Greenstone had been without his prosthesis in jail.

"Oh man," said James, stretching out on the rock. "You have every-thing you need." James thought it was comfortably messy, a bache-lor's place. Not a monk's cell, not a jail cell, but more of a boys' fort in the woods.

"That is right, James. Better than fulfilling many desires is to have few desires." He turned off the radio.

James was looking up at the roof of the cave, and he saw that it yawned open to the sky, a dark turquoise. "You probably could use some protection when it rains, though."

"Oh it's not too bad. I've got tarps." James saw the water stains flow-ing through the sleeping area and imagined the misery of a cold spring rain or melting snow.

"I thought they evicted you," James said.

Greenstone fixed him with a disbelieving frown, as if the thought dishonored him. "I'm about to celebrate my eighth year living in this place, excluding the brief period of incarceration. Including the time in my summer place, a little farther up the mountain. Hey, did you notice all the dead trees in the path of those microwaves on the summit? Just imagine what they're doing to your mind. That's in the Hopi prophesies, too, by the way. Just like the jet contrails, the coal mine . . ."

"So you got off?"

"A slap on the wrist. They know I do good work out here. And there's the sympathy factor." Greenstone patted his prosthesis. "How about you? I expected great things of you. Presumably you are accomplishing them."

"Oh, I don't know. It's only been nine months. I feel pretty good, generally. No more jail, just doing probation, taking pee tests."

"Nine months! So much can happen in nine months. An entire gestation."

"Well, speaking of that . . ."

Greenstone started in as if he had read James's mind. "Bringing up a child is many people's only accomplishment. I never had progeny, and I have to admit it seems like a somewhat neutral accomplishment. There's overpopulation, of course, though nobody includes their own kids in the problem. People talk about raising kids like they're paying back some kind of debt. Someone had to raise *them* so maybe it zeroes them out. To get to a positive balance they are going to have to do more, like help stop global warming or promote world peace."

"I don't know if I believe in global warming, or world peace."

"Well, there you have it, my young friend. And your urinalyses, are they coming out clean?"

"Sure. I never smoked that much anyway, and I hate tweak."

"So it's not a burden."

"It's a pain in the ass. I hate having to piss into a cup when some asshole tells me to. How about you? You declare world peace yet?"

"Alas, no. I have been offering my philosophical seminars again, though."

"That's where you fly your prayer flags and the kids ditch high school to shoot the shit with you?"

"I use the Socratic method."

"Well, good. The mind is a terrible thing to waste."

"And you? Playing any chess?"

"No, my mind isn't wasting, but I haven't played chess since I got out of jail. I got a job, which is starting up again in a month or so. I give tours at the historic site and I'm getting ready, reading up on local history. And writing songs. I'm in a band."

"You told me once: jazz?"

"Hell, no. Death metal."

"And what else?"

"Had a girlfriend. Don't know if that's over."

"This the pregnancy you were referring to? You can't just walk away from it."

"I wouldn't walk away from it. It's not mine." He explained the situation with Malcolm. "What really bothers me is that she tried to lie to me about it, to trick me into it." Somehow James felt it was easy telling Greenstone. He might never see him again.

"Ah, the plot thickens. Don't get me wrong, James. I didn't mean that bringing up a baby is *not* an accomplishment. And what choice do you have?"

"Maybe that's not my problem."

"Are you going to let the kid bring himself up?"

"He'll have a mother."

"Ha. Doesn't sound like the real dad will step up to the plate. You might as well make a prison cell for the kid right now."

"Well, that's harsh. And we've both been in jail."

"But we ain't criminals, James, you better remember that. They can't make a criminal out of you; you got to do that to yourself."

James wiggled away from a knob on the boulder that was pressing on his spine. "When I thought I was the father I was blown away. In a good way. Then when I found out she tried to trick me, I still wanted it."

"Maybe you still do."

"Her husband isn't going to raise it. He hasn't been there for his other two kids."

"So I don't see what the dilemma is." Greenstone was staring at him.

James shifted his weight. "Well, I hate that she tried to trick me."

"She was probably just looking out for herself. And the baby."

"You're sure free with your advice, man. I believe you told me you don't have any kids."

"So far as I know."

"Never married?"

"Almost. Once."

James waited awhile for the beginning of a story but it never came. It must have either amounted to nothing at all, an idle boast that he had almost led a normal life, or something too painful to talk about.

Finally Greenstone said, "You're right. You shouldn't listen to my gladly given advice. You didn't ask for it, and I'm not qualified."

"That's not it, man, I appreciate your concern; it's just that I don't have any idea what to do."

"Actually, I find that people know what they should do most of the time. It takes waiting awhile and letting it settle. Just sit there and think or just sit there, and sooner or later it comes to you."

"I hope you're right."

James and Greenstone lay on their backs on the rock soaking up the sun, their straight bodies at forty-five degrees to each other, closest at the feet, looking like two o'clock. The air was cool, which made the warmth of the sun on James's face even more welcome and peaceful, and he drifted into a dream.

Sometime later, as the sun dropped farther in the sky and the air grew cooler, Greenstone lit his stove and boiled water, then put James's cup of tea on the rock beside him. The camp was now in the shade, and the light had traveled up the steep bouldery slope above them, shining a deep pink gold. James drank his tea and Greenstone said, "You don't want to be wandering around in the dark."

In fact there was no moon that night and he could hardly see where his feet fell. He had calculated that by the time it was completely dark he would be out of the woods and onto the lighted streets of town. He had misjudged, since the range of color was already rapidly narrowing to dark gray, then dark brown, with a little shine from the patches of snow on the ground.

"Where have you been?" his mother said as he walked in the door. "You didn't say where you were going or anything. I looked around and you weren't there."

"Went walking in the woods. Saw a friend."

"A friend? Well, sit down and eat."

His father was already sitting at the table carving a roast chicken. "What's the news from the reservation?"

"Oh, you know. Nothing new. Can't really go anywhere."

"Is there still snow?"

"Mostly mud."

"Oh, you know, your brother sent us a copy of the *Stanford Law Review* with his article in it. It's in the living room."

"I've seen it. He sent it to me as a manuscript. I wrote a song from it."

His father looked at him and laughed. "A song? About his law paper?"

"Yeah, about water rights."

"That's nice," his mother said. "Have some potatoes."

His father said, "Didn't know you were interested in that kind of thing."

"There's lots you don't know about me, Dad. I've been reading a lot. Long winter nights. That's one of the reasons I'm here; I want to go to Special Collections at the university to see what I can learn about Hubbell and the Republican Party."

"Was he a Republican?"

"Oh, yeah."

"Well, back then it was the party of Lincoln."

"No, Dad, that was over twenty years after the Civil War, and by then it was already the party of business. New York and London investors financed the rape of the grasslands in the 1880s. Shipped out thousands of cattle. Let them loose at Pinta and Adamana."

"Interesting. Maybe you should go back to school and study it."

"Don't need to go to school to study it. Just as soon stay out of school so they don't brainwash me. I mean, nobody knows this stuff."

James spent a couple days at the university library, and the librarian was falling all over herself to be helpful. In numbered boxes he found all kinds of things besides books: brittle notebooks from Hashknife foremen about rustling by Navajos in the very same area they were rustling Max's cattle now; letters from Hubbell opposing legislation that would expand the reservation.

Walking from Special Collections, where they treated him as if he were some sort of maverick scholar, through the main area of the library, James felt like an imposter or alien, a stranger among all these students. There were plenty of brown faces; it wasn't that. It was that they were all so young. When had that happened? The girls were mostly slender, their breasts, he was sure, so firm. Some were chewing gum. Guys sat around a study table, talking and guffawing without restraint. The younger they are the more they think they know it all. The last time James was on campus he had also felt like an alien, but for other, more familiar reasons: he had not been a student, not even a student type. Not Joe College. Now in a matter of a few years, how had James gotten to be so old?

It had gone beyond curiosity, this need to know the history. President Jefferson wanted to make sure Indians didn't know their history, and no doubt President Bush felt the same way. Perhaps they were right, because it didn't make James any happier. Yet he was obsessed. He needed to know more. Of course the victors wrote the history books, but there was much to learn between the lines from the oral underground that knows better. Independent illiterates. In another month, when they were both working again, James would have another talk with Littlesunday.

Meanwhile, back on the reservation, the mud was drying in the lengthening days. He wanted to continue his research in the archives at Hubbell's but was worried that he would run into Angie before he was ready to talk to her. He practiced what he would say if he did, and thought about what Greenstone had said. "She's probably just looking out for herself and the baby."

He needed to get permission from Gabaldon, who was sitting at his desk with a bowl of soup, his family pictures facing James.

"How are you, James? You should have some of the posole I brought in. Fresh pork from my brother in Texas. Can't find good fresh pork around here. I don't know why you johns don't try it; you can eat 'em when they're only a few weeks old. Tell your cousin."

"Max doesn't know a thing about raising hogs and neither do I."

"*Por eso . . .* that's why I'm telling you. You coming to work April 16?"

"Of course. Actually, I'm wondering if I can use the archives. I'm looking for material for the tours."

"Sure, help yourself. Of course you're going to have to stick to the official text."

"Official text?"

"I should get the draft next week from Washington. It's been updated."

"The history's been updated?"

"Constantly, constantly. I thought maybe you'd come in to see Angie, poor girl."

"What do you mean? Is something wrong with her?"

"Not *wrong* exactly, but . . . I thought you knew."

"I try to mind my own business."

"I thought it might be your business."

"It isn't any of yours."

They kept the old Hubbell office period-correct, with a big rolltop desk and a huge panel of pigeonholes. Inkpots and leather-bound ledgers and kerosene lamps. James had unlocked the adjoining room where the archives were kept in a semijumble, and he sat looking through boxes of letters and notebooks when Angie rapped lightly at the open door. He was surprised at her shape. How long had it been?

"Hi." He couldn't keep the question out of his voice.

She put her hands over her swollen front. "Hi."

"Aren't you supposed to be on maternity leave or something?"

She smiled. "Nice, James. The first thing you say to me since before Christmas is shouldn't you *not* be here? I'm thirty-two weeks. I'm not due until May."

"Yes, I know." He was smiling, too, though it spoiled the effect he had been intending.

She looked over his shoulder at the photograph he was holding of two dozen men in suits standing behind a fat man with a mustache. "Who are all the bilagáana?"

"President Taft signing Arizona into statehood. That's J. L. Hubbell right behind him. Wow, you're big." She was practically shoving her abdomen into his face. He reached up and, despite himself, put his hand over her belly and felt the baby kick. She laughed.

"I'm supposed to have a labor coach, my doctor says."

"Ask Malcolm."

She turned away. "Everybody has been saying how happy he must be he's having another baby. He doesn't even know."

"Are you divorced yet?"

"Yes."

"Do you have papers to prove it?"

"Never mind." Should he be surprised she resented his asking? Just like he resented taking a pee test though he knew it would come out negative.

"How's Winona?" he asked.

"She misses you. She was asking for 'Amos' the other day."

CHAPTER TWENTY-SIX

 MAX WORKED AT the refinery but he didn't work for the refinery, thank God. He worked for a company out of Houston that the refinery contracted for certain jobs, like the one he was trained to do: inspect welds. He'd been with the company for over ten years in various places in Texas and New Jersey, and even spent nine months in Malaysia where he ate all kinds of weird things at Chinese restaurants, vegetables and animals he'd never heard of. The work gave him a chance to see places he would never have seen before, though they were all full of men from Texas and Oklahoma with their toxic petroleum chemistry, and he was glad to be in his home area the last two years.

The refinery managers had decided that it was finally time to fix all the aging equipment that had led to the failures, and Max was out of work until the crew from Houston redid their shoddy job and he could take his radiographs and point out all their mistakes. He probably had another month before they called him in.

He thought he might just kick back, see some movies, maybe strike up a friendship with that teacher at the community college or go out again with the nice-looking alcoholic he was sure he could find at Dancing Mothers. It took just one day trying to help his mother to change his mind. She asked him to ride along when she took his father to dialysis so they could run some other errands while he was getting his blood cleaned. Max sat in the back seat. His father was still not used to getting around on one leg, so Max had helped him into the front seat, where he complained about her driving, about the route she was taking, and needed to know why she had to stop at this store or that house. As far as Max was concerned, she had divorced him for plenty of good reasons, and he never could figure out why after all that she would spend her time taking care of him. "He can't do it himself," was her way of explaining it.

"You never could do a damn thing right." His father actually said this as she was driving him around, spitting out the words like sunflower hulls. "I don't know why the hell you take the long way around. I should have just drove myself."

"Go ahead and try," she said. She was doing way more than she should, Max figured, but at least she wasn't going to be nice about it.

"I should just take off and live on my own."

"You were living on your own, you mean old man, and see what happened to you?" His mother was laughing, and his father didn't think anything was funny. "You been telling me the same thing all these years, and you might as well admit you can't take care of yourself."

"You just want me to die. Okay, so I'll die."

Max couldn't stand it. "Dad, just shut up. She's trying to help you out. I don't know why. But the least you could do is shut up, if you can't be grateful."

"Talk about grateful," his father said. "You can't say a thing to me. I gave you the gift of life."

"I never asked you to."

But if he had to judge whether his life was worth it—with two parents who hated each other, two ex-wives who hated him, and allowed no contact with his kids—he wouldn't turn it down. He wanted to live, but he'd be damned if he'd thank his dad for anything. Last time his father did anything for him was close to twenty-five years ago when Max won the state high school bull-riding trophy. And the next year, when he came in third, his father had told him that he was useless, never listening to the pointers he had tried to teach him.

His father was true to grumbling form all day, and they never did get to run errands because he complained so much when they tried to leave him at the dialysis center. "What am I supposed to do here by myself?" His saliva tended to spray with the words when he was feeling resentment.

That's when Max decided he had to go somewhere while he was waiting to get called back to work. He had thought of various ways to spend the time, including trying to see his daughters in Colorado, but he'd abandoned that idea: he felt bad every time he thought about them, which was often, but it had been so long now, and he couldn't face another round of Siri's bitterness and spite, which would probably end anyway in her refusing to let him see the girls all for very noble and totally phony reasons. He wanted to be a decent father, given his previous mistakes, but if the bitch wouldn't let him then maybe he had to accept that fact.

There was plenty to do at the ranch, but he always ended up putting off any project he thought of, sometimes because he couldn't do it himself, and James was getting tired of being bullied into helping him, even though he owed it to the family. And sometimes he lost heart about these improvement plans because he started thinking, *What good is it going to do? Everything is falling apart and it's going to keep falling apart.* He could keep fixing fences and chasing after the cows, and Beebee or someone else would keep stealing them from under his nose. Until he solved that problem there really wasn't any point in the rest of it.

There were two ways to go: east or west. He already knew Beebee was involved, and there might be some way to shake it out of him. Some kind of blackmail, maybe, but it was hard to blackmail someone who had no shame. Anyway, most people knew most of what should have been his secrets: his drunkenness, that prank at the emergency room, his moronic siblings. If not blackmail, some direct threat. Get the law on him somehow.

The other way was to follow up on the little clues he'd come across and travel to the nearest meat-packing plant and see what he could find out. It was a long shot; he didn't know anyone in Amarillo; and they weren't likely to be slaughtering stolen branded stock in plain view. But it was a trip, a way to get out from the confinement of his motel in Gallup and the mud of the reservation (though it was drying fast), and if he didn't do it now he'd be wishing he had when he was working overtime inspecting welds.

So he packed a duffel and a sleeping bag and bought a bucket at KFC in Gallup and headed east beyond the refinery listening to country on the radio—James was right, it was all corny stuff by these new guys, who all wore hats—and then his old tape of Merle, who could make corny sound real. Going where the lonely go.

The highway from Gallup to the refinery was too familiar to him, and it produced a mild version of the daily dread and discomfort with which he faced work each day. But beyond the plant's silent pumps and tanks and the stack now without its nearly eternal flame, the highway stretched up toward the low summit of the Continental Divide, south of steep red cliffs on the way to a horizon more full of mystery than the successive billboards advertising "The Thing" with giant question marks. And onto the east slope, across the fields of clotted monster blood, the strange country of the Acomas, little peach orchards blooming prettily—the blooms would probably be violently scattered on the next windy day—the ancient enemy Indians were living in modest houses and working in the ridiculously sparkly casino in the middle of nowhere, huge neon panels waving and flashing neon fantastic luck to idiot truckers and tourists. There were plenty of stupid people on the highway with him, Max knew, but they needed to be enticed by their own delusions. He wouldn't be sucked into a casino, but he knew he was not free of delusions and vices—consider his wives and the lure their fingers and mouths had been.

Then the swells of yellow desert, past the Canoncito Navajos who were trying for their own casino, across the dry Rio Puerco of the east, and finally onto the crest of the hill overlooking Albuquerque and the greening strip of the Rio Grande and facing the upended slope of the mountain on the other side, as pink in the last light as a slice of watermelon. A web of lights gradually appeared below, and the rough and dusty city presented some promise of adventure and novelty, like a whispered offer at the Indian bar near the fairgrounds. He wondered if it would be too early to find her there, or someone like her.

Instead, he stopped on Central for gas and a pint of Jim Beam, seemingly at the intersection of bum and student. One carrying a grimy paper bag, the other a backpack, neither with his hair combed.

The first stars appeared over the pass at Tijeras, and by the time he was out of the pines and onto the prairie there were no shadows and no light, just a deep black sea all around him, his fellow travelers encased in their own vehicular worlds. He wanted to stop before he got to Texas: it was a part of a persistent superstition that at the state border cops ceased acknowledging Indian humanity, and he didn't want to deal with it, so near Santa Rosa he took a dark exit onto a graded road, and then turned south onto a smaller road until he found a dirt turnout near a clump of junipers. He got out of the cab and the silence assaulted him after the hum of the highway. He could see nothing except what was directly in front of him: the truck, the gravelly packed ground, the clump of junipers, and above, the familiar pattern of the stars, so clean and ancient. Max took a drink of whiskey. The air was not cold and he could lie outside and watch the stars twist over him. He threw down a blue plastic tarp and his sleeping bag. Another drink.

When he was young—younger, maybe fifteen years younger, around the age James was now—he wasn't as free as he was now, but he felt freer. He had a wife, a son, not much money, but he enjoyed where he was, making a life for the future. Now there didn't seem to be a future. He knew more now to worry about. He remembered the years between wives when he shared an apartment with another Navajo guy in Houston, entertaining girls sitting on the kitchen counters in their underwear. He couldn't remember the girl's name and that made him sad. He took another drink. Not remembering her name made it seem that much longer ago. They fucked their girls in separate rooms but with the doors open, just for the energy. Would he ever be that hot again? No.

He hated losing his hair. At first he thought he had some terrible disease, then he figured out that it was the inheritance from his father and every time he'd look in the mirror that was whose face he saw. Now he wore a hat. It was beside him, his head on his duffle. He took a drink.

Youth was wasted on the young. James didn't know how lucky he was. He could do anything, yet he seemed to be going after that girl again, the one with all the kids and ready to foal again. Guess in ten or fifteen years it'd be James lying out in some prairie night somewhere thinking the same thing.

Max recognized he had drunk to the point where he had drawn his boundary line, where he began to think there was no future. He had been here before, and had crossed it; but when he had crossed it, it had been a mistake. Soon he'd be thinking that the earth was in the middle of its destruction and that it was better to die than to live. He had to get his mind on the moment. He had to find the goddamned rustlers and bust them. He had to do that to make himself feel better, to brighten up the future.

He had to get up and walk around. He was hit with a touch of the spins when he stood up, the stars leaving little tracers behind them. The Pleiades were about to set in the west. It was dark, but he could move on instinct, on drunk radar. One foot in front of the other. The ground was flat; there was nothing to it. He looked back and could make out his truck in the starlight. Walking would clear his head. The earth wasn't destroying itself, and if it did the stars would still be there.

His boot struck something: a metal fencepost. There were strands of barbed wire. He thought at first to cross it, as walking was feeling good. Then he looked back, unable to see his truck. He recognized this objectively as a time that he might panic if he had not been drunk. Equaminity. No, equanimity. Better get back. Turn exactly a hundred and eighty degrees and go back. Same number of steps, however many that was. He should remember not to go wandering around strange places in the dark. Maybe ought to call it a night. But he was okay, it wasn't too cold. If he wanted he could just sleep where he was and find his way to the truck when the sun came up.

When it did get light, in fact when the actual rays of the sun rose over the flat horizon and hit him full in the face and woke him, he was in his sleeping bag on the tarp and felt okay. He didn't have to remember how he'd gotten there. Just had to figure out how to find the rustlers. He bought two big cups of coffee in Santa Rosa and as he pulled into Amarillo in the late morning he had figured that if the packing plant were slaughtering stolen stock then no doubt they were cautious of strangers asking questions, and the best way to get into it would be to pretend to be looking for a job. It wouldn't be that hard, because he'd had a job in a packing plant years ago. It was when he and Siri were first married and she was in school at Fort Collins and that was the best-paying job he could find. He was about the only one there who didn't speak Spanish. He was the one who got to kill the cattle with the nail gun. One after another. Then wash all the blood off at the end of the day and kiss his wife.

He didn't have to even set foot inside. He ordered a turkey and Swiss from the quilted-aluminum sandwich truck outside the plant and sat on the concrete wall near a Mexican guy who asked if he was Navajo. Mexican as in Mexico, what cops called a "national." Wore a plaid western shirt with snaps that Max would bet was made in Monterrey.

"I didn't think you Texans knew there is such a thing."

"I don't know how I tell, but I can. Yá'át'ééh."

"Yá'át'ééh. You married to a Navajo or something?"

"No but I herd sheep three four years ago." He said it like it was one word: yearssago. "I like it. First job I have here on this side. It was nice, quiet, peaceful. But no money. Like Mexico."

"You're right there," said Max. "No money. They hiring here?"

"Probably," the man said. "Always somebody's quit. I don't work till three."

"So you lived out on the rez, huh?"

"Rock Point."

"Damn, that's out there all right. What'd your sheep eat, tumbleweeds?"

"Yeah, everything. One time somebody try to take some sheep, pay me some money. One of the neighbors. I say I don't want to cheat my boss. You want to buy sheep, you talk to him. He say we don't have to talk to him. But I say no. There's a lot of people steal animals, you know, especially cows and calfs."

"Yeah, I know," said Max.

"I think that's what this guy's doing, the manager's brother or cousin or something from out your way somewhere, brings in these animals at night sometimes. I don't think nobody check brands."

"Who's the manager?"

"Mike Gabaldon."

From the time he'd finished his turkey and Swiss and shook the Mexican's hand and got in his truck and headed back west, he kept thinking, *That's way too easy. Just way too easy, nobody will believe me. The kind of thing you read in a bad detective novel, where he just stumbles on the important clue.* He'd even considered going through with his plan of applying for a job in the packing plant just to make it harder, but then what for?

He spent the night in a motel in Albuquerque that looked and smelled like its carpets and leaky faucets had survived half a sorry century, but he wasn't up for more stars and Jim Beam. He was at the ranch by early afternoon and caught his horse by evening. At dawn he saddled up and headed west toward Beebee's. He took a rope, a water bottle, a pair of binoculars, and his .357.

In just a few days the weather had gone from cool and wet, with rain turning to snow and back again the week before, to the hot dry windy days he would have to expect until the summer rains. It was early in the day and fresh, and mourning doves and meadowlarks were cooing and burbling as he headed down into the desert and to the land of the crazy Beebee who had once threatened him with a cast-iron skillet for broaching the subject he was about to raise again. His plan wasn't well formed; he thought it would eventually come to him what he should do; he would perhaps start by telling him that he already knew who he was stealing cattle for and that Gabaldon would take the fall. But that was not even remotely true. Max hadn't gone to tribal or federal law enforcement, and without evidence and cooperation from people like Beebee, Gabaldon probably didn't have a thing to worry about. He thought for a short moment that what he should tell Beebee was that if he stole another cow he would kill him. This time he had a gun he could show.

It would have been better to have come with James, a kind of fiercer repeat of the visit last fall. But James hadn't been around. Perhaps he was chasing that woman or visiting his folks in Flagstaff, getting soft, no doubt, as a consequence of lovers and parents who don't hate each other. He said he was about to start work again at Hubbell's. It had always been Max's job to teach James a thing or two, especially about cowboying. Gave up with Ben, and apparently he was right to, since he was on his way to be a big lawyer with a pretty blonde wife. Their father certainly wasn't going to teach them reservation ways, and their mother . . . was a woman. Not that James would ever be much of a cowboy, though he could still stay in the saddle and wasn't afraid of horses. There was a certain gameness, even eagerness to him, and Max knew how to use it. James always worked hard, wanted to show he could do it. Lifted weights. Big muscles by the time he was fourteen. Should have brought him as backup, but it was too late now.

He was wearing his polarized sunglasses, which helped him pick out the dust devils forming up and down the valley. There were wide spaces between the clumps of grama grass, which were barely greening up. The sky above was clear turquoise except for the contrails stretched in all directions like a poorly spun web. A single-engine plane crossed east-northeast, perhaps a track from Las Vegas to Window Rock, some mobster paying off a tribal official.

Far down the valley, past Beebee's house and Chester's ranch, Max could make out some activity that was raising dirt. At first he thought it was another dust devil, but this was thicker at the ground, and he made out a stock trailer parked by a red clay hill. He kept his eyes on it as he approached. Through the binoculars he could see cattle and someone on a horse. Someone big. This was his chance to catch Beebee red-handed.

He kept watch for other people, as loading cattle was not an easy job for one man, and slowly approached the trailer. It was empty, the back open and the ramp down. Three cows crowded the trunk of the single rugged cottonwood, which still had not leafed out enough to give much shade. From nearby but out of sight he caught the sound of a horse: not a single snort or neigh but a shrill and sustained cry of panic. Above it was a human sound, a loud "Aiii" not far from the pitch of the horse's whinny and just as desperate. Max rode around the clay hill and saw Beebee flailing. He was on horseback facing away from him, but the horse looked oddly dwarfed, as if he were riding a Shetland pony. Beebee was yelling at the horse, pulling hard on the reins, but its legs were gone, sunk in the ground.

He knew this was the dry quicksand that he had heard of but never seen. As kids they were familiar with the idea of quicksand from old movies on television, something that existed in wet jungles, and that a person could save himself from only if there was an overhanging vine or a nearby hero. But this was not the same as the mysterious local peril of *nahodits'ǫ́*. It featured in many stories, like the bolt of lightning out of the clear blue sky that sent his uncle's horse down the escarpment, and like the raging sheet-flood that stopped the escaping skin-walker in his tracks. It was an old myth like the underground creature who surfaced from time to time to devour children, yet he did believe it. He had seen evidence of the hidden tracts and tunnels in the clay hills, where slabs of petrified wood sat heavily in a gully one day and were gone the next. Chester once claimed to have landed in a patch of it and nearly lost his horse. "Sometimes you can tell by the way it looks, but this place looked like any other place." Where Beebee sat on his sinking horse was simple flat ground, only slightly below the crescent of rockier land from which Max watched them with dawning horror and understanding.

The struggling horse and rider spooked Max's horse and he dismounted, running along the rocky rim to where Beebee could see him. "Help!" the big man cried.

"Get off the horse!"

"I can't," Beebee squealed. "I'll sink in."

Max stepped toward the horse who was tossing his head frantically, the only thing he could move. A grinding sound came from the ground Max had stepped on and he found himself almost immediately up to his knee in sand. His other foot was on solid ground and he was able to pull the sunken leg up. He sprang to his horse and snatched his rope, flinging it to Beebee. The fat man clutched at it and dove off the horse and Max dragged him in as if from a lake. The horse, now up to its chest, could no longer breathe, and the two men watched from solid ground as it jerked in agony. "I almost sunk just like that one!" Beebee said, panting.

"Wow," said Max quietly. Without warning Beebee's arms were around him and his fat wet lips were kissing his cheek, reeking of alcohol. Max pushed him away.

"I'll never do that no more," said Beebee.

"You better not," said Max, referring to the kiss.

"I'll give you money and I'll never steal your cows no more."

"You do and I'm going to throw you back in there. Too bad about your horse."

Beebee started to cry. "And I'm not going to drink no more. I told Gabaldon I wasn't going to do no more of his stealing. He said he'd turn me in if I didn't. I said that's not right."

"I'll help you get back at him," said Max. It would be funny when he told the story. Right now it made him feel sick. Dead horse, wet cheek, exhausted on a warm spring morning.

CHAPTER TWENTY-SEVEN

⌇ **NOLAN DASHED OUT** of the back room in the chapter house as James went in, and he gave him a sign, crossing his eyes and sticking out his tongue and inscribing a triple circle with his finger in the air above his ear.

Something about Wesson had changed since their last visit. He was smiling and friendly, offering his hand as if James had come to visit an old friend. "Sorry I missed you the last couple of months."

It had been since January, and it was the middle of April, James's second day back at work. "That's okay," said James. It would be fine if he never saw his PO again. But this was interesting: Wesson had his feet up on the desk and wobbled a little when he stood up. Although it had been annoying in February and March to have made his way into Ganado just to wait around the chapter house, James hadn't expected an apology. He didn't expect to hear the word "please" from Wesson, or even to see him smile.

The smile James did see was crooked. Wesson's hand was clammy. James sniffed the air for alcohol, but didn't find it.

"How you been?" said Wesson.

"All right."

"Staying out of trouble?"

"Your spies tell you otherwise? Your buddies Austin and Gabaldon feed you some gossip?"

Wesson's face fell. "It's really rotten what they're trying to pin on Gabby. Besmirch the name of a good man."

Max had told James that Beebee was talking to the tribal prosecutor, but he hadn't heard anything since then. The few times he had seen

Gabaldon in the last couple of days he hadn't picked up signals that anything was wrong. James waited for Wesson to elaborate but he was on to something else.

"What's a positive for this week?"

"Well, I'm back to work. And friends with my girl again, I think."

"Negative?"

"Don't get paid for two weeks."

"Stinkin' thinkin'?"

"What?"

"We never talked about that? It's the kind of thinking that encourages bad behavior, like for instance, *My wife doesn't understand me so I should go get drunk.*"

"Well, I'm not married."

"Or, *My girlfriend thinks I ought to go to church every Sunday so I'll go to the bar instead.*"

"And I don't have an alcohol problem."

"Denial is not a river in Egypt."

"Do you remember what this was about? Misdemeanor possession of dangerous drugs, so-called. I'm not you, Mr. Wesson."

"Things would be a lot easier for you if you weren't so resistant."

"You want a pee test? I'll do a pee test. You want me to show up? I show up more often than you do. You want me to say I'm powerless over alcohol and my life is unmanageable? What good will that do?"

"You won't be the first person it's helped."

"I'm glad it helped you, Mr. Wesson."

"It did! And it keeps helping. I still have to call my sponsor sometimes."

James watched Wesson get in his car to leave, then unbuckle his seatbelt, open his trunk, and bring out something wrapped in his jacket. He left it hidden but within reach in the passenger seat, carefully buckled himself in again, and backed out.

Angie lay with her head in James's lap and panted. The Lamaze instructor was a white woman who assumed that he was her husband. She chirped, "Just look in each other's eyes, concentrate, and pant. This is what you'll be doing when it's too soon to push."

It wasn't a safe assumption, as there was only one other so-called husband there, a skinny seventeen-year-old with his chunky girlfriend. All the other "coaches" were aunties and sisters. It looked like Greenstone was right: there were few fathers anymore.

Looking into Angie's eyes was like looking into a pool too deep to see the bottom of. She panted and he stroked her hair and thought of the panic that would surely be added to the scene when it actually occurred. "Coaches, don't let her hyperventilate. Very shallow panting for ten breaths, then take a deep, long breath. Then pant. Pant like a puppy dog."

The instructor had the kind of cute, breathless voice James associated with blondes, although her hair was dark brown and cut in such a perfect wedge that it looked like a wig. These chicks were coming in from town to teach Navajos how to give birth, just like the old-time missionaries James was reading about, the prim men and women in the historic photographs lined up outside the Presbyterian church at Ganado with their uncomfortably dressed Indian students, hair cut and parted, eyes cast down. "*Look* in her eyes. Don't let her loose." Like the deep water under a waterfall.

It was as intimate a scene as he thought he would ever again have with Angie, although he often imagined having sex with her, as huge as her belly was. He wasn't sure it was possible, and wondered if that were part of the reason most of these women were without male partners. You would have to lie on your sides, but even then it might be hard to keep it in at that angle. What about her on top? Or doggy style? Funny how he'd never thought much about this before. And was any of it safe for the baby, who, he understood, was wrapped in a kind of clear balloon? Would it cause infections? If she came, would she go into labor?

When the class was done the women struggled upright and their coaches helped them waddle off slowly, pillows folded under their arms. What a pitiful bunch, like rain-bugs on their backs. "Practice, everybody! See you next week!" the instructor called.

"I hope so," one of the women said.

James had helped Angie up from the floor and she was still holding his hand when they walked out the door. "Thanks for coming," she said.

"Don't get the wrong idea, Angie. I don't really think I can start up again where we left off. I don't think I can trust you."

She let his hand drop. "I'm not asking anything from you. Or not much. I'm glad you're willing to give me a ride to the hospital and stay with me when I'm in labor. Or if you don't want to, I'm sure they have nurses."

"It's not like that. Actually, I can't wait to see the baby. The whole labor thing and the water and the blood and the placenta and all that grosses me out, but it's the baby I want to see."

"What you're saying is that you care about the baby but you don't care about me."

That wasn't true, either, but he wasn't going to let her trap him into answering.

It was like some of the questions tourists asked when he was giving his tour. They almost never asked anything directly about the standard spiel, like, "How long did it take them to deliver wool to the railhead?" or "Who paid the men to burn the irrigation ditches in the spring?" This is what convinced James that people showed up for more complicated reasons than historical curiosity.

"Would you say that most Navajo young people have contempt for Western culture?" This was one of those trick questions from the other day.

He was learning how to respond to such questions without actually answering them. Not responding meant that the questions defeated him, but answering them was also a defeat.

"I'm not sure. What do you think?" This was one strategy. Another was to call over to Angie and say, "Let's ask our resident expert on local young folks." And she would respond by blushing and giggling.

Now she was frowning at him. "That's the way people treat you when you're pregnant. They're all concerned for your safety and comfort, just so you're cushioning the baby, nourishing it. Then when the baby's out, everyone's attention is on it. They don't need you anymore."

"You don't think the baby's going to need you after it's born?" he asked.

"Babies need parents, yes."

He was getting better at his job; when people asked him what he did, he could say "tour guide" without a smirk. He tried to tailor his talks to his audience, and this required sizing them up quickly. It wasn't hard when it was a group of seniors from the Memory Unit at the upscale nursing home in Flagstaff, even though they were groomed and dressed like the retired academics they may have been. This was a group that never nodded. They never smiled at his amusing comments. There was no point in deviating from the standard text, the approved script Gabaldon had passed on to him, no reason to waste his own creative variations on it because their eyes were blank and their expressions were flat. This was one time it didn't matter that he performed the requested duty.

At other times, when the tourists were listening, it seemed important to take Greenstone's advice about not being a part of the problem and give them some truth rather than the official lies. Like malicious gossip, it was better not to say anything at all. When the tourists had memories and spoke English, they gathered together and looked at him expectantly, and he couldn't keep his mouth shut.

The day after the Lamaze class it was a mixed group: some families, the usual retirees stepping carefully out of their mammoth RVs, and a couple from California James thought he had seen in the movies. The guy reminded him of some sidekick in an action movie, or maybe some pop star who sang weak stuff. He was wearing a bandana and a white shirt and khaki shorts with lots of pockets. His girlfriend was also generic L.A.: blonde, thin, frowning, wearing sunglasses and a silk scarf that covered her head and neck, which she kept readjusting to cover her mouth as if she were afraid of breathing in some dangerous rural air.

"Okay, you guys, everybody ready for the tour? I'm supposed to teach you something. So if it's all right, I'll go ahead and tell the truth rather than just give the standard tour. Okay?"

A brother and sister who were elementary-school age looked up at him with big eyes of the same pale blue and both said, "Yeah."

"Good. Nice to see some enthusiasm. My last group forgot where they were. Okay! My name is James Claw and this is the historic Hubbell Trading Post, founded by Juan Lorenzo Hubbell, friend of presidents— friend of Teddy Roosevelt, that is, and while we're talking presidents, who can tell me which president advised against the Indians' learning their own history?"

"George Washington?" the boy said.

"You might be right. But I'm thinking of Thomas Jefferson, another founding father and slave owner. But we're not going to take his advice, okay?"

The Hollywood guy was smiling. "Say that again."

"He was writing to the governor of Virginia, telling him how he was planning on tricking the Indians out of land somewhere in Ohio or Kentucky." Although he had committed it to memory, James looked at the scrap of paper and read, "You will also perceive how sacredly it must be kept within your own breast, and especially how improper to be understood by the Indians. For their interests and their tranquillity it is best they should see only the present age of their history."

"I love it," the Hollywood guy said.

"I hate it," James said.

The guy was maybe in some detective series, but James couldn't place him since he hadn't seen much TV lately. The guy was looking at him like he thought James recognized him, and James was glad he didn't. The girl put her arm around his waist and pulled the scarf up over her nose.

They were still outside, and James pointed out the extent of the Hubbell homestead. "So not a bad little ranch. Especially as it had the only perennial stream for miles. Which brings us to presidents again: Hubbell was able to keep title to this land even as the Navajos got back control of all the area around it, because Hubbell was a personal friend of Teddy Roosevelt. It wasn't like Jefferson's big old plantation, but it was your standard colonial enterprise. Hubbell was an entrepreneur, and I don't want to short him for it. He was looking for business opportunities every day. He had the ranch business; a little orchard, though conditions were lousy for an orchard; his ranch, with beef, wool, mutton, cheap labor. Some of the laborers brought women: sisters, wives . . . the weavers."

Now they were in the weaving room, and the children knelt down next to Mabel and watched as she pounded her loom. The boy started to roll one of her balls of yarn and she smiled benignly as she took it back. "*Doo 'ájít'įįda,*" she admonished, and he seemed to understand.

In the hallway hung a couple sketches of local women, signed by Maynard Dixon and labeled "Ganado 1906," James's favorites. One of the women, whose children had by now probably died of old age, reminded him of Angie, with a shy smile and downward gaze. "Dixon was another one of don Lorenzo's guests. In fact he was the friend who introduced him to Charles Lummis, the Los Angeles writer and activist who was a college classmate and friend of Teddy Roosevelt. You ever hear of him?" The others were slowly moving into the dining room, including the L.A. woman, and James found himself talking directly to the guy, the actor or singer, whoever he was.

The L.A. guy nodded. "He founded the Southwest Museum."

"That's right. He's a great example of how it's ambiguous—friend of Hubbell, pro-Indian activist. Was he a good guy or a bad guy? He opposed forcing Hopi men to have their hair cut. This was good. In his opinion Hubbell did 'more for the Indians than all the missionaries and Indian agents.' It was the Indian agent who was forcing the haircuts and banning the ceremonies. According to him, the Indians loved Hubbell so much they would walk a hundred miles 'to be silently in his presence like an intelligent dog.'"

"Jeez. You've got a bunch of great quotes."

"It's interesting stuff."

Gabaldon appeared in the doorway. "Interesting, but not necessarily the opinion of the National Park Service."

"Well, duh," said the Hollywood guy, and James laughed. Gabaldon's smile was fixed under a nose wrinkled as if it had smelled something bad.

After the tour the Hollywood guy gave him his card, but James still didn't recognize the name. He told him that lately he was into animal rights and electric cars, but he also had an interest in what he called the Native renaissance. "I really respect what you're doing here, trying to make sense of all this. I had to study some of this for a project I'm involved in. And it isn't easy to find the truth."

"Especially if you're supposed to be promoting the old myths."

"Exactly. To the victor goes the narrative. So I appreciate it." His girlfriend sidled up to him and James noticed the big concho belt she was wearing, the one that had been in the case for months. She looked good, but belts like that needed a bigger waist, James thought. And she ought to take that scarf away from her face.

"What do you think, honey?"

"You want it?" He reached for his back pocket.

"See you, man," said James, leaving them in the gift shop with the mystical flute CD playing away. Might be a good idea to slip one of the early Deicide CDs in there someday.

Gabaldon was scowling when James met him in the parking lot. "You must know from the material I gave you that don Lorenzo provided economic opportunity, respect, protection from unscrupulous agents . . ."

"There were plenty of those, all right. Still are. A steady stream of them. People who enrich themselves, steal livestock . . ."

"Let me remind you that we have an approved text," said Gabaldon, who was now red.

"You need to stick with the approved text, too."

"You think I don't know who's behind this harassment? Why would anyone believe that fat moron? When I think of how much your father helped my family, when my daughter was going through her difficulties, I have a hard time squaring it with this . . . persecution. Now I have to go on leave while they go through their mock investigation, all because you and your cousin have a taste for communist revenge."

"Hey, Mr. Gabaldon. It's not me, okay? You did something wrong; I guess you got to take responsibility for it."

"I gave you this job because I thought I owed your family something."

"And you still do."

The evenings were longer and warmer now, and as he left Hubbell's, walking through Ganado toward Angie's house, he watched the light on Round Top shine gold, then magenta, and felt a gradual reawakening of energy and strength. Somehow nothing could go wrong.

CHAPTER TWENTY-EIGHT

▨ **THE SOUNDS FROM** the Bouncy House were of alternating happiness and misery, the children's giddy whoops and shouts followed by angry complaints and choked tears as they jumped and jostled inside it. Reeba had put on weight and every time she made a big jump the smaller kids were thrown up like confetti. Angie and James tried to keep Winona out because among all the bigger kids she continued to fall down in the corners and be squashed. But there was no keeping her out. Every five minutes she would present her smudgy self to James—wearing the Vile T-shirt James gave her, even though her favorite music was Raffi—to be lifted up into it again. "Just *stay* in here this time," he said.

The first-laugh party for the baby, Rosie, was bigger and more complicated than it needed to be. All you really had to do was feed some relatives and give out salt, just the bare essentials. When Chief Manuelito had his first laugh, his parents hadn't rented a balloon house shaped like a castle from the party shop near the mall, and most people now didn't either. It was Angie's doing, encouraged by her sister and James's mother, and once they started planning, it rapidly got out of hand.

It was James's idea to have a keg, and this was a matter of disagreement.

"They'll arrest him," Irene had told Angie on the phone from Shiprock. She was going to come down with Evangeline and Reeba, who was going to move in with James and Angie and Winona and the baby in their much-too-little rented house in Sunnyside. She said she didn't want to go all that way to watch the baby's father being hauled off to jail and all the children taken away by Child Protective Services.

"That's not going to happen," Angie said. "It's perfectly legal." She wasn't actually sure of this, since she'd lived so long on the reservation where you had to hide your beer or you *would* get hauled off to jail.

When she checked again with James he tried to be patient. "Yes, it's legal and I'm off probation. If your sister doesn't want to drink beer then she doesn't have to."

In their next conversation Irene complained to Angie that it was the baby's party, not a chance for the adults to get "all drunken and passed out in your front yard."

When she conveyed this to James he pointed out that the idea behind *ch'ídeeldlo'* was to encourage the baby to be a generous host, and he intended to feed her guests well and to provide beer if they wanted it. "I'm going to decide this," he said finally, "since I made her laugh. And I won't let anyone pass out on the front yard."

Angie had suggested live music also, meaning Putrefaction, and this, too, became a subject of discussion. His mother asked how he expected to look properly after the guests if he was going to be on stage. "Ben and Francine are coming all this way. Don't you think they'll want to talk to you?"

"They're going to be here a few days this time," James said. "And Ben told me that for sure he wants to hear us play."

It had become more difficult getting the band together since James had moved to Flagstaff, but they had some gigs planned and were doing some recording with a black musician, Nathan, in his kick-ass studio. They had decided to take advantage of the occasion by having Nathan set up his recording gear at the party to try to get at least a couple of songs for a live CD. Even though their music was getting better, the audiences were declining, even on the reservation. The kids were into hip-hop, and James couldn't rap. Just couldn't do it.

The sky was totally clear at dawn but soon the clouds appeared, not from west or north but from the air itself, like the community that had formed around baby Rosie. It was overcast by late morning with those dark gray clouds that in this season meant rain by evening. By the time the party started they had already heard distant rumbles, a sound as welcome as the sound of the first laugh itself.

Rosie's first laugh had happened earlier than they expected it to, which is probably always the case since it is always a surprise. She had been smiling for a while and following Angie and James and Winona around with her eyes, those two black dots above her fat cheeks, and every day there seemed to be more and more of an appreciative glimmer behind them. That morning, not long after she had awakened from a short nap, James was dressing and unpacking some of the remaining boxes into his dresser. He could tell she was watching him. He deliberately pretended to ignore her, then stole a look, and she smiled. Then he ignored her some more, then stole another look, and she smiled again. Then he put his face up to her as she watched him as if to suck him in, and she let out a full, perfect, amazing laugh.

That was a few days ago; they had planned the party quickly, called their family and friends from all around, and here they were, a varied group that started out a little stiff around each other, now loosening up. Nathan was setting up his equipment while hitting on Shondeen, a pretty Navajo woman from the neighborhood with two unwanted children. Both Nathan and Shondeen were on the verge of being drunk. He was telling her about another band that was producing a CD with him. "Death metal, I mean *dark* death, one hundred percent satanic shit, and their outfit, it's these matching powder-blue cardigans." Later on James heard Shondeen threatening to smack her five-year-old.

"They'll be sending out CPS and taking your children away from you," Nathan told her, and James thought, *Good, somebody told Shondeen.*

But by that time she had drunk another big red cup or two of beer and said, "Let them. I wouldn't have to worry about these brats then, ruining my life."

James got away from there. He didn't want to hear that kind of talk.

Nolan was sitting in one of the lawn chairs next to Angie who was holding the baby. James took the empty chair on the other side of him.

"How's it going?" James asked. Nolan was drinking a Diet Coke, and there were two empty cans under his chair. "How about a beer?"

It was a joke but Nolan gave him a pained look. "Six more months."

"That's when you're off probation?"

"First day off I'm likely to have a beer. And a poppy seed bagel. We should throw a party. Get one of those Bouncy Houses and all jump in there naked."

Nolan told him that his meetings with the new probation officer were over in five minutes. "This guy is all business. 'Got a job? Get in any trouble?' Not like Wesson with all his . . . issues."

"Wonder where he is."

Nolan shrugged and said, "Still in fucking rehab. Six months residential. He's on disability, courtesy of you and me."

"You? When did you start paying taxes?"

Winona and the Beast showed up together, faces both sticky, hair flying up in tufts, begging. "Up?"

"All right, doggone it," James said, walking them over to the balloon castle and lifting them up one by one. "Stay in there!"

Nolan took a peek at Rosie, who was asleep in Angie's arms with a pink knit blanket partly over her face. He touched her cheek lightly and watched her lips twitch and suck. He laughed, and his gold tooth shone. "Whatever happened to *my* pretty baby?"

Two white cops glided by slowly, staring. The driver was so big it looked like his head must be touching the ceiling of the squad car. James stared back at them, feeling just a little uncertain about the keg. His mother and his aunt Thelma and Angie's sister Irene were saying that they should really hide the beer. Irene said, "I don't know about bringing up a baby in town."

"*Eii lą́ą́*," Thelma agreed. "All these gang peoples, bi'éé' daalzhinígíí." She had come to help with the food, but Max had stayed behind, supposedly to drive his father to and from dialysis. James knew the real reason was that he was angry at James for leaving the ranch.

"What'd you come back here for, anyhow?" Max had asked. "Just to find a woman you can take back to town? You could make a life here: you've got a baby, a wife—what I call a wife—a job, a house."

"I'm sure I'll be back," James told him. He tried to cheer up Max by sharing his plan to return to open a bed and breakfast on the reservation. "Build a kind of Victorian hogan, maybe blue with white trim. After a comfortable sleep on *yaateeł* on the floor, quilts, nice fire in the stove, we serve them a fine breakfast of pancakes and Spam. Then we tell them, 'Now go let out the sheep.'"

The Park Service had made it easy for him to transfer to Flagstaff to a permanent job at the Anasazi ruins at Wupatki, since he was a whistleblower and they didn't want the whole story about Gabaldon to come out. He guessed they also figured he couldn't sabotage the Park Service message where ancient cultures were the focus, but he was finding out a thing or two about the Navajo and Hopi claims in the area. It was secure work all year long with benefits, including paying for him to take a class every semester at the university.

Five minutes later Nolan was urging the band to get ready, tuning his bass. The same two cops cruised by as James was changing Rosie on her baby blanket spread out on the patchy grass. He loved the folds and dimples in her thighs. Somehow she always managed to cross her legs when he was trying to put a diaper on. Resistance was the name of her game. Her arms, too, were soft and round, almost as if there were no bone under there, just those squeezable fat muscles. He kissed her shoulder.

Rosie had changed so much in her short life. The laughter was just one marker. Her first hour, when she lay on her back wrapped like a burrito in a pink blanket with her eyes wide open, before she had tasted milk, before she belonged to anyone, she had seemed somehow wiser and less human than ever after. The next day, when the three of them woke in Angie's bed, she stretched and sighed and fell asleep again, and when she opened those eyes once more they seemed not to really see him, nor to be the beacon of her former secret knowledge. And she whimpered as she began to nurse.

James guessed most humans started out in a scene of chaos, if you considered birth the beginning, but Rosie's was strikingly confusing, with the shouting and banging in the hospital corridor along with Angie's screams and the doctor's fumbling. Maybe for Rosie it wasn't chaotic at all, as all she had to do was emerge.

It happened right on the due date, May nineteenth, so they should have been expecting it. James had been staying at Angie's for two weeks or so, sleeping together and doing various things that were more or less equivalents of sex. That morning he had gotten a little carried away and didn't realize what was happening when his whole face was covered with fluid. He thought at first he had really accomplished something, and when she told him to stop he thought she was playing a game. "My water broke," she said, pushing him away. After a couple of hours she was complaining about the contractions.

No one came to the door of the emergency room, though it was the middle of the afternoon on Saturday. Angie was hardly able to stand, leaking fluid in dribbles and gushes, and he was sure from her moaning that he would have to deliver the baby himself, a possibility he had driven from his mind weeks ago and now wished he had thought through and studied up on. Then when the doctor showed up—it wasn't the nurse practitioner Angie knew, but someone who had arrived the previous week from Pennsylvania, someone who looked about twenty—he was flustered and confused, and after Angie was led to a bed he admitted he was a medical student and might be able to summon the real doctor before the baby came.

Angie was swearing the baby was going to come right then and there, yelling at everyone that she knew what she was talking about because it hadn't been that long since her last one. But she was only dilated three centimeters, the medical student said, then an hour later two centimeters. "How is that even possible?" James said. They'd talked about centimeters in Lamaze, and if he remembered right it went from one to ten without going backward. "Did you call the doctor yet?"

So before long the medical student checked her again and declared that she was back at three. "Are you sure?" said James. He couldn't get the fetal monitor to work, then there was a power outage, then the student disappeared for two or three hours. No real doctor showed up. "I don't know where he is," the medical student said. James suggested that he take her to Fort Defiance, but she swore she couldn't move.

Then, when she was eight centimeters and yelling to push, there was a big commotion somewhere outside labor and delivery. Some guy was shouting, "Let me in!"

"Oh my god," said Angie between pants, in a different kind of tone.

"What?"

"It's Malcolm."

"What's Malcolm doing here?"

"I don't know. Someone must have told him."

"Who?"

"I got to push!"

"Not yet, not yet," said the medical student, who had big dark spots on the armpits of his green scrubs.

"I don't know. Someone."

"She's having my baby!" they heard him holler.

James thought, *Your baby?*

They heard other voices shouting Malcolm down and yelling to call security. Very briefly Malcolm's face appeared at the delivery room door as the student was telling Angie to push, but he was yanked back and the yelling was drowned out by Angie's screams. "Just get it out!" James had maroon nail marks in his forearms, crescents of fire.

James turned his head toward the door just for a moment and called into the hall. "Call the police! She has a restraining order." Then to Angie, whose face was a fiery grimace, he asked, "That's still in effect, isn't it?"

She didn't answer but clutched his arm again and gave a fierce grunt. He uncurled her hand as he slid down her side to look at the crowning head, black curls matted down with the white waxy stuff, this incomprehensible swollen ball between Angie's legs. Then he returned to her side and she dug into another part of his forearm, leaving four more angry crescents.

Then it occurred to him that the baby wasn't going back in. And his life couldn't go back to what it was. The student was saying, "Don't push, don't push," as he tried to get a glove on, as if she were really able to obey that command.

The baby was born with no participation from the so-called doctor until he clamped and cut the cord. The nurse blotted the baby, who was gasping and blue. When she told him the baby was fine he believed her, bathed in relief and love for the squinting face.

He had told himself he would withhold his commitment until the baby was born, and only then he would be able to tell by his feelings what he would do. Now that he was looking in her eyes he knew he was lost. A man's life is a progression of weakenings or defeats, and he had no strength to resist her.

The Beast was running in her clumsy way toward her father, who was still tuning his bass, and put her hands on his shins and told him urgently, "Nona fell down!" James popped up out of his chair and walked quickly to where the Beast was pointing, just outside the doorway to the Bouncy

House. Winona was face down in the dirt, crying. He clutched her under her arms and lifted her up. No marks on her face but a lot of dirt. "Hurt!" she said and he walked around with her over his shoulder, way too heavy, patting her back. He asked himself if he had made some conscious choice, or had he simply ended up as an instant father of three?

He found a piece of watermelon for Winona, who stomped over to the Beast to share it with her. He stood with his mother and father and his brother Ben with Ben's girlfriend, Francine. They had flown down the day before, and James and Ben had spent hours talking about bands and listening to new music James had discovered. He had told James he was envious of his musical skill, but even more of his being a father. He seemed amazed by Rosie, but Francine wouldn't hold her. "I might enjoy it," she explained. "At this point in our careers . . ."

There were enough non-Navajos around for James's mother to feel she owed them some kind of explanation. "It's the baby's party, really," she said more or less toward Francine, who stood picking at potato salad on her paper plate, but Nathan was sitting nearby and she aimed her little tour guide talk toward him as well. "Even though her dad is here with all his friends drinking away. It's like she's saying, 'Come and enjoy the company; it's my treat. My daddy has to pay for it, but it's my treat.'" Ben and Francine laughed and James smiled, looking down at his plastic cup. "Because if we don't do it, she's going to grow up all stingy and grouchy. Not what we call *k'éí*, which has to do with being a relative, meaning friendly and generous. It's true, too. I did know people, when their babies laughed, they said, 'Well, let's just save the money, or maybe we'll do it later,' and never did. Those were the babies who turned out really mean."

"What about Ben?" Francine had a sneaky smile on her face. "Did he have a first-laugh party?"

"Sure, but he was old, maybe four months old, and then it was kind of an old man's heh-heh-heh when his dad tickled him."

His father said, "Sardonic is the word I'd use. And Ben was late with everything. He didn't talk for the longest time, then used whole sentences."

"Yeah," said James, punching his brother's shoulder. "Your first word was 'egregious.'"

Angie carried the baby to James's mother's side. "How about James?"

"He was early, and he laughed a lot. Sort of a mischievous laugh."

Most of the guests were listening to James's mother, and James thought she was cute, performing happily for them, flushed with pride in her grandchild. He didn't think she knew about the paternity issue, as she had already said a dozen times that Rosie looked just like he did, that she smiled lopsided like he did. She raised her voice in a kind of announcement. "She's going to give out some salt now. Everybody come get some. We use salt because in the old days it wasn't that easy to get, and people had to travel a long way for it or trade valuable stuff for it, because it's something you have to have."

Angie held the baby as James put a few crystals in the chubby hand, which couldn't even grasp them without help, and gave them out. Then other things were given to people: toys, flashlights, candies, Cracker Jacks, other little things Angie got, including little statues of pigs and princesses that she picked up at the dollar store down the street.

When Angie got tired she handed James the baby, who had slept through the whole process of giving things out. The tiny breath in and out of tiny perfect lips, even the pink stippling on the nose was somehow perfect. It hadn't taken James long to learn to carry his daughter like a football, to lose his fear of dropping her. His hands, rough with calluses and eczema, didn't seem to bother the exquisite skin of his daughter. He continued to have dreams of terrible mishaps—he had grown up hearing about infants' flaccid necks and disastrous punctures of the soft spot—but when she was awake he found her nearly indestructible.

James's father touched the baby's cheek, and her face twitched. "I remember having the babies, especially you, James. All of a sudden I couldn't do what I wanted to just when I wanted to." The pitch of his voice went up a seventh as the baby started to open her eyes. "Ball and chain, baby, aren't you a ball and chain."

The band finished tuning their instruments and fiddling with the amps. Nathan gave them the go-ahead. He was at the panel with his earphones on but didn't seem to be paying proper attention, as Shondeen was standing behind him, playing with his dreads. Before the first song Nolan growled a dedication to the baby. In a few measures the kids peered out of the Bouncy House and started bobbing their heads. Putrefaction played a couple more of their standards, but that was enough. Leon had been downing cups of beer for hours, and it was clear that Nathan wasn't getting much of a recording. They would sound better inside some dark basement with an audience that didn't look so content.

The cops had drifted past a third time before Leon decided he was going to drive his truck back home. He wobbled when he stood. Irene stared him down. "Give me those keys," she said, and before he knew what she was doing she had put them in the pocket of her jeans.

"I drive better when I've had a few," he said. "I'm more careful." The cops made one more pass from the other direction and he sat down, letting out a resigned sigh.

The clouds darkened. A little shuffle of wind blew paper plates off the table. In the breeze the baby gasped. A fat raindrop landed on her blanket, and by the time they had rescued the remaining food and covered the musical equipment and taken shelter in the house, water was crashing down in sheets with a sound like a tall column of cymbals, bouncing off the streets and filling the air with a metallic smell. The guests who didn't fit in the small house ran into their cars or into the Bouncy House. James, Winona, Angie, and the baby crowded together in a corner of the couch and watched the storm through the open door.